Theatre for Early Years

# Kinder-, Schul- und Jugendtheater
## Beiträge zu Theorie und Praxis

Begründet von Charlotte Oberfeldt† und Heiko Kauffmann

Herausgegeben von Wolfgang Schneider

Band 13

PETER LANG

Frankfurt am Main · Berlin · Bern · Bruxelles · New York · Oxford · Wien

# Wolfgang Schneider (ed.)

# Theatre for Early Years
Research in Performing Arts
for Children from Birth to Three

PETER LANG
Internationaler Verlag der Wissenschaften

**Bibliographic Information published by the Deutsche Nationalbibliothek**
The Deutsche Nationalbibliothek lists this publication in the Deutsche Nationalbibliografie; detailed bibliographic data is available in the internet at <http://www.d-nb.de>.

Gratefully acknowledging financial support by

Education and Culture

**Culture 2000**

EUROPEAN NETWORK FOR THE DIFFUSION
OF PERFORMING ARTS FOR EARLY CHILDHOOD

ISSN 0723-8312
ISBN 978-3-631-59259-5

© Peter Lang GmbH
Internationaler Verlag der Wissenschaften
Frankfurt am Main 2009
All rights reserved.

All parts of this publication are protected by copyright. Any utilisation outside the strict limits of the copyright law, without the permission of the publisher, is forbidden and liable to prosecution. This applies in particular to reproductions, translations, microfilming, and storage and processing in electronic retrieval systems.

Printed in Germany 1 2 3 4 5   7

www.peterlang.de

# Table of Contents

## Preface by the editor

*Wolfgang Schneider:*
Theatre for Early Years?
Questions about Qualifications ............................................................................ 9

## Reflections

*Gerd Taube* (Germany):
First steps
Aesthetic peculiarities of the "Theatre for Early Years" ...................................... 15

*Carlos Herans* (Spain):
Why "Theatre for Early Years"?
Memories and highlights of artistic experiences................................................. 25

*Ana Lúcia Goulart de Faria and Sandra Regina Simonis Richter* (Brazil):
Education meets theatre
Pedagogical remarks about the role of arts in early childhood .......................... 29

*Geesche Wartemann* (Germany):
Wechselspiele – Playing with interplay
Staging the theatrical structure, and the fragility of the ground rules,
in "Theatre for Early Years" ................................................................................ 49

*Ute Pinkert* (Germany):
Starting all over again?
Changing ways of perception through theatre – not only for young children .... 60

*János Novák* (Hungary):
The joy of re-discovering the world
'Communitas' and streaming in the performances made for babies................... 68

*Wolfgang Schneider* (Germany):
The category of simplicity and the complexity of the theatre
Art education requirements, neurobiological justification and cultural policy
considerations for the dramatic arts beginning with earliest childhood ............. 79

## Reports

*Dan Höjer* (Sweden):
Big drama for small spectators
*Unga Klara's* Swedish experiment ................................................................. 89

*Charlotte Fallon and Michel van Loo* (Belgium):
Babies and theatre
Notes about the imagination on stage ............................................................. 94

*Agnès Desfosses* (France):
Little ones and adults, alive and aware
Theatre brings together .................................................................................. 99

*Stephan Rabl* (Austria):
Surprise
Creating "Theatre for Early Years" between everything and nothing ............. 105

*Ivica Šimić* (Croatia):
"Dance and movement is a natural choice of language"
The art of making theatre art for small children ............................................. 109

*Cate Fowler* (Australia):
Installation theatre
Creating a performance space for babies and toddlers ................................... 113

*Megan Alrutz* (USA):
Visionaries wanted!
Theatre for *very* young audiences in the United States ................................. 119

*Gabi dan Droste* (Germany):
Distinguished theatre for young children
About the European network *Small Size* ....................................................... 127

## Experiences

*Roberto Frabetti* (Italy):
Does theatre for children exist?
An unlikely model ........................................................................................... 135

*Myrto Dimitriadou* (Austria):
Theatre and children are beautiful and 'ding dong'...
Artistic processes in theatre work for the smallest of the small
(A letter to the editor) ..................................................................................... 146

*Melanie Florschütz and Barbara Kölling* (Germany):
The discovery of the small child as a spectator
The performer Melanie Florschütz and the director Barbara Kölling in a discussion on "Theatre for Early Years" ............................................................. 156

*Jo Belloli* (United Kingdom):
Unearthing the potential
Exploring "Theatre for Early Years" in the UK ................................................ 160

*Sarah Argent and Kevin Lewis* (United Kingdom):
"I was struck by the difference in age between us, but by the similarity in hairstyles"
Journeying out of the blue ............................................................................... 168

## Appendix

Credits ............................................................................................................... 179

Plates ................................................................................................................. 181

Authors ............................................................................................................. 197

Supporters ......................................................................................................... 199

# Theatre for Early Years?
## Questions about Qualifications

*by Wolfgang Schneider*

There is an old phenomenon in the arts: Education! And there is a new tendency: Arts for the very young! The relationship to education is clear, but what about the profit for the arts? Theatre for Children started in former times from six years, since a couple of years there is a kind of theatre for children between three and six, nowadays we find examples on stage for babies – from birth to three! What does that mean for the theatre arts?

### First

– The world of children as the horizon of experiences? To duplicate the images: The Teddy bear as a Teddy bear, the duck as a duck, and the snowman as a picture of the snowman? Where is the new experience?

### Second

– The role of music as a dramaturgical element? Could you see the music, could you feel the music, could you recognize the music? – Songs as literature art? – Melodies from the record?

### Third

Is the performance divided into two pieces – the actors and the spectators, the stage and the audience, the one who tells the story and the one who is told the story? Why do we need the traditional confrontation? Are the very young children much more interested in the whole situation, with other very young children, with the mums and fathers, with the nursery nurse, with the lighting-system and so on?

### Fourth

Is there a special age for a successful reception of a performance? How could children be satisfied with something like theatre, if they are not able to follow the performance? Do we need standards for a better reception? Or do we need such adults who accompany the children with gestures to be quiet, to sit down and to look at the actors, don't push the neighbours, don't steel the requisites, and don't play your own game?

**Fifth**

What does it mean; theatre is art and education in another world? How much theatre artists should be informed about the physical and psychological development of children? Why do children have to understand everything in theatre? Do we, as adults, understand everything in Shakespeare's dramas, in Goethe's "Faust" or in Peter Brook's "Maharabata"?

Questions, questions, questions, good to ask questions. It seems that "Theatre for Early Years" is a work in progress. It means that theatre for human beings from birth to three should be evaluated in the practice. It is a question of theatre art: What is the communication between the actors, the children and the adults? And nothing makes me angrier when theatre artists play childishly, forget me as a companion of the children and don't take the chance to use the whole theatrical system. Maybe there is a new challenge for Theatre by "Theatre for Early Years", a challenge to renew the language of theatre, to establish an art of simplicity for the complexity of theatre.

I would never have believed that theatre like this for Early Years works, if I had not seen it with my own eyes. And I do not know whether theatre means anything to the youngest children. But the way they are treated, what is shown to them and the intensity with which a person – the actress, the musician, the dancer – pays attention to them must have a positive impact on their life.

The discussion about the phenomenon of "Theatre for Early Years" proceeded, the examples are more and more on the stages of the world, and the artistic development is collecting experiences: In Europe, in the States, in Australia. A variety of different perspectives are included in this research in performing arts from birth to three. The authors are reflecting their work, their observations, and directorship. The articles show us the practical "How to do?" in Wales, England and Scotland, in the Nordic countries, in Austria and Germany, in France, Belgium and Italy, down under and between the Pacific and the Atlantic in Northern America. Some of the remarks are answers to our questions, but most of the artistic work the authors talk about poses new questions. This book is written for this discussion: To discover a new audience, to educate from the beginning, to accompany the new generation in aesthetics, to understand the signs of the time, to make our globalised world transparent. "Theatre for Early Years" is another piece in the mosaic of arts education which is an assumption for the rights of the children to take part in culture as the United Nations promised it. More and more the cultural policy and the educational system have to take care of all children that they use theatre: Children need theatre – from birth to three, and so on! From the moment of the beginning of this movement this book could help to find an orientation in this new phenomenon of theatre:

Theatre for Early Years!

Thanks to all authors, to the photographers, to the translators! Thanks for the initiative of the European Network of *Small Size*[1], especially to my friends Valeria and Roberto Frabetti and their wonderful 'family' of *Teatro Testoni Ragazzi* in Bologna. Thanks to Stephan Rabl and Julius Stieber from the Theatre Festival "Shäxpir" in Linz; thanks to Anna Lena Schanz, Lydia Baldwin, Meike Fechner and Paul Harman for their help, thanks to Robert Peise for the editorial assistance.

---

1 *Small Size* was funded thanks to the *European Union*s programme *Culture 2000* (See Appendix "Supporters"). *THE EUROPEAN UNION – CULTURE 2000*: "The responsibility for this publication lies with the author and the *Commission* is not responsible for any use that may be made of the information contained therein."

# Reflections

# First steps
## Aesthetic peculiarities of the "Theatre for Early Years"

*by Gerd Taube*

Based on the theatre for the youngest substructures of the theatre acting and dramatic communication may be discussed.[1] The reception of the situation isn't affected by civic theatre conventions, because the young spectators aren't yet exercised in those conventions. But even the children's theatre substructures at large may be reflected and defined. Such a constantly used and never challenged doctrine says: Children's theatre has got a special connection to its audience. It provides a cause to confine the children's theatre from the 'ordinary' theatre, although there are many professional children's theatre companies in Germany where this cause doesn't apply. Therefore it's necessary to analyse what makes the connection between children's theatre and audience so special.

Neither there is the eternal children's theatre nor could any other kind of theatre be reduced to an aesthetic canon.[2] The characteristics are as different and multifaceted as the characteristics of other kinds of theatre. Even though it's impossible to deflect statements about aesthetic principles for theatre for the youngest only by watching several performances, there are however different phenomena in different performances to be seen. On that account, the consideration about an aesthetic specific of this kind of theatre may firstly be arranged via specific aspects and categories. This effort should not be misunderstood as a canonisation of those aspects and categories. The point is to arrange the first perceptions in this process of discussion which takes place in Germany since few years[3], so the aspects and categories can be discussed further.

---

1 Intrinsically the concept of practicability – in conjunction with the theatre for the youngest – should be discussed and applied to this kind of theatre. But theoretical discourse about practicability in dramatics and cultural studies hasn't been noticed previously but perceived as foreign by the scene of children's and youth theatre related to their opinion about theatre. Therefore I renounce to broach the issue of this discourse in my essay, which has got the purpose to pick out the actual discussion about the theatre for the youngest as a central subject.

2 The determination is one result of the congress "Theater von Anfang an" ("Theatre from the Beginning") which has been arranged by the *Children's and Young people's Theatre Centre in the Federal Republic of Germany* as a component of the "International Guest Performance Main Focus" at the 8th "German Children- and Youth-Theatre Meeting" in May 2005 at Berlin.

3 Therefore, this essay examines both the results of the symposium "First Steps" (2005 at Hamm) and the discussion aspects during the 8th "German Children- and Youth Theatre Meeting" in May 2005 at Berlin and of earlier discussions, for instance the symposium "Unter dem Tisch" ("Under The Table") at the *Schaubude* Berlin in 1999.

The discussion process in Germany has reached a point where such an interim result is getting necessary to bring the practical examination and the theoretic reflection to a new quality. It may no longer broach the issue of legitimating the theatre for the youngest – it already exists. The discussion has got to change from the pure description and reflection to an analytic-systematic level.

Different from many other discussions about (children's and youth) theatre, it should not be distinguished between the discourse about social condition and aesthetic aspects because they are dependent on each other. Below, they will be displayed separately. They wouldn't be analysable and presentable in their own specifics.

## Image

More than other forms of children's and youth theatre the theatre for the youngest is depending on the society's attitude towards children – in this case towards very small children. Meanwhile, the ordinary children's theatre for children up from five or six years has become socially accepted. Coming along is an acceptance of the children's right to enjoy theatre art. The right of art for the smallest children from zero to three or four years is generally challenged. Even in the ranks of the committed children's theatre maker's strong rejections concerning theatre for the youngest are not rare – mostly as a result of aesthetic convictions. Inherently, this fact necessitates asking some questions about the childhood image which forms the basic of such convictions.

What does a small child figure? The answer to this essential question is a key to the attitude towards theatre for the youngest. Are they 'human beings' or 'human becomings'? The perceptions are lying between these two poles. Are they regarded as premature beings, as good because ingenuous humans, as human beings on a certain level of development or as human beings with a special expertise? What do we expect of small children? When are they taken as 'human becomings' – what or how shall they become?

In Germany there's a discussion in progress at the moment in which nursery and kindergarten deemed to be places where education takes place. Whereupon in the most formal curricula for children of the age from zero to ten years that exist since the eighties of the twentieth century, the educational function of these institutions is codified. But in practice those concepts haven't been or have hardly been realised, and to take care of the children is still more important. The question about status and function of nurseries and kindergartens comes up, because in every country that has convincing examples for theatre for the youngest, the status of infantile educational institutions in the whole educational system is different from ours. In Norway, Italy or France those institutions are part of the educational system – in Germany it's preliminary. Whereas in Germany the education career starts with the school enrolment, the children of the named countries are already starting their education in the nursery or kindergarten. I am firmly assured this fact is a very important assumption to create a dramatic art for the youngest.

Therefore, the discussion about theatre for the youngest in these countries is mostly of an aesthetic matter. Consequently this form of theatre has got to legitimate itself in respect of aesthetic by the quality of the artistic work. In Germany the legitimation of art – especially dramatic art for children – takes place via the educational (and thus also a political) discourse in Germany.

**Perception**

In Germany, the corporate discourse about the legitimation of art is held within the two poles: the art as a kind of cultural-aesthetic education versus the autonomy of art. The assertion of the functional aspect of art (in this case its educational function) confronts the assertion that art has to be art – and nothing else. Even though this pointed description had to be distinguished in practice, the tendency towards either direction seems problematic to me; certainly, dramatic art educates just because it's art. Education and art are connected in a dialectical relationship. This seems to me to be the more productive approach if we intend to talk about the coherence between education and art.

The answer to the question of the children's right of art is depending on the kind of the corporate accepted image about childhood. In this coherence even those theatre makers who are endued with experiences about theatre for small children (up from three years) – such as puppeteers – confirm the opinion that theatre for children under three can't work. This dogmatic opinion is reasoned by experiences with performances for older children where children under three have been attending. The estimation of these theatre makers are based upon an opinion about theatre which applies to the model of the civic representation theatre. In this respect their opinion seems to be confirmed, as this kind of theatre in fact doesn't work for children under the age of three years. Last but not least the dissection of the theatre for the youngest is imperative because it still has to legitimate its existence. We have to deal with legitimation during the dissection and the wider reflection of this form of theatre, but it may not dominate, as the underlying discourse of the progression of this kind of theatre is still the aesthetic discourse.

At present the following basic aspects are weighed to different degrees. For example, the first aspect to be mentioned – the communication – has to be further distinguished in later discussions due to its complexity.

## Communication

As any dramatic communication, the communication in a play for the youngest is based upon the common presence of players and spectators and their direct or indirect interaction. However, the dramatic communication in play for the youngest is especially fragile. By constantly balancing this communication it is obvious much earlier when and how it works – and when and how it doesn't. If the communication between stage and auditorium in the course of an urban theatre performance of Schiller's "Räuber" does not work, it usually doesn't appear directly during the performance. At the ordinary theatre, the reception of the audience is in such a way conditioned that the missing balance of communication hasn't got an immediate effect and will be barely noticeable neither.[4]

Communication is based upon reciprocal perception. For our examination, the reciprocity of perception is crucial – the players and spectators betake themselves in a special relationship. Firstly, no part is dominant in this relationship. The eye contact – for many players of theatre for the youngest a basic requirement for the performances' success – is one approach of the reciprocal perception. Perception is not reduced to hearing and seeing. It means perceiving with all senses. The touching, fumbling, fondling, – for example in the performance "Sous la table"[5] – has got a special importance. As a matter of course, the physical contact has got communicative aspects because the kind of contact – forcible, rank or hesitant – coevally transmits information. And the reaction to those physical contacts – defence, affright, retreat, snuggling – also carries information.

As a further example of the specific perception with the whole body the performance "Uccelini"[6] has to be mentioned. In that play the actress stands quite a long time with her back towards the audience, drawing onto a canvas. But she describes she is continuously perceiving the audience. She hears it and she feels it in her back. As an actress she has to perceive with the whole body.

The tactile aspect is insofar a matter of particular interest as it is considered as an exception for the conventional theatre where usually the spatial separation and physical distance between players and audience prevails. With the description of the perception in theatre for the youngest as a physical matter, we coevally describe an expansion of the restricted conventional perception (seeing, hearing, and possibly smelling) at the ordinary theatre. At this point it gets in

---

4 Exceptions could be those productions which intend to activate the spectator to break his conventions he was conditioned on by the civic theatre. This mobilisation is effected by pointed taboo breaks and a deliberately breaking of conventions with the intention to provoke the spectator.
5 "Sous la table", *Compagnie ACTA*, Val d'Oise (France), Concept and Direction: Agnès Desfosses, Players: Anne Cammas und Thierry Gary.
6 "Uccelini", *Association Skappa!*, Marseille (France), Production: Paolo Cardona, Isabelle Hervouët, Players: Isabelle Hervouët.

touch with advanced contemporary forms of theatre, for instance the performance which widens the possibilities of perception, but with the motivation to break conventions to re-perceive what is thought to be familiar.

At the theatre for the youngest this motivation is irrelevant because the children don't dispose of such conventional conditioning. The reference to performance is based on an analogy of means, but the impact concepts behind the use of those means are entirely different.

In this context materiality and physicalness of the artistic means of expressions are decisive. The dancer and the musician who palm across the wood of the red bus in "Bussen"[7] let me feel like touching the wood with my own hands – the reason for it is my remembrance of the contact with ply wood.

Another example may be the player who is digging in the soil "Earth, Stick and Stone"[8] where I felt a sense of dirt under my own fingernails. Even the light has got its own materiality. That makes up the absurdity and poetry in the scene of the production "Hase Hase Mond Hase Nacht"[9]: The actress tickles the moon (the pool of light from the reflector) and the moon responds to it. Even the materiality of things and the players' physicalness on stage demands the physicalness of perception.

## Participation

The theatre for the youngest always needs to be a common artistic experience for the players and the children. This sentence may be the aesthetic imperative for the theatre for the youngest. Even if the observation of different performances brought more differences than similarities there is a basic assumption for successful working within theatre for the youngest: The necessity of a common experience of player and children. Particularly the player's attitude towards the audience comes to the fore.

Some theatre makers who are working for the youngest children have got experience in street theatre for example, and consequently a certain routine with the direct contact to a previously unknown audience that often comes together by accident. From this fact one could derive an ability which is a must within the theatre for the youngest: The ability to react on the slightest fluctuations of the spectators' mood and to re-build the communication balance. There from, the player has got to be skilled in terms of a specific sensibility for his audience.

---

7 "Bussen", *Whispering Space*, Oslo (Norway), Production: Bibbi Winberg, Dance: Hilde Rustad, Music: Joakim Strand.
8 "Erde, Stock und Stein", *HELIOS Theater* Hamm (Germany), Production: Laurent Dupont, Player: Michael Lurse, Music: Roman D. Metzner.
9 "Hase Hase Mond Hase Nacht", *Theater o.N.*, Direction: Andrea Kilian, Player, Scenery, Sound: Melanie Florschütz, Michael Döhnert.

Starting from this basic assumption there are many open questions that cannot be answered properly until today. How do players and spectators come to an interaction? Does it require a collective space where players and spectators interact (also physically)? [Can this 'playing together' also take place by the spatial confrontation and separation of the players and the spectators? Are there special needs concerning the scenography in the theatre for the youngest?]

Roughly speaking theatre returns to its origin, for instance to the 'ritual' from which yet in the ancient world some kinds of theatre originated. The occidental theatre has always been relating to those kinds of theatre. An example is the tendency to abandon the dissociation between player and spectator in the theatre for the youngest – a parallel to pre-civilizing kinds of theatre with their permanent changes of the roles between players and spectators. Insofar answers could be found by examining the phenomenon 'ritual'.

**Player**

It's noticeable that in the theatre for the youngest the actor is named as a 'player'. This indicates a basic activity especially for the theatre for the youngest: the play. In the performances usually no special motive is designed for the player's entry like in the exposition of the drama, e.g. The Player is just there. He is present on the stage or in the performance space. And he should be serious, real, honest and present according to artists who are doing theatre for the youngest.

From my point of view there are two possibilities. The first: The player doesn't personify any figure – he's just himself. The other: The player creates a figure but not of a dramatic kind. Such figures often have clownish traits but don't conform to the popular stereotype of a clown.

During the performance the spectator opens up himself to a presence of another being. He perceives this other being like he is being perceived himself. And his imagination allows him an access to the player's activities. The spectator does not identify with the player or the figure he meets. And that is indeed not the aim.

**Language**

The theatre for the youngest (like any theatre) is endued with many languages[10] and it is not reduced to the language of words. In the hierarchy of artistic means the verbal language is in most cases not the dominating one: this is a further difference compared to the text and literature dominated civic theatre. It is similar to everyday communication where only 15 percent of information is transmitted

---

10 Adequate to the hundred languages of children's, mentioned by Malaguzzi.

verbally. The biggest part of information is said to be transmitted by different forms of non verbal communication. This experience shows that the fact that the basic mastery of 'dramatic trade' alone can't be a guarantee for a felicitous performance in the theatre for the youngest.

Pictures, tones, sounds, movements, materiality and the body are emancipated means of expression in the theatre for the youngest. But often other means are dominant, like e.g. physical movement, dancing or musical forms. The hierarchy of the artistic means of expression is, even in the theatre for the youngest, not repealed. The medium of those forms of expression is the player. Thereby the theatre for the youngest is an art of minimalist kind, an art of the concentration of means but not an art of simplification.

## Rules

Every game needs rules! These rules of the game have to be flexible in the theatre for the youngest. There are stops and turns within the performance where those rules might be negotiated or set new completely by the players. An example could be the performance "Sous la table" with changing rules related to location and behaviour of the spectators. At the beginning the spectators are taking a seat on red pillows on the floor. They already have in view the oversized table which serves as the space for the performance. Later they have to sit down at this table to finally scrambling underneath of it. But the centre of the space remains reserved to the players who may be moving freely among and around the spectators.

In conjunction with the rules the limits are decisive as well. We have to distinguish between the limits which are apart from the performance's aesthetic and those which are set by the aesthetic. Both kinds of limits are defined externally by the players. They can't be manipulated by the children; but they are different in the way in which they will be communicated to the spectators.

The overall situation is set and can't be negotiated or be changed by the children. Therefore for the makers of theatre for the youngest the following questions might be of particular importance: How are the children received in the theatre? How are their parents who are both, spectators and those who accompany the children[11], familiarised with the rules?[12] If the observing of certain rules is the assumption for a successful collective artistic experience for players, children and parents, it's necessary to communicate those rules because they are

---

11 I am using the item in terms of 'leading the children' as to help and support them in their reception.
12 An approved method is, like in the theatre for children in general, the announcement before the performance, providing flyers or the personal conversation before the performance.

different from the conventions of the theatre which may be familiar to the parents.

In most production for the youngest children the rink (as the area for the performance) is clearly limited. However, the conventional theatre room, with its separation of the stage and the audience room, seems to be improper for this kind of theatre. So how can the limitation get perceivable and consequently accepted? Which conditions in respect of the room are necessary for an efficient theatre for the youngest? How does the room correlate the audience to the players? What is the importance between closeness and distance between players and audience?

The player provides first indications to the children about the limits which should be respected by the way he relates to the audience. Thereby, the most important question seems to be: How can the aesthetic communicate the limits which are inherent in the performance? This is at the same time a research assignment for the artists. Only they are able to define the rules and limits for their own chosen form and level of communication. So they are saving their own form of communication and respecting the child as a spectator.

Thereby, the question about the means of expression which are claiming distance and limits should be posed, like for example a poetic language which is totally different from everyday language or a pictorial abstraction. How does the performance's aesthetic claim the area for the players, the area for the children and the common area? This could be a clearly limited rink, a sound area (created by music) or the player's presence in a certain cruising radius. All those artistic means are setting psychological barriers which usually will be respected by the children.

The parents are the crucial instance that decides about the acceptance of those rules and limits. The mother, who decides that her weeping agitated child with its movements in the performance area is disturbing the collective theatre experience, feels it and is respecting these limits. The father who enters the stage area during the performance to take a photo of his child as a spectator misunderstands or does not understand at all the rules – he is ignoring them. The parents' behaviour is as an example for the children's behaviour during the performance.

Time and time again the question appears: When is a child disturbing the performance? This question acts on the assumption of the conventions of the civic theatre which requires the devotional and quiet spectator. But the question should be another: Where is the limit of the audience's attendance to keep the communication balanced?

In a different systematic, much of the described aspects may be assigned to the thoughts about the spectator's specific of the theatre for the youngest.

But it is interesting that the chosen focus on the aesthetic is bringing up discussions about the role and the specific of the spectator, each in a situation where it is demonstrative.

## Story

It's noticeable that the most productions of the theatre for the youngest can be described by means of the categories of the conventional dramaturgy (suspense, surprising turn, conflict). But they won't be used in their primal dramaturgical meaning.

The category of conflict is rather used in its general meaning. A dramatic conflict as a collision of two figures' interest (or groups of figures) hardly exists or doesn't exist at all. This fact is not astonishing because this category assumes figures and action that only exist contingently in the theatre for the youngest. The question may be: Are there no figures because there is no story? Or is there no story because there are no figures? How many stories does the theatre for the youngest need? How many stories do the little spectators need?

The theatre for the youngest is no theatre of illusions. The created artificial worlds are visible as art spaces. The creation of this special world are not veiled, they are rather shown. The players suggest a world and this suggestion is accepted by the spectators. Coevally, these special worlds form the basic and the foil for the spectator's imagination and fantasy. However, the theatre for the youngest doesn't miss the stories and neither the creation of illusions. But the stories are not told straight-line. They are based, more than in other kinds of theatre following rather conventional dramaturgies, upon the spectator's imagination.

Insofar the dramatic signs in the theatre for the youngest don't intend to constitute a special meaning. The soil in "Erde, Stock und Stein" is just soil and doesn't represent anything else than soil. The bowl in "Al di La"[13] is a bowl and doesn't mean anything else. The objects don't stand for anything else than as what they really are. But it's possible to make something else out of them. The soil is becoming a cake of sand; the reflector light in "Hase Hase Mond Hase Nacht" is becoming the moon. In both cases the material was used as means of expression to figure something.

Anyhow, every spectator (the child and the adult) faces his or her perception of things and objects with its experiences. Everyone sees a different story. There is certainly accordance if a means is used so clearly that it is not possible to interpret it elsewise. That can be shown explicitly in the performance "Gribouillie"[14]. We see the clownish figure on a journey, coming from elsewhere with his small cart, saying hello. And after drawing for us, cleaving some points on our noses and saying goodbye she is leaving to somewhere. What we all experienced has only been possible because our ways had crossed and we had stayed

---

13 "Al di la", *TAM Teatromusica*, Padova (Italy), Direction: Laurent Dupont, Players: Favia Bussolotto, Marco Tizianel.
14 "Gribouillie", *Compagnie Lili Désastre*, Marcé (Frankreich), Player: Francesca Sorgato.

together for some time. From where the figure comes, to where it leaves, who it could possibly be – everyone has to invent his own story about it.

The hands of the player in "Erde, Stock und Stein" digging in the soil are suddenly turning into two figures. And the suddenly they have appeared, the suddenly they are leaving and at the same time this episode is ending. I have seen primeval dinosaurs discovering, destroying and rearranging the earth. I assigned that meaning as a spectator with the corresponding experience. Somebody else might have seen something else. The player's and director's assumption of this scene was – as I heard after the performance – the description of ants.

Maybe a story will be necessary at the point when – in which way ever – figures are (episodically) established on stage. Someone who likes to tell a story is in need of figures. The production "Al di La" plays with the absence and presence of players and things. From its presence and absence the spectator may imagine a story. We can conclude that the theatre for the youngest has got an own dramaturgy.[15]

## Time

The theatre for the youngest has got its own handling with time and its own rhythm corresponding to the audience's rhythm. The rhythm of the players and the spectators is connected by the breath. A collective breath, especially to be taken up by the players to harmonise with the children, gives them a sense of security. Breath is keeping the suspense between player and audience. Suspense might be a further dramaturgical category which is realised in a different way in the theatre for the youngest than in the conventional theatre.

Besides the action following a special rhythm even the silence belongs to the theatre for the youngest – both the acoustic and the temporal silence. The repetitive moment, the repetition of scenes or of verbal answers is often to be found in the theatre for the youngest.

Theatre takes place in a new way and differently with every performance. No performance is like the other. That is true for every kind of theatre. While it is imaginable that the stage dominates the audience room in the ordinary theatre (also seen in practice), this may not happen in the "Theatre for Early Years". Neither the player nor the spectator may visit the performance with the attitude that they know how the communication between these both sides works. It will always be a common risk with the assumption of productive doubt.

---

15 In this case dramaturgy means the entirety of the performance structures.

# Why "Theatre for Early Years"?
## Memories and highlights of artistic experiences

*by Carlos Herans*

An old countrywoman talks to the prince. The action takes place on a stage, with a paper prop representing a house in the countryside. At a certain point a panel of the house, that corresponds to a chimney, falls towards the audience, the prince catches it and pushes it backwards and the action continues.

I ignore what was going on during that scene, but soon after this, the prince gave the old woman a bag full of money and she said: "Thank you, with this I will be able to fix my house, because it is falling to pieces".

I was five or six years old. It is one of my first childhood memories of theatres. And in my mind, this scene is very, very vivid. Why? I have wondered so many times. The answer is difficult. But some possible answers are: I was totally fascinated with the magic of the scene and I was witnessing real life and an imaginary reproduction of it.

Actually, I remember nothing of that show but that anecdote. I think that this intense impression can happen quite frequently when we perform for children. I also think that when we work for the early years, we place them within a sensible and symbolic universe that is related to their need of playing and exploring, which, in turn, plays a major role: it makes situations and characters, conflicts or fiction come true, and they develop in the present tense and allow young boys and girls to carry out an experiment on how to control that 'reality' emotional.

In that game, the universe is inhabited by characters, sounds, movements and plastic art, and everything is made for the children's fascination. We cannot forget that psychoanalytic theories have stressed the importance of such elaborations to build and maintain the Ego and as a way out of unconscious drives.

Even today it is plain that theatrical games during childhood are social games. According to several researchers, between two and five years children play following a non-written rule that is based on cooperating while playing, both while planning it and when players exchange their roles, as well as in the changes made in its structure. Isn't this the basis of many creative processes carried out by adults? As a consequence, symbolic games take social themes as a starting point: doctors, teachers, shops etc. And we should not forget that particular moment in children's development when the first steps in social exchange originate from self-centred games in which, through the imitation of manners, young boys and girls reproduce the behaviours of the adults that surround them.

In these age groups, the game played is deeply rooted in life itself. Acting – this is what we are talking about – is a way of living, a way of acquiring knowledge about life, neither for free nor taking the concepts conveyed by teachers as a starting point.

This game implies commitment among people. From one's self to one's self. From one's self to others, learning how to be ourselves and how to relate to, understand and get to know the others.

**Being someone else and telling it to others**

Being ourselves, pretending to be one or someone else, stems out from this 'being another' game, which is the basis of theatrical acting. At the beginning, we generally pretend to be those who surround us. We are mothers and fathers reproaching their children-puppets because they got dirty; feeding red brick dust or wet sand to their children with plastic spoons or with the bad mood of those who stand us, with the love with which they lull us – imitating our parents' arguments. We learn to be those who surround us through these elements of life, not only in a descriptive sense, but also in a symbolic and 'played' one.

Such fictional creations typical of childhood, such anxiety to disguise ourselves to be someone else and then become ourselves represent the root that nourishes theatre. Being someone else and telling it to others. It is a way to go beyond ourselves and enter spaces of game-fiction provided by the hole 'under the table'. Fantastic scenarios created from a chair in the kitchen turned into a space shuttle, a house, a table, a ship, – inhabited by the characters we have been building since we were very young "with the matter of which dreams are made", as Bogart would say in "The Maltese Falcon" (quoted here with Shakespearean certainty).

This matter and these characters, always the same and always different, will end up building our own character one day. Let me conclude this statement with a commonplace: this game is very important.

When I entered the theatre world I was engaged both in education and life – if they have ever been separate entities at any point, no matter how much educational systems actually invest on it. My theatrical experience was influenced by a direct contact with young boys and girls, having dedicated over ten years of my life to creating and developing theatrical workshops, games and dramatisations in an educational centre for different age groups.

The fact of being in touch with 'their' productions and the processes that follow their development is, together with the memories previously mentioned, part of that baggage of experiences, discoveries and emotions that led me to commit my efforts to staging, translating and adapting texts and to other theatrical tasks during the past 25 years, after teaching in schools.

Now I would like to briefly comment on a topic that in classrooms first, and, later, in the courses I held in professional training and other fields, was often discussed: children are so imaginative!

What meaning do we assign to the term 'imagination' in common language? It is generally intended as the ability to invent, imitate public figures (let us say artists), draw inspiration from daily events to create and tell imaginary situations.

Behind these phenomena there is the need to be like someone successful, socially acknowledged, loved, and the elaboration of situations children usually would like to live. In front of these events, adults, especially parents and some teachers, describe these events using the word 'imagination', adding that it is their children's or pupils' 'ability to imagine, to invent' and commenting on the fact that it disappears in adulthood.

It does not seem to me that this can determine the fact that a child is imaginative; we simply can deduce that there has been an imitation process, mainly guided by visual impulses, since they are usually fed TV characters who repeatedly appear on the small screen with all those linguistic and gestural clichés that can be easily mimicked.

## Playing the 'game of telling'

To elaborate concepts in an 'imaginative' way is instead a very different process, difficult to find in these age groups. What we usually witness in theatrical workshops is a first approach to this type of work; they are generally elliptic elaborations, with a very simple dramatic structure and they usually originate from the reality that surrounds them: family, school environment, other children, – all situations about which they can fantasise, normally within the boundaries given by their observations and experience.

This process cannot be objectively reproduced, because it is triggered unconsciously.

It is essential, however, that the reference framework is clear: we are playing the 'game of telling', which does not require major artistic skills. On the contrary, it simply means to put different and coherently developed stages together, relating to evolution, observation and expression. It is within this ever-enriching framework that, I believe, theatre for children plays an essential role.

Firstly, because it places the audience/children in front of a direct phenomenon that, by 'playing with fiction' and through its specific codes, can convey a whole universe of elaborations, – which in this case are, in fact, imaginary. That has a 'true' dimension because it is being reproduced here and now. Because from the point of view of both the themes treated and the elements staged, a show for this particular age group is an invitation for them to process what we are offering them, in accordance with their needs and abilities.

As far as I am concerned, I can say that I do not owe what I have learnt to the things I have studied; on the contrary, it has developed thanks to the fact of being in touch with the early years: *they* have been my teachers, the boys and girls that had to put up with me.

## Creating 'artistic creations'

The emotion that the theatrical performances and work I experienced with them has provided me, the same emotion an audience of children conveys when watching a show cannot be found in any of today's show for adults – apart from some rare exceptions. Perhaps this is because when I was working with them, we were not doing theatre. They were showing me how they fully live their life.

I also think that the role of parents and society should be to convey this emotion, to encourage the contemplation and observation of aesthetic and ethic proposals. Paying attention to the 'creations' of young boys and girls should be the public administrations' primary objective, in order for them to find their own cultural framework and take it as a starting point for building 'their' culture and enter it as adults with their own critical eye and ability to judge by themselves. We, the adults, like to call this 'artistic creations'.

If we follow this path, – a difficult one, especially for its limited social acknowledgement and for the frequent lack of acknowledgement among theatre professionals –, it is because in an ocean full of doubts, every time we start putting into practice our projects there is the intimate certainty that – to paraphrase a poet from my country – *theatre is a weapon loaded with future.*

# Education meets theatre?
## Pedagogical remarks about the role of arts in early childhood

*by Ana Lúcia Goulart de Faria and Sandra Regina Simonis Richter*

"In the unbeginning there was the verb.
Only later on came the delirium of the verb.
The delirium of the verb was at the beginning, there where
the child says: I hear the colour of the birds.
The child does not know that the verb 'hear'
does not work for colours, but for sound.
So if a child changes the function
of a verb, it delirates.
And so.
In poetry, the voice, which is the voice of the poet,
which is the voice that brings about births –
The verb has to get a delirium
...
Science can classify and name the organs
of a song thrush, but it cannot measure its enchantments.
Science cannot calculate how many horses
of power there are in the enchantments of a song thrush
Who accumulates too much information
Loses the power of guessing: divinare.
The song thrushes divine." (Manoel de Barros)

We will discuss here the emergence of a pedagogy which contemplates very early childhood as a subject to rights and therefore, as a subject having the right to be educated by graduated professionals in the children's collective of day care centres, through the recovery of art, which is already present in the Greek *paidea* (science, art and technique). We will first discuss 'the early learnings', as considered by philosophers and thinkers, who are interested in human life and in its overflowing art. We will make a criticism of the scholarising of pedagogy, which is grounded on regular sciences, focused on analytical teaching, centred on the teacher and on the transmission of knowledge as the only way of guaranteeing the right to education.

The highlight here is given to poetical imagination, to the pleasure and to the complexity of learning, to the right to beauty, to non-verbal communication. This evokes a pedagogy which does not separate experience from knowledge, nor the body from the mind, thinking, and action in the world. Problematising the scientific bases of pedagogy and its structural technicism – didatics –, we are trying, with art, to fill the gap of teacher training, aiming at early childhood pedagogy.

Therefore, this text, written by two women researchers of children up to three years old, aims at creating the interlocution between art, education and very early childhood, and aims at overcoming our own gaps of pedagogical training as well. But this encounter also seeks to problematise the myth of free imagination as an ornament of pedagogy, as well as the myth of neutral science, which guarantees the right of children to education and their recognition as a citizen even without being aware

> "that it can be a manner of capturing and of premature scholarisation, in the sense of disciplinarisation, normalisation of the body, of the words and gestures, in the production of a determined type of apprentice, and bringing, thus, a rejection to the alterity and to the differences that children announce, as such." (Abramowicz 2003: 16)

## Poetry and Interpretation

A child coming into the world soon launches into the insatiable movement of learning: invention and existence adhere; the unpredictable happens, makes and forms itself. Since the child is deprived of concepts and ideas of mundane things, the child establishes a direct relationship with its surroundings. The child develops a primal, poetical look, seduced by admiration, enchanted by novelty. Imagination becomes an intense desire to see and integrate ordinary details, which, by defying the familiar, demands becoming a fabulous operator of languages. The fictional emerges, thus, as an amplification of the act of deciphering and interpreting the world to make it intelligible. Thus for Gaston Bachelard, a poet is one who preserves the direct manner of a child in his mind. In each poet is a childhood preserved in language. In a child, the poetical emerges as the act of learning to question and value what has been lived, to fictionalise it; as a gradual – multitemporal – manner for the body to complexify language experiences of belonging and participating in the world.

Approaching childhood and art is simultaneously fascinating and tense. Both configure the shadow that pursues and corrupts the clarity of logos in its oppositions of the sensible and intelligible, between body and intellect, between the playful and the lucid. The ambiguity of both seduces reason, in the uncomfortable permanent conflict which theoretical rationality maintains with the imagetic universe, and their diverse ways of happening. Childhood and art, sympathetic in their respective movements of opening themselves to life, to the unpredictable, and the novelty of initiating movement in the world, both question pedagogy in its generalized disenchantment, through the poetical power of the body to produce, borrow, extract, invent, multiply, attribute, magnetise the world with significances.

Disenchantment with mundanity, and with the dimension of shared life, emerges from the pedagogical belief that a child must be taught to listen and look, without learning to feel and to have 'spontaneous ideas'. Seriousness and boredom, ways of pedagogising the sensible and simplifying the intelligible, make childhood education converge in a moment of learning to stanch what is lived, turning it into an immovable, unchangeable reality: an absurd realism against the turmoil of life, which reduces the real to the word that names and explains it. A mostly cognitive pedagogy forgets that, from birth, the body is already irremediably committed to the complexity of learning to extract and formulate senses, since it must imagine, must run risks of exposing and signifying itself in mundane living. What is important to retain here is the poetical power of imagination, mobilising the body and favouring constitution of thought into act, complexifying the body in the alternation of the real and the fictional.

The phenomenologies of creative imagination in Gaston Bachelard, of the body in Maurice Merleau-Ponty and of action in Paul Ricoeur, enable us to affirm that imagination is not disordered – a ghostly vestige of visual perception. Rather, it projects dynamics, finds all of its transfigurative force as it places the body in languages, and engenders narratives which mould actions into mundane living. From this perspective, imagination does not end in the mind; it is an act fed by the operating body at the instant of taking the initiative in action: a mode of the body to learn to complexify experiences, which can perform the coupling[1] between imagination and reason, between the sensual and the mental (s. Richter 2005).

The phenomenologies of body, image, and action, point to the formative importance of the enchantment experience of the first learnings; a 'know-how' – fingere[2] – which, from childhood, constitutes the boundary from which we learn to interpret and engender actions to give things another course. This is a matter of denying the reductive scission between 'I think' (mind) and 'I can' (body), pointing to childhood education as a time and place to learn enchantment with the power of operating languages; as a formative space of temporalisation of the childish body, as it learns to complexify itself in and with the world, through the different ways of recounting and redoing with others what has been lived. Learning, thus, implies not only exploring, but also reconfiguring reality, being able to remake our own steps, to retell something we want to share.

For Ricoeur the common character of human experience emerges from its temporal quality. Just as everything we tell and retell takes time and arrives in time, so everything that is developed in time can be retold. Narrative marks us, articulates us, makes us understand and take hold of temporality, because the early learnings result from fictional reports. The importance of the first learnings

---

1 The term coupling here is used to affirm the inseparability between the relational and the existential senses contained in the act of settling, transforming and transfiguring images through the operating body in the world.

2 Etymologically, fiction originates from the Latin term 'fingo', which means figurate, format and model clay with the hands. Fiction is fingere, it is to make. Fingere (pretend) does not mean to deceive or to lie, but rather to elaborate intelligible structures.

is in the emergence of a complex process of learning to disclose the secrets of languages, as they arrange and rearrange the real through the narrative intensity of a body enacting the world.

> "Every thought that results into an act capable of transfiguring reality, as it animates things and lends them a poetical existence, transforms the thought and the mundane happenings: in the simultaneousness which engenders thoughts, invents realities. Poetics emerges precisely in the daring or in the astuteness of a thought which is not pleased by re-enacting – or re-producing – the world, but rather rejoices in improvising other worlds as it takes the initiative in acting and as it elaborates coordination between actions which produce effects in the real by the poetical power of opening to other dimensions of reality. Here is the compelling commitment of pedagogy to favour learnings which retrieve the productive power of poetical imagination to rationality." (Ricoeur 1986: 14)

When we withdraw from the term 'art'[3] the cultural varnish, which has reduced 'art' to only the realised works and the contemplation of beautiful works, we achieve a broader sense – a poetical sense of moulding silent worlds – related to the lucid and playful power of different languages, engendering unique senses in the collective, regardless of their ways of manifestation and concretization. This involves removing from the notion of art the historically demarcated pertinence which is limited in space and time to European civilisation between the seventeenth and eighteenth centuries and today: so as to reclaim the vibrant link between languages and life.

Both art and childhood point to a radical beginning which gives things another course: a gesture, a mark, an incision in the already interpreted world. By acting as if there were not already a signalised sense, it is invented in the amazement and admiration of what has not been felt, or seen or named. Therefore, the intention is not to hold a discourse on art and childhood, but rather to establish a closeness of mutual learnings. And thereby, to re-learn the poetical pact of bringing about birth: through this, to recover the delirium of the beginnings in the human adventure, of facing the unknown and uncertain.

Reaching back to repercussions of the first learnings in the childish body requires a physiological return to the experienced domain, of the pre-reflexive, of the immediate: the operating sensible body as a link which launches us into the unpredictable and shared experience of our corporal existence in only one world. Observing the efforts of the newborn's body in its eyes opening for the first time, the beauty of the silent experience of this primal look, the slow movements, the hesitant attempts to accomplish the mysterious launching into the world, causes us therefore to question: what does the child see?

---

3 The term art here refers to the gestural material action which makes things appear in the world, the captured action executing itself as a transfigurating transforming of materialities through the sensory operating body; capable of making it into what it is not through the different languages.

Perhaps this is the first act to demand the initiative of turning the halo of visibility into images of what has never been seen, to extract senses from the seeing body, which sees itself seeing: the action of being born unto things, which in itself is the action of mixing with the world. Mixing with the mundane visibility of light, colours, reflections, and shadows, requires a whole visibility to be created in the body. In order to make these visible, it is necessary to learn to see, to take hold of vision, welcoming its echo in the body, in the very act of redoubling it into another visibility: that which makes me seen from the outside, which settles me inside the visible.

**Miration and admiration**

The first act of approach is transformed by irremediable distance. I take distance, but not without my temporality. Opening the eyes, and looking, with all the sensations of a body inaugurating into the world, as it puts into motion images already extracted from pregnancy and birth. It is the first initiative, after the intensity of the body's exigencies for the effort of being born: the intense movement of leaving the womb. It is always the body that learns. And before vision, it is through hearing in and from the uterine space that the first images emerge. For Bachelard (1989: 9), "it is in the flesh, in the organs, that the early images arise. These early material images are dynamic, active; they are linked to simple wishes, amazingly rudimentary" which cause something to begin, to initiate; to enter the world and inscribe thoughts and actions in it, producing links of belonging and participating.

The decision to start something points to what Merleau-Ponty (2004: 16) highlights as the interlacement between vision and movement, which makes the operating and actual body a part of the visible world. It is about 'lending the body to the world', since seeing is not a decision from the spirit, it does not emerge from 'conscience', but rather it originates from the body as a sensation which, silently, says "I can" to the world. Vision is the conquest of a body coming into being, and sliding along the surfaces of an inalienable presence, which is already always 'there', before reflexion, before problematisation. – It is the undivided being. Therefore, as opposed to the Cartesian belief, Merleau-Ponty (ibid: 30) states that, if there is no vision without thinking, "thinking is not enough for seeing", since vision originates from thought initiated with and by the body. Here the act of looking – gazing, *miration* or *admiration*[4] – emerges

---

[4] According to Chauí (1988: 36), there are variations in the look: "de mirus (amazing, strange, marvellous) come from mirari (get amazed, look with amazement, gaze, look and admirari (look with respectful amazement, with veneration). Here, paralised with astonishment, the look sees a miracle, miraculum, and prodigious wonders, mirabilia. By its very name, a miracle belongs to the field of looking and is destined to vision".

from inside the body, is born at the instant of taking the initiative to become gesture in the world.

In this powerful act of looking, the baby encircles the things and approaches them, at the same time that it withdraws from them in order to scrutinise the sensations in its body, which arouse the fact of being inextricably mixed with the world and with the others. In this sensory movement, which makes it simultaneous to things and to others, there is always something that comes before: the experience of deciphering. We do not have another way of learning about the world, other than affirming its indetermination at every moment it turns into us. As Deleuze (1998: 10) said, "there is no learner who is not 'the egyptologist' of something", who does not face enigmas without deciphering them, since it is the enigmas which give meaning to the solutions, and not the opposite. From this perspective, learning is an infinite task, as there is nothing prefigured, foreseen, predetermined to learn.

With first vision, for Merleau-Ponty (1999: 146), "there is the initiation, that is, there is not a position of a content, but rather the opening of a dimension which can never be closed again", since it will be texture which will tone the existence from then on, as it will turn the body into a measurer of captive things in the world. Here, learning is not a synthesis, let alone the cumulative process of what is perceived, but rather a bodily metamorphosis into the temporal experience of becoming in the simultaneousness that the world gradually becomes for the child and for the others. This is a metamorphosis which extracts learning as it forges thinking, in the opening of a beginning to achieve the limit of the visible and enlarge the field of visibility.

Such an opening supposes learning to have vision: namely, learning to operate vision silently, in order to open nameable and sayable languages, engendering a particular historical process as it emerges as corporeal temporalisation[5]. Time happens in the body and modifies it. For Agamben (2002), that is why we have a childhood: because we are not born already speaking and we have to learn to install a language history in the body. In-fan is the one who does not have a voice, who is not born speaking; who is learning to speak and to be spoken of, to see and to be seen. Only in this condition, can history not be the continuous progress of speaking humanity along linear time: it is an interval, discontinuity, interruption of the thought, of the future. Since we have to learn to be in languages, we have to learn the actions of the body: which means collective existence.

In Agamben (2002: 93-94), lack of language is the condition of our emergence and, thus, the course of learning is the same for every child: all of us have

---

5 The enactive focus of Francisco Varela (1997), inspired by Merleau-Ponty, affirms the cognition as a corporalised act where the body is conceived simultaneously with the physical structure and as a lived experiential structure, that is, both biologically and phenomenologically.

to learn to speak (and to project vision) with others. Freed from subjective conditioning which defines origin as a point in a chronology, as an initial cause devising a time before and a time after, "the origin of a certain being cannot be historicised because it is itself historicising; it is this that founds the possibility of something as 'history'" (ibid: 91). Everyone has to engender speech, since everyone has to learn expression in speech. Childhood is not natural or universal.

## Speaking and acting

Agamben (2002: 103) highlights childhood as a condition of history, starting from the difference between language and discourse, between semiotics and semantics; in which man cannot enter language as a system of signs without radically transforming it into semantics, without constituting it into discourse. This radical transformation, which affirms childhood as an original dimension of man, as a human power of speaking and being spoken, implies denying a politically dominant view based on the chronological axis, and on rationalist discourse of a progressive psychological process which places children on the zero pole. Such view allows division into different groups – which vary according to the theory – towards the end of life. This point situated at zero legitimates not only engendering phases and developments, sustained on the deficit plane in relation to the logical-mathematical adult plane, but also authorises 'specialisation' of areas of knowledge in order to 'administer' these age groups.

Arendt (2004) contests this naturalisation of the chronological time course, arguing that the only resistance to the fatality of a life limited by birth and death is action. Acting is capable of interrupting the inexorable and automatic course of everyday life towards death, because it can interrupt it, and begin something new: "a perennial contradiction in which man, despite being bound to die, is not born to die, but to begin" (Arendt 2004: 258).

Action – speaking and acting – while a regularity of the infinitely improbable (S. ibid), releases us from condemnation to the unceasing cycle of the vital process and its inexorable laws, since it is exercised directly among humans in mundane living. The wish to be among others, in action and in discourse[6], allows us to initiate new, endless processes, which make plurality the condition of human action[7]. This capacity of initiating something, with all the surprise and unpre-

---

6 For Arendt (2004: 191), "if action, as a beginning, corresponds to the fact of birth, if it is the effectuation of the human condition of natality, the discourse corresponds to the fact of distinction and it is the effectuation of the human condition of plurality, namely, of living as a distinct singular being among equals".

7 It is worthy pointing out that in Arendt (2004: 17-19), "The conditions of the human existence – life itself, natality and mortality, the mundanity, the plurality and planet Earth – will never 'explain' what we are, for the simple reason that they never condition us in an absolute mode."

dictability inherent to everything that begins, has its in birth. Only the newcomer, the newborn, has the capacity of initiating something, namely, of initiative. For Arendt (ibid: 259), it is the birth of new human beings and their new beginnings – the actions that they can have as a result of having been born – that can render faith and hope in the world. The promise is in the rupture of continuity. Each child who arrives in the world maintains it and alters it, is part of it, as well as a foreigner. Each child to be born introduces discontinuity in the narration of the human time: every beginning – or irruption of existence – is delirious.

It is what Valéry (1999: 203) reaffirms as he points out that a child at birth brings along several possibilities. After a few months, the child learns to speak and to walk: two types of action which to which he can resort, in accidental circumstances, extracting what the child can do in response to his needs or to his imagination. In learning to walk, the child will also discover how to dance. The child has invented, and at the same time discovered, a second order utility for his limbs, a generalisation of the formula of movement. While walking is, in short, a very monotonous and not especially perfectible activity, this new form of action, dancing, effectively allows an infinity of creations, variations, and configurations.

The poet questions whether an analogical process could not occur with the word. He thus concludes that the child will discover and invent the power of reasoning. The poet points out that children, having a different language-corporality, do not imagine or perceive things as adults do.

**Experiences and learnings**

Because the body brings a history – a corporalised time – one cannot 'teach' children to see, let alone imagine, think and act like us, adults. This requires differentiated times, since children approach the world and the unknown in a different manner from adults: in their inexperience – another temporality – they approach it enchanted, amazed, surprised, and investigating. They approach it in the scope of sensory knowledge, which emerges from corporal roots: a primal knowledge, founding, corporal, direct, prior to the processes of reasoning and reflexion, which requires encountering the qualities of the world. Sounds, colours, textures and odours put us in the world, and are made corporeal by us. To provoke sensory excess, a direct relationship, it is necessary to share the experience. Sharing the experience is being together in a certain time; it is sharing a determined rhythm, its intervals, its resonances and repercussions.

An affirmation like Merleau-Ponty's (1999: 23) that a child can act and perceive prior to thinking, that a child can begin to place his dreams in things, his thoughts in others, and to form a common block of existence with them, – where the perspectives of each one cannot be distinguished yet, since they are mixed in the encounters of the bodies – cannot be ignored by pedagogy in the attempt to elucidate experience analytically. It is not important here to know how to elucidate dilemmas, but rather to highlight the opening to thinking, without excluding the concealing of the world (ibid: 38).

To underline that not all the learnings are on the same plane, Francastel (1993: 12) calls attention to Valéry's observation on the distinction of the first step, over all the following ones. For the poet, the "first time" not only implies lengthening previously prepared gestures, but introducing irreversibility in the child's conduct. Walter Benjamin (1995: 105), in "One-Way Street", contributes to our comprehension of the unrepeatable, as learning something that 're-dimensions' us, when he says: "I can dream just like in the past I learned to walk. However, this does not help me at all. Today I can walk; nevertheless, I will never learn it again".

The time of childish corporality[8] is the place of intense learnings. It is here, and at no other age, that a child will learn to move, walk, hold and touch things, like and dislike, cry, laugh, run, jump, fall, fear and marvel. Fundamental learnings of a body, that will also learn culturally to look, speak, sing, hear, draw, mold, dance, paint, count, make-believe. Rapidly or slowly, the child will learn the complexity of acting and being moved, in touching others, learning to interpret and to make decisions, to imagine and to narrate, to relate and to value. The child learns to turn into what it is and can become, within the flow of living with others. The child intensely experiences privileged moments of learning – for this is the moment of extreme plasticity – unique in its happening: the moment of the first time!

A happening for the first time is distinct from others, in that it cannot be learned again! The first time is irreplaceable in its singular corporal happening, for the intensity of expectation, of novelty, of the unexpected causes the emergence of a rupture with what is already made corporeal, renewing it. The body is always a reservoir.

The first learnings are irreversible; they can only be repeated. Repetition, here, is not used in the usual sense of doing the same thing, but rather as a re-feeding, which implies the continuous re-elaboration of what has happened before. Experiences are not only immediately present in repetition, but they also re-feed other coming experiences. In the philosophy of difference, "repetition is only a necessary conduct and it is fundamented only with relation to what cannot be substituted" (Deleuze 1988: 22). From this perspective, it is not the mere addition of the second and the third experience to the first one, but of "raising

---

8 For Merleau-Ponty, as well as for Francisco Varela (1997), the term corporality has a double meaning: it comprehends the body as a lived experiential structure and the body as a context or a scope of the cognitive processes. It is to affirm the body as a dimension which is simultaneously biological and phenomenological.

the first time to any 'power'. Under this relation of power, repetition is reverted, interiorising itself" (ibid).

If there is something every child does on a regular basis, it is to resort to the conduct of repeating movements, gestures, sounds, and words. This is a behaviour which, in Deleuze's words (1988: 22), may be "the echo of a more secret vibration, of an interior deeper repetition in the singular which animates him/her". This conduct arises in the flow of the bodies' encounter, invigorating and impregnating the history of a body constituted by the repetition of gestures that were already there in the first place.

To be involved means to be taken in by the occurrence. We only learn when we are entire in what we are doing. And to be committed also involves pains and frustrations. Therefore, it is worthy of notice that involvement is not supposed to be a motivational approach for learning; that is, one does not learn only what gives pleasure or is pleasant. Deleuze (1998: 46) understands that disappointment – itself plural and invariable – is a fundamental component of search or learning, since every learning is an interpretation of signs or hieroglyphs. This implies understanding that "we do not become carpenters unless we become sensible to the signs of wood, as well as doctors to the signs of illness" (ibid: 10). Therefore, in each field of signs we become disappointed when we do not reach the expected secret. For Deleuze, only a few things do not disappoint us at the first time we do them, "because the first time is the time of inexperience; we are not able to distinguish the sign from the object: the object interposes and confuses the signs" (ibid: 46).

In childhood, says Bachelard (1989: 122), the fear blocks curiosity. This relationship between fear and curiosity, accompanying every initial action in the world, is reactivated or restructured in the very act of ingenuity; that is, it is revived in the first observations, those which start something. The sensible threshold of knowledge is paradoxically situated between the intense interest in acting and the fear of acting. On this threshold, interest wavers, is disturbed, returns, and reveals strange subtlety, when the waves of fear and curiosity are amplified by imagination and reality is not present to moderate them.

Observing the tension, in this moment of the entry of the first learnings into the collective, involves considering and welcoming the difficulties lived, the obstacles each child faces, the attempts and efforts to surpass and overcome them, the necessary and the needless mistakes, the fear and happiness before the astonishment of novelty, which is the unknown. In this experiential process of the conducts in living together coming into being, the child learns to re-dimension what has already been felt – what has been made rhythmic in the body – fabricating and fictionalising. The child learns to make a decision to begin something to become a gesture in the world.

In Merleau-Ponty (1999a), the operating sensory body – the "I can" – is not open by itself, but through its own opening to other bodies and to the world, since pure acting would be contradictory. I am settled in mundane experience before I can think. In this sense, I do not represent the world, I am adhered to it. We gradually become, within the simultaneity that the world becomes for us and for others. The world will not remain quiet: it disquiets us, forces us to touch it, to move it, to make it within ourselves. It is because children like and need to move and touch things, to fiddle with and provoke the world, – to name it again, through gestures and words which open fractures in it, baptising and engendering senses when they still have none, – that artistic things are so relevant in the everyday life of early childhood.

## Questions and investigations

The poet offers the educator another voice, another look at educational acts and at the pedagogical word. He offers another discourse which seeks to show – but not say – against the distinct dominantation of scientific and technological reason. Poetical logic does not suppose explanations of the world, but rather actions in the world. It establishes a happening in the world, not a discourse on the world. Creating and inventing presupposes questioning and not answering, supposes investigates and not explaining, demands actions in the world, not only its contemplation. To consider learnings which can emerge from a poetical relationship with the world and others, is to make a claim for educational actions which will allow children joy first and 'understanding' afterwards. The affirmation denies the conception of a given, fixed reality, which must be consumed in order to affirm it as a temporal dimension of living, co-produced from the unpredictability of the transforming encounter between body, words and images of the world. This affirmation does not consume knowledge of is the world, but rather favours learnings which act in the world.

As Merleau-Ponty (1999) observed, a child understands much beyond what it can say and responds far beyond what it can define. Also, with an adult, things do not happen in a different fashion. Agreeing with the statement that we can understand what we cannot know yet, supposes that decisions and hesitations can both be formulated within the operation of the body coming into being over the world. However, this also implies facing, beyond the rooted conception of childhood as a chronological "phase" to be modelled and overcome by the accumulation of "teachings", the whole of a philosophical tradition sustained by the suspicion of sensory experience, of the enacted body, of imagination, of daydreaming, of the distracted look and of the marvelled hearing.

In opposition to the pedagogic sense, it is not the mind that accumulates learnings! It is bodily metamorphoses coming into temporal being which actualise learning. Here, learning is not a performed synthesis, let alone a cumulative process of past perception: it is, rather, a metamorphosis as the body opens to the temporal experience of its own beginning. It is worth emphasising that the metamorphosis process is delicate, as it implies a radical bodily change, though without loss or destruction: the whole being transforms itself even as it is maintained and preserved. It is a temporal, historical, never-ending process of the movement of the body in its conquest for other movements.

This transfiguring dynamic makes the body learn to act in other ways because it has been altered in its metamorphoses. Metamorphosis, in Bachelard (1997), is a way of immediately concretising a vigorous act: the conquest of another movement, another time. Therefore, they are not acts of overcoming, but rhythmical acts, which last in their discontinuities. Only by being discontinuous can they be rearranged; they can always start 'again', and thus inaugurate other gestures. The body moves, dislocates, invents, and sediments gestures. The recursiveness temporalises in the repetition itself: it invents, restarts, resumes, reinvents, complexifies into updates which engender gestural – and imagetic – repertoires, bringing movements into being, which gradually differentiate us. Here there is no symbolism or reduction of the psychological; the individuation process originates from the dynamics between repetition and difference (s. Deleuze 1988). It is the body before the verb.

In Bachelard's words (1994: 132), "the large rhythms mark human life": they mark it and sign it. This rhythmic mark of ours, this temporal accord which links us to the early learnings in childhood, the first-time world, Bachelard (1988: 119) designates as a poetical accord, demonstrating that "childhood remains in us as the beginning of profound life, of a life which is always related to the possibility of restarting. Everything that begins in us in the clarity of a beginning is a craziness of life". Childhood remains in us, because the poetical accord between primal images connects us to the world when revived by our reserves of enthusiasm, making us trust in the world in order to take the initiative to remake them. Poetry remains, because it reforms the discontinuities to which our affective resonances-repercussions render coherence, or continuity. Thus images, which become enlaced and lost, are elevated, presenting the realism of the fictional. For Rancière (2005: 58) "the real must be fictionalised to be thought"[9] and it is only through this reference as a producer of fiction, that the human experience, in its profound temporal dimension, does not cease to be refigured.

---

9 Rancière (2005: 58-59) warns that "this proposition must be distinguished from the whole discourse – whether positive or negative – according to which everything would be 'narrative', with alternations between 'big' and 'small' narratives. ... It does not mean that everything is fiction. ... It does not mean, thus, that 'History' is only made of stories that we tell each other, but it simply means that the 'reason for stories' and the capacities of acting as historical agents are interconnected. Politics and art, as well as the knowledges, build up 'fictions', that is, material rearrangements of signs and images, of relationships between what is seen and what is said, between what one does and what one can do".

Through imagination, we reach fiction as an astute and subtle antidote for the inevitable disjunction between the limits of our reality and of our excessive appetites. Thanks to imagination, we can be more, and can be others, without failing to be ourselves. We can dissolve and multiply, living many more lives beyond the ones we have, and beyond the ones we could live if we remained confined to only one reality. Daring – and running risks – belong to thinking, through the craft of languages; never pure or isolated from temporal presence in the world. As Serres reminds us, (2001: 354), "when language is transformed, everything is transformed", namely, the conquest of another movement or gesture, another image or word, broadens our comprehension of things, as it forges a widening of the horizon of existence.

From this perspective, *how* one imagines is more instructive – or formative – than what is imagined. Not so as to "acquire" or "accumulate knowledge", but rather, so that we learn other fashions of shaping fictions, which allow us to overcome the contingencies given by the place or time of our birth. As Pascal Quignard states,

> "I do not know anything more despicable than a man who is not able to escape his place of birth and detach himself from the ties that have been imposed on him by obedient, family, social, impersonal and dumb terror of his early years." (apud Bárcena 2004: 13)

Here, perhaps, is the most disturbing challenge children pose for pedagogy: the right to animate things and render them a poetical existence, in their language conquest of gaps between real life and fabricated life. In this opening space, a child learns to resist to what is excessively real, to initiate gestures that expose the child to the unknown and the uncertain. It is in this opening space to bodily metamorphoses that the poetical resides, with its power to expose us to the invisible – to the shapeless, to what has not yet been thought.

To recover the productive power of imagination for rationality, for deciphering and engendering senses which produce effects on the real, from learning in early childhood, is to emphasise the formative dimension of the processes of learning, to fictionalise what has been lived in order to put oneself into motion and to move toward a future[10]. It is to reclaim the right to experience a marvelling – a fascinated happiness – in early admiration of the plasticity of the world, which convoke the child's body to move, to launch itself into action as a strategy of a shared thought with the world. Above all, however, it implies a courageous critical attitude, which is our very challenge as teachers and researchers of very young children.

---

10 Bachelard (1989: 18), maintains that "with its living activity, imagination detaches us at the same time from both the past and reality. It opens itself to the future".

## Philosophy and aestetics

> "The opposite of a truth is not necessarily a lie"
> (Bohr)
> "Art exists because life does not suffice"
> (Ferreira Gullar)

The right of young children to education is a different right from the right to obligatory education. Different, as well, was the struggle to achieve it. The most recent right to education in day care centres for children up to three years old has innovated teacher training. Until then, those who exercised this position were informal child-care workers, nurses, social welfare assistants and, sometimes, even pedagogues; but these, who only cared for and looked after the children, were educating them without any scientific (or artistic) references of education. Therefore, on the one hand, pedagogy was not seen as an applied psychology; on the other hand, those pedagogical informal practices were gradually developed by professionals (with or without a degree) who very often focused on animation and manipulation, as opposed to didactics and the mere transmission of knowledge. Since then, it has become possible to think of a pedagogy of process, rather than a pedagogy of result.

Childhood education is not centred on the lesson, on teaching, on the figure of the teacher, on the binomial teaching-learning. Childhood education is focused on childhood experience, on the process, rather than on the product. The day care centre teacher is a teacher of children, not a teacher of school subjects.

What do we learn and what do we teach in pedagogy courses so that we can work and deal with children who do not yet speak, or walk, or read, or write? What do we learn about zero- to three-year-old children, beyond the scientific approach, which is predominantly psychological and usually isolates mind from body? How do children, from a very young age, build up knowledge and speech among themselves? How does the production of children's peer cultures happen, in this collective space of education in the public sphere (complementary to the private family sphere), with professional teachers who create appropriate conditions, organising space and time? In actual fact, our profession is being invented: the teaching profession in early childhood education should be integrated into science, art and technique, thus overcoming a pedagogical scientific technicality, without falling into pragmatism. Therefore, it is important to rescue its philosophical and aesthetical bases.

This has to do with constructing a childhood pedagogy from within the collective of very young children, which is based on the characteristics they project. Pedagogy, as a science of practice, demands an interdisciplinary effort, overcoming fragmentation of thought, permanently articulating theory and practice.

Research on the children's collective in day care centres, – and this is the great discovery of the twentieth century, carried out since the 1970s –, demonstrates that children learn even when adults do not intend to teach (s. Gunnarson 1994). Therefore, there must be a curriculum for childhood education in continuity – day care centre (0 to 3 years old) and pre-school (4 to 6) – and also it is necessary to integrate with primary school education and build a curriculum for a childhood pedagogy focused on children up to ten years old, taking into consideration their age specifics. Teacher theoretical training must be widened, without antagonising playful culture and the cultures of writing; there must be deep training in art, as well, which will provide attention to the several sophisticated forms of organisation of the body and thought during childhood, different from the powerful organisation achieved with writing. This must be simultaneous in the graphocentric societies.

> "We must stop thinking of educating through the teaching of ready curricula. We should privilege the self-learning of children and find with them the curricula and the fields of experience[11]. And, in this pursuit, have the contributions from the families. If we, adults, collaborate by discussing, thinking and researching detached from any sort of acquiescence, then we can offer our children a valuable model. This is what we try to do. ... *Seeing, touching and demonstrating is something extraordinary for a pedagogy which, frequently, on the contrary, simulates, conceals and limits itself to words only.*"
> (Malaguzzi apud Ambeck-Madsen 1992: 19 [Highlighted by us]).

In the 1960s, working, educating, and observing very young children, the late Italian Loris Malaguzzi sought from other fields of knowledge new dialogues and interpretations of the world of the children, and the world of the adults. Thus, he retrieved the aesthetic dimension in the form of production of human knowledge, and proposed the creation of the atelier for the organisation of pedagogic work in day care centres and pre-schools. One can say that this pedagogy has its fundament in art, in addition to science, which is permanently problematised[12]. For this purpose, Brunet and Dewey (among others) are his interlocutors.

> "Art is learned outside art, drawing is not only learned by drawing – certainly there is the need for learning techniques; however, one can learn both by drawing or by doing other things ... and, on the other hand, logic is also learned through drawing, projecting and building ... Art wears everyday clothes, not Sunday clothes." (Malaguzzi apud Rabitti, 1999: 149)

---

11 These are the fields of educational experience, according to the new trends of Italian children's schools in 1991: A) body and movement, B) discourses and words, C) space, order, measurement, D) things, time, nature, E) messages, forms and media, F) the self and the other. For children aged 0-3 years old in day care centres, the Italians Borghi and Guerra propose: A) perception and movement, B) gesture, image, words, C) problems, attempts, solutions, D) society and nature, E) the self and the other.
12 On art and education, Malaguzzi maintains a permanent interlocution with Bruner, who is still a friend of Reggio Emilia's children. He also maintained a dialogue, among others, with Dewey and Freinet.

## Relations and differences

From this perspective, in which pedagogy shows its political side, the atelier updated the Italian culture of image, – generating, not a separated space where it is comfortable to paint, to draw, to sculpt, to build gadgets, etc., and where one can get dirty and messy, but rather – generating the conjunctive work of the *atelierista*, the teacher and the children. In this tripartite, there is potential for the integrated development of the hundred languages, as Malaguzzi would say. That is: the construction of all human dimensions and, hence, of all forms of expression and communication of being in the world. This process represents a break in the methods of traditional pedagogy, which must be revolutionized in order to contemplate the broadness of childhood: observation and documentation are inseparable in the atelier.

> "The atelier supposes a physical transgression: according to Rodari's idea, it would be '... a dialogue which interrupts the so-called educative normality'. Malaguzzi had already commented: there is too much normality in the school. The atelier invites children and adults to try, to provoke, to search, to play with madness." (Hoyuelos 1998: 7)

The modernists, in the early twentieth century, already said that children are inventive; that when they express this inventiveness, for instance, in drawings, they (re)invent even perspective (Gobbi 2004). Recent researches have shown that children are communicators *par excellence*, they are story and culture builders, they are capable of multiple relations and are not *alumni* – without light –, rather, they are capable of sophisticated forms of organisation of thinking, and of manifesting different manners of expression, even prior to reading and writing. Therefore, another, just as sophisticated, form of teacher training is necessary (training + research = innovation), as well as a childhood pedagogy which is not only synonymous with reading and writing. A pedagogy which will not use the word as a path for knowledge (Malaguzzi 1998), with teachers who are capable of working mixed ages, in pairs of adults without a hierarchy, 'literate' in the hundred languages, critical of spontaneist and cognitivist pedagogies, overcoming binarism (as well as adultcentrism, sexism, racism, homophobism), in short, every prejudice. The teacher does not teach, but rather, with educative intentionality, a teacher plans, organizes and makes time, space and material available to children, so as to encourage imagination and challenges to reasoning, giving room to curiosity, providing amazement, discovery, marvelling and all the forms of expression in the most varied intensities. Intelligence is acquired by using it (Malaguzzi). Therefore, the organisation of time and of the physical space also has to be reviewed, in order to allow for the unpredictability of the child protagonists; and thus a pedagogy of listening, relations, and differences may be built, in continuity with obligatory school.

"The malaguzzian pedagogy is complex: it 'allows itself' subjective, divergent and independent interpretations of the world, in contrast with an idea of linear, cumulative progress. It is sceptical about the past, present and future beliefs; it is prepared to break free from the hegemonic canons of pedagogy and psychology. The malaguzzian pedagogy is also aesthetical for its capacity of showing the essential through new relations, with apparently remote proximities. It lives in tension, transgressing itself, though without betraying itself and, at the same time ... a metaphorical and symbolic communication which multiplies our image of the world and of childhood" (Hoyuelos 2004: 7).

Experience with differences will allow children from different social classes, from a very young age, to learn about the origin of inequality, and thus they will find possibilities for overcoming it. Therefore, we will have a teacher who is committed to knowledge, to the creation of it, and closely connected with the invention of childhood knowledge. Without teaching classes, teachers will act like scenographers, like creators of environments in which childhood can happen, as in a performance. As Walter Benjamin says, the teacher of children is like a play director: the teacher invites children to feel, think and act simultaneously, without separating head and body, creates conditions to act and to express oneself within the collective, having a good time, and communicating (S. 1984).

We have been very creative and invented many manners of educating young children, without becoming didactic about playfulness or pedagogising art. Now, so as not to lose all this, it is necessary to integrate with obligatory school. Day care centre, pre-school and first grade teachers must be allied in this process. Art will be the great agglutinate. The construction of the individual as the central axis of school, which usually becomes individualism, can be overcome through construction of the children's collective, of diversity. Articulating the teaching/educational national system, along with non-formal education, may favour the construction of a childhood pedagogy focused on children and, especially, on the human dimensions which are neglected in obligatory school: the playful, imagination, the unpredictable, the aesthetic and fictional sense.

Therefore, this is about a new teacher training, which will guarantee the continuity of education in the collective of children at every age. The commitment to knowledge in the scientific and artistic preparation of childhood teachers, will favour the building of a pedagogy capable of educating young citizens focused on integrated actions of being, such as playing, along with the artistic manifestations, human actions; where feeling, thinking and doing may not be detached, as long as the educative intentionality of the adult professional wishes it. Such actions will correspond to another "humanity rehearsal" (Milton Santos), since we are far from establishing it fully. *"They are an irradiant confirmation of the possibility of man."* (Gardner 2004)

We end this paper without a conclusion, raising many questions and the will to continue this interlocution between art and pedagogy, on the perspective of teacher training and of pedagogical practice. Nevertheless, we will interrupt it with the strength of the voice of the Brazilian poet Mario de Andrade, who, in 1929, in the same period in which Benjamin writes about childhood, says[13]:

"A child is essentially a sensible being in search of expression ... he/she is much more expressively total than the adult. Before a pain: he/she cries – which is much more expressive than to withdraw: 'I am suffering'. A child utilises indifferently every means of artistic expression: he/she uses the word, the beats, singing, and drawing. They will say that his/her tendencies have not become firm yet. I know. But it is the same vagueness of tendencies that allow him/her to be more total. And besides, these 'tendencies' often originate exclusively from our intelligence" (Mario de Andrade, 1929).

## References

Abramowicz, Anete (2003): O direito das crianças à educação infantile, (The right of children to childhood education), in: *Pro-posições*, Campinas: v.14, n.3 (42), p. 13-24, 2003

Agamben, Giorgio (2002): *Enfance et histoire,* Traduit de l'italien par Yves Hersant, Paris: Payot & Rivages 2002

Ambech-Madsen, P. (1992): Attività prescolastica: Reggio Emilia, Italia: non si deve porre limite all'infanzia, in: *Il premio Lego*, Ygdrasil 1992

Arendt, Hannah (2004): *A condição humana,* Tradução de Roberto Raposo, posfácio de Celso Lafer, 10.ed., Rio de Janeiro: Forense-Universitária 2004

Bachelard, Gaston:
1988: *A poética do devaneio*, Tradução Antonio de Pádua Danesi, São Paulo: Martins Fontes 1988
1989: *A poética do espaço*. Tradução Antonio de Pádua Danesi, São Paulo: Martins Fontes 1989
1997: *Lautréamont*, Traducción Angelina Martín del Campo, México, D.F.: Fondo de Cultura Económica 1997

Bárcena, Fernando (2003): *El delirio de las calabra,* Barcelona: Herder 2003

Benjamin, Walter:
1984: *Reflexões: a criança, o brinquedo e a educação*, São Paulo: Summus 1984
1995: *Rua de mão única*, Tradução Rubens Torres Filho; José Carlos Martins Barbosa, 5. ed. São Paulo: Brasiliense 1995

Borghi, Battista Quinto/Guerra, Luigi (1999): *Manuale di didattica per l'asilo nido*, Bari: Laterza 1999

---

13 In 1953, when he was director of the *Department of Culture* in São Paulo's city council, Mario de Andrade created playgrounds for children of working-class families who, without attending classes, were raised in the Brazilian cultural diversity, in art and playing.

Chauí, Marilena (1988): Janela da alma, espelho do mundo, (Window of the soul, mirror of the world), in: *NOVAES, Adauto (org), O olhar (The Look)*, São Paulo: Companhia das Letras 1988, p. 31-63

Deleuze, Gilles (1988): *Proust et les signes*, Paris: Quadrige, PUF 1998

Faria, Ana Lúcia G. de (2007): Loris Malaguzzi e os direitos das crianças pequenas, (Loris Malaguzzi and the rights of young children), in: Oliveira-Formosinho, J.; Kishimoto, T.M.; Pinazza, M.A. (orgs.): *Pedagogia(s) da infância: dialogando com o passado, construindo o futuro, (Pedagogy(ies) of childhood: dialoguing with the past, constructing the future)*, Porto Alegre: Artmed 2007, P.

Francastel, Pierre (1993): *A realidade figurativa*, Tradução Mary Amazonas leite de Barros, São Paulo: Perspectiva 1993

Gardner, Howard (2004): I cento linguaggi di una riforma educativa di sucesso, in: *Bambini in Europa*, anno 4,N. 1, p.16-17, feb. 2004

Gobbi, Márcia A. (2004): *Desenhos de outrora, desenhos de agora: Mario de Andrade e seu acervo de desenhos de crianças pequenas, (Drawings from the past, drawings from the present: Mario de Andrade and his collection of young children's drawings)*, Tese de Doutorado, *Faculdade de Educação da Unicamp* 2004 (Doctoral thesis, *Faculty of Education at Unicamp* 2004)

Gunnarson, Lars (1994): A política de cuidado e educação na Suécia (The care and education policy in Sweden), in: Rosemberg, Fulvia / Campos, Maria M.(orgs.): *Creches e pré-escolas no Hemisfério Norte, (Day care centres and pre-schools in the Northern Hemisphere)*, São Paulo: Cortez 1994, p.135-188

Hoyuelos planillo, Alfredo (2004): *Loris Malaguzzi: una bibliografia pedagógica*, Bergamo: Junior 2004

Malaguzzi, loris (1988): Intervista a Catini, E., in: *Bambini*, N.12, 1988

Merleau-Ponty, Maurice:
1999: *O visível e o invisível*, Prefácio e posfácio de Claude Lefort, Tradução José Artur Gianotti e Armando Mora d'Oliveira, São Paulo: Perspectiva 1999
2004: *O olho e o espírito, seguido de A linguagem e as vozes do silêncio e A dúvida de Cézanne*, Tradução de Paulo Neves e Maria Ermantina Galvão Gomes Pereira, prefácio Claude Lefort; posfácio Alberto Tassinari, São Paulo: Cosac & Naify 2004

*Nuovi orientamenti per una nuova scuola dell'infanzia*, Italia, 1991

Rabitti, Giordana (1999): *À procura da dimensão perdida: uma escola de infância de Reggio Emilia*, Porto Alegre: Artes Médicas Sul 1999

Rancière, Jacques (2005): *A partilha do sensível: estética e política*, Tradução Mônica Costa Netto, São Paulo: EXO experimental org.; Ed. 34, 2005

Richter, Sandra R. S. (2005): *A dimensão ficcional da arte na educação da infância, (The fictional dimension of art in childhood education)*, Tese de Doutoramento, *Faculdade de Educação, Universidade Federal do Rio Grande do Sul*, Porto Alegre: 2005

Ricoeur, Paul:
  1986: *Du texte à l'action*: essais d'herméneutique II. Paris: Éditions du Seuil 1986
  1994: *Tempo e narrative*, (Tomo 1), Tradução Constança Marcondes César. Campinas, SP: Papirus 1994
Serres, Michel (2001): *Os cinco sentidos*, Rio de Janeiro: Bertrand Brasil, 2001
Valéry, Paul (1999): *Variedades*, São Paulo: Iluminuras 1999
Varela, Francisco/Thompson, Evan/Rosch, Eleanor (1997): *De cuerpo presente*, Barcelona: Gedisa 1997

# Wechselspiele – Playing with interplay
Staging the theatrical structure, and the fragility of the ground rules, in "Theatre for Early Years"

*by Geesche Wartemann*

## The experience of community as a potential of theatre

"The primary player in theatre is not the actor, but the audience," claimed Manfred Wekwerth in the nineteen-seventies (Wekwerth 1974: 101). A theatre theorist and long-term collaborative member of Berthold Brecht's *Berliner Ensemble*, Wekwerth indicated as evidence for his thesis an experiment going back to Stanislavski, in which an actor is directed to do 'nothing' onstage. The audience members, unaware of this acting task, watch the actor intently and describe in detail afterwards what he has performed; or rather, what they have seen and experienced. Wekwerth depicts their reception as an active process, which expresses itself in silence or in clearly perceptible reactions. In each case, the audience's behaviour "confirms to the actor onstage that the particular situation he is presenting has become a real circumstance for the audience: that he and they are now in a human relationship." (Ibid: 102) This interchange between performers and audience members is at the heart of the experience of collective creativity. This special quality of interaction is still often highlighted in current discourse among theatre theorists and practitioners. Jason Cross, artistic director of the *16$^{th}$ World Congress and Performing Arts Festival for Young People* held in May 2008 in Adelaide, Australia, wrote in the festival's programme booklet: "The desire for humans to gather together in the same place at the same time to share stories via song, dance and storytelling is an ancient pastime, which can be dated back to the earliest human history". (*16$^{th}$ World Congress ...* 2008: 5) In this need for communal production of song, dance, and story "in the same place at the same time", Jason Cross recognises an anthropological constant. And finally, the German theatre theorist Erika Fischer-Lichte also emphasises "bodily co-presence" as a defining moment within her "Aesthetic of the Performative" (S. Fischer-Lichte 2004).

## The asymmetry of theatrical interaction

The ubiquitous assertion, or even sometimes invocation, of the collective participatory nature of theatre, clearly calls for further analysis and critical examination. For instance, Wekwerth's formulation of the "*primary* player" describes not only a desired "human relationship" between actors and audience, but also an underlying dispute. With his telling formulation, he positions the audience as an important part of the theatrical performance, and thereby polemicises against self-referential egotism among politically- and socially-disinterested theatre producers. Then, too, the previously sketched anthropological motivation as worded for the occasion of the *World Performing Arts Festival for Young People 2008* earns its special historical relevance solely with respect to a youthful public recently socialised through new media. In an age marked by the disembodiment of social relationships, the theatre becomes a compensatory location where such bodily experience can be found. Lastly, the theoretical conceptualisation of theatre as a place of "bodily co-presence" must be more precisely rendered. Concurrent physical presence, in and of itself, does not guarantee a successful interchange between performers and audience. As early as the nineteen-eighties, Manfred Pfister voiced critical concern about the 'feedback loop' in theatre performances:

> "Despite the feedback effect, this can never, even potentially, become a symmetrical two-way exchange with reversible sender-receiver relationships, such as in ideal cases of *face-to-face communication*; because here, an institutionalised asymmetry is present. This asymmetry is clearly historical, and varies widely according to type ...". (Pfister 1988: 65)

Elsewhere I have already argued that in children's theatre, the recognisable lack of practice with audience conventions, along with the nature of the audience's psychological development, work against this asymmetry on the one hand while intensifying it on the other; in theatre for children, a generation gap exists between the interactive partners as well (S. Wartemann 2005). To describe how the potential quality of theatre as a space for an experience of community might develop, there must be more detailed consideration of the relevant conditions and staging strategies. Which activities can especially invite (or on the other hand, frustrate) the audience's participation and productive reception? What specific strategies and ground rules can promote an exchange between artists and children up to age three?

## The "dramaturgy of the audience"

To describe the proactive inclusion of the audience in concepts of plays and stage production, to the degree that the audience becomes a (fellow) player, Volker Klotz has found the elegant notion of a "dramaturgy of the audience". What is meant by this idea?

> "Under a broad umbrella, any such activities may be understood as a 'dramaturgy of the audience': theatrical actions undertaken among, and by, the audience members. The audience becomes an object of dramaturgical arrangement – for the purpose of having it take part as a dramaturgical subject." (Klotz 1976: 17)

Beyond this, the concept of a "dramaturgy of the audience" also emphasises the theatre producer's responsibility to set up preconditions for a productive reception process. Volker Klotz names two basic conditions that lay the foundation for the audience's participation. One of them is that "this dramaturgy must keep in mind, to a wide extent, the viewing resources that the audience itself brings along" (Ibid: 17). In this respect, in theatre for children aged three and under, artists often arrive empty-handed. In Germany, interest in early-childhood pedagogy has enjoyed an upsurge only within the past few years. With recent public attention directed toward these very youngest audience members, it is now possible to focus upon what they can do and what they know. From an artistic perspective, this is an inspiring situation. Along with this new target audience group follows a new line of inquiry and discussion about the medium of theatre, at the level of specific content as well as in formal discourse. Substantial periods of research thus accompany many theatre productions for the very young. The second essential prerequisite for a successful interactive theatre piece, according to Klotz, is the recognition and observation of particular conventions of performance. Theatre

> "lives or dies according to an unspoken agreement to bring the audience along from the very outset. If those on the stage don't hold to this rule, they [the audience, G. Wartemann] cannot appropriately take part, because they have no idea how to begin to approach the content, nor the means, nor the purpose of the scenic representation." (Ibid: 19)

This position should be viewed from the critical distance of the nearly 40 years since its formulation. Today, particularly in theatre for children aged three and under, it is no longer assumed that such "unspoken" agreements can be taken for granted "from the very outset". In contemporary theatre, especially for the age group of three and younger, with absolutely no previous experience with theatre, the question is turned around: When, and how, can each of these agreements be established within a particular production? For the idea of necessary, transparent, basic ground rules for the playing situation, so that audiences of every age group may "appropriately take part", is still valid. The intent here is not to add some desired 'supplemental feature', just for the benefit of the audience. Rather, this is a matter of a fundamental condition of theatre. Compared to other media and art forms, theatre is constituted by the simultaneous nature of its production and reception, a point which Klotz expressively emphasises: "The occurrence of the theatrical production, however, requires… that the audience respond to it, here and now." (Ibid: 19)

At this point, it should be noted that a lasting, or even increasing, significance for successful interactive theatre has come be linked with the "dramaturgy of the audience". This revaluing may be due to the ever-greater heterogeneity of the theatregoing public, and of performance and production forms; it may further serve to address an audience's age-based lack of experience with theatre. The German theatre system allows for this area of production, framed in terms of 'audience outreach', to be separated from the artistic process. Today, every German municipal and state theatre has theatre educators offering a comprehensive audience-education program. This effort to involve the audience has found expression through the establishment and professionalisation of theatre education in these theatre venues for the past 15 years, and naturally it can be valued as a very positive development. Within the very spirit of the arguments in this essay so far, a good theatre educator can contribute fundamentally to successful interaction. What seems increasingly questionable to me, however, is the accompanying isolation of this task, and the detachment of "the dramaturgy of the audience" from the artistic production process. Max Schumacher refers to this phenomenon as well, in his consideration of an "over-all-dramaturgy". He broadens the concept of a "dramaturgy of the audience" by underscoring how audience members' attitudes of expectation are decisively awakened and determined *at the outset* of a performance. At the same time, he states: "Artists concern themselves often far too little with this part of their performance." (Schumacher 2008: 74) Thus Schumacher closes with a stirring appeal to artists: "Generate your own expectations among audiences, if you want to be convincing to them, so that the theatre experience as a whole becomes the one you envision for yourselves!" (Ibid: 84) In theatre for children, this awareness is obviously not new, and now, theatre artists design even the entrance setup with great consciousness, often using elements of the production staging (S. Wartemann 2009). In regards to theatre for the very young, however, these considerations bring a specific challenge to the foreground: Children aged three and younger usually have no expectations of theatre at all, since they have no previous contact with this art form, and thus no concept of it. The task and challenge for a "dramaturgy of the audience" thereby take on much more radical form: How does theatre for these very youngest audiences become theatre in the first place?

Thus, I come to the description of my example: the production "Holzklopfen" ("Knock on wood") for children aged two and up, at the *Helios Theatre*, Hamm, Germany. Working within the scope of the project "Theatre from the very start!" of the Theatre Centre for Children and Youth of the Federal Republic of Germany, I accompanied this production via ethnographic camera, together with Bina Elisabeth Mohn, in January and February 2008. During its so-called 'field experiments', *Helios Theatre* incorporated children into the development of its production already within the rehearsal process. Each week, children were invited to an open rehearsal, in order to present the production's current status to them and observe their reactions. In this way, the theatre artists could continually test out their ideas and performances in the presence of their intended audience. The 'field experiments' were not viewed as some kind of tiresome obligation, but rather, as a welcome chance to develop knowledge early in the creative process about the effect of the staged action; and in conjunction, to develop greater precision in performance. During the rehearsals, ideas for staging were tried out, changed, or discarded. With regards to the question of how theatre for these young children becomes theatre, it must be stressed that the 'field experiments' were not aimed at placing an established concept of theatre in front of the children and introducing them to it. The 'field experiments' are not a method of audience development. Quite to the contrary, the artists of *Helios Theatre* envision the encounter with the children as an opportunity to test out their own understandings of theatre and open them to discussion. What performances prove to be interesting? How does the theatre piece begin and end? What room do the children have to take part in the action? The basic ground rules of that which can be understood as theatre – how performers and audience members take on their roles, and what are the associated possibilities to take part in the action – are not simply assumed; in the 'field experiments', they are examined and tried out instead. Each of these 'field experiment' rehearsals was followed by thorough reflection and discussion of the children's reactions, so that the insights could be fruitful for the further production process.

During the ethnographic camera recording of the 'field experiments' of "Holzklopfen's" production at *Helios Theatre*, the following focus areas developed from the observations:

1. How are actions framed as theatre?
2. For the children in the audience, where is there open space to take part in the action? How physical is the reception in the theatre? How do the children act, collectively or individually, in the performance?
3. How are the adult chaperones involved in the interplay between the artists and the children?
4. How do the theatre artists manage the shifting focus between the action happening on stage, and the extroverted bodily responses of these smallest audience members? How do they handle the resulting fragility of the ground rules of theatre play that can arise from this interchange?

As it is not possible within this article to go into all of these observations in detail[1], I would like to single out two aspects here. In the first place, through a detailed analysis of the beginning phase of the children's theatre visit, I will demonstrate how the framework of theatre is set up through a process of transformation. Next, in writing about a problematic rehearsal and the following controversial discussion within the *Helios Theatre* team, I aim to show the fragility of this

---

[1] In spring 2009, a German-language DVD by Mohn and Wartemann entitled "Wechselspiele, Experimentierfeld Kindertheater" ("Interplay, field experiments in children's theatre") will be available.

theatrical framework in theatre for the very young, and the challenges and decisions related to this, for the theatre artists.

## Designation of the theatre framework

The ethnographic camera observations show how, through multiple markers, the events in the foyer of *Helios Theatre* were transformed into a theatrical situation, with adults presenting and children attentively observing. Four stages of this transformation process can be distinguished in the course of the 'field experiments':

(a) *Preparation*: The children and their adult chaperones are situated in the foyer. The door to the stage is still closed. They remove and check in their jackets and bags, and place themselves on benches that have been set up for them. Some kindergarten groups arrive at the theatre so early that they eat breakfast in the foyer. If there is nothing else to do, the children begin to lie down on the benches, to run around them, and to vigorously explore them with their whole bodies. At length, this free play is interrupted by a verbal announcement from theatre educator Matthias Damberg. He points out that now is the last opportunity to visit the toilet. The caretakers present immediately pick up his cue and take action upon it with those children who are already toilet-trained. Until this announcement from the theatre educator, the time in the foyer is filled with a variety of activities. Only with his address does the preparation phase begin for the coming "main attraction". At this point, the children still have no clear idea what this entails, but they now have a notion that it will require a certain amount of physical self-control.

(b) *Welcome*: In the next step, the director Barbara Kölling makes herself known to the children with a short speech. Collected on the benches again, now for once in an orderly fashion, the children give the director their interested attention and wait for the next thing to happen. "Soon we will be going into the theatre over there," Barbara Kölling says, pointing her hand toward the long, dark aisle, now visible to the children through the just-opened door to the stage. With the words: "This is Michael. He performs. You'll be seeing that next," the performer Michael Lurse comes forward for introduction. The musician Andrés Cabrera is made known by name to the audience as well. Through this spoken explanation, the events to take place in the stage area are labelled as theatre, and the participating players are introduced to the children. A central aspect of this brief pre-show talk is the welcoming of the children. The gestures and tone of voice the director uses to introduce herself, and the other unfamiliar adults present, can inspire trust, and thus contribute to the children's willingness to go along with the uncertain situation: this unknown called theatre.

(c) *Invitation*: Performer Michael Lurse and musician Andrés Cabrera step out in front of the children and lead them in the change of location. Whereas in the earliest rehearsals, wooden shavings or wood chips were presented and then laid out to mark the path, in the final setting the signals are primarily acoustic. The actor places himself with a Chinese gong at the threshold between the foyer and the stage area. An adult can immediately recognise the conventional opening ritual. For the children, the invitation issuing from the bang on the gong to now adjourn from the foyer to the stage area is also reinforced through gesture by a wave from the actor. The musician remains standing closer to the children, smiles invitingly at them, and begins to beat his wooden snare drum, which will be sounding from now on until the end of the performance. Making music throughout, he then moves into the playing area, thereby offering the children an orientation and an acoustically marked pathway. Some children understand this acoustic and gesticular call right away. Other children wait until their adult chaperones begin to move. They stay close to the adults, take hold of their hands, or let themselves be gently pushed in the right direction.

(d) *Changing spaces*: The fourth and last stage of the transformation from an indeterminate, non-theatre situation, into a theatre, with its division of performer and audience roles, starts with the crossing through the doorway from the foyer to the stage area, and lasts until the moment when the children take their places on the audience benches. In the *Helios Theatre*, an aisle some ten meters long leads from the entrance door to the rows of audience seating. During the 'field experiments' the *Helios Theatre* team continually tried new design variations for this aisle. After an early pathway of wood shavings, which also mark the playing area onstage, also wooden logs were placed in the middle of the walkway. In the end, they settled upon wooden sticks at roughly adult height, edging the walkway to the left and right. In their reflective sessions, the considerations of all those involved kept revolving around this pathway. Since it is already part of the stage area, but does not belong to the playing area itself, the question was whether and how this intermediate space already represented the theme of 'wood'. Throughout this process, the theatre artists' reflections on this passage's design displayed a high awareness of how even methods of presentation lay the early groundwork for a desired spirit of receptivity. So it was very important for the theatre team, for instance, that the laid-out pieces of wood retained their openness for individual interpretation, which each child was welcome to discover. For example, the wood pieces could be read as markers along a pathway to be followed. But they could also be taken as obstacles in a game-like course, to climb over, to kick out of the way, and so forth. Barbara Kölling distances herself from the idea that something should "function" here. For her, the 'field experiments' serve much more as observations of "what happens".

In the team conversations afterwards, Michael Lurse also stresses that this first passage into the stage area hopefully will not be understood as a means of restriction, but rather, as an 'installation', to do with however one pleases. A basic challenge of this entrance setting thereby becomes clear: as I have shown, the action is precisely structured, using verbal, musical, gesticular, and spatial designations to stage a framework which spotlights the production as a special event called theatre. Alongside the explicit directions and explanations given in the foyer, fears must be overcome, and an atmosphere of willingness created to join into the upcoming event. Furthermore, the audience members' role, particularly in a process of collective response, requires certain rules of behaviour so that attentiveness to the play is even possible. During the theatre piece, personal, and especially physical needs, and natural urges to move, must be disciplined. At the same time, there is a basic artistic understanding that this situation calls for something more than simply providing of rules of behaviour and controlling adherence to them. In anticipation of the theatre production, therefore, *Helios Theatre*'s entrance setting attempts to release modes of thinking from categories of 'right' and 'wrong'. This is a valuable stimulus for other entrance situations as well: What attitude, and in relation to this, what image of theatre is being set in these moments right before the opening of a performance? Often enough, children are confronted at exactly this time with prohibitions: Eating and drinking are not allowed; for older children and youth, this is followed by the direction to turn off their cell phones. *Helios Theatre* has found another possibility here. It makes its audience into more than solely the object of a "dramaturgy of the audience". Through the entrance setting, even the small children become dramaturgical subjects – according to Volker Klotz, the second dimension of the "dramaturgy of the audience". As subjects, audience members can determine for themselves where to focus their attentions and how to make their own meanings of events. Thus the asymmetry of theatrical interaction is reduced, and the theatre becomes an equal partner in the interchange. The theatre artists also maintain their positions as observers. "What is the impulse that makes them begin to move?" the director asks in the evaluative conversation, for example, rather than just stating an obvious indication. However, allowing for this autonomy and individuality presents special challenges. In the closing section, I would like to report on one such challenge.

**The fragility of the ground rules**

On this particular Friday to be described, a blond little girl becomes conspicuous shortly after the start of the rehearsal. She slides back and forth fitfully in her seat, then stands up and moves slightly in the direction of the playing area, only two meters away. In her hand she holds a stuffed animal, which she drops on the floor and then picks up again. A caretaker signals to her to sit down. She complies hesitantly, but soon gets up again and is visibly drawn to the music. Finally she follows this impulse. She goes all the way around the playing area and comes to stand at the back edge of the stage, directly in front of the musician and his instrument. She listens to him and shows him her plush toy monkey. When the musician changes his position, she follows him. The other children are astonishingly unaffected, only glancing briefly in her direction early on. Otherwise, they are following the actor's performance with interest and concentration. As an adult observer of this occurrence, I sense an increasing tension. The child's activity is taking on a dynamic of its own. What will she do next? At last, a theatre educator starts toward the girl to put a stop to her independent actions. Yet the director waves a hand to indicate that she should let the child be. So the girl serenely accompanies the musician for a long while, until she moves back to her seat. But just as quickly, she turns around and heads back to the musician again. This time, she is not only listening to the music, but also stamping her shoes to produce her own sound and rhythm. This is the point at which the theatre educator does intervene, speaking to the girl gently at the very back edge of the stage. The girl pauses for a moment, then joins the musician again as before, and remains near him until the end of the rehearsal.

What happened here? In conversation with the caretakers following the rehearsal, it was revealed that this girl is almost blind. She had done nothing other than to follow the stimuli that were most attractive to her sense of perception – in this case, the music. To the artists, who were not aware of the special needs of this child, her behaviour was irritating. A situation thus arose, in the event with this blind girl, which makes a very common phenomenon in theatre for children especially clear. Focusing attention on certain actions on stage – generally, on the actions of the actors – does not result from audience conventions established *in advance*, in theatre for the very young. Young children are attentive and focused on particular stage actions, only if, and when (for any length of time) these actions can spark their interest. Their level of interest is clearly exposed through their reactions, whether vocal, verbal, or physical.

Following the rehearsal outlined here, a spirited discussion broke out among the involved artists on this question: Was this event a disturbance? The ensemble of *Helios Theatre* is basically united on the matter of incorporating children into the rehearsal process within the 'field experiments', and letting them examine and question theatre. In this ensemble, theatre's claim to be a process of collective creativity between the performers and the audience is taken very seriously. This understanding comes to bear upon the theatre visits and in the evaluation discussions afterwards. The behaviour of the blind girl, however, makes clear a basic problem within the participatory ideal. In the willingness to give the children no strict rules of behaviour, but rather to take them seriously with their various responsive skills and receptive needs, much room for interpretation appears: within the manner of the content, at the level of the story being told, within the characters, and beyond. Openness occurs at the level of the so-called external communication system as well; that is, at the level where all those present encounter each other as actors and theatre visitors. This means that during the performance, the general rules of interaction are negotiated once again, corresponding to the actual situation and actual needs. The director of *Helios Theatre*, Barbara Kölling, emphasises her underlying interest in a theatre that can encourage and adapt to the unpredicted and individual reactions of the children. Especially in the theatre for the very young, she finds little focus on these reactions. The director would like "to learn how to handle this fragility", as she says. Her response in that rehearsal confirms this: she put off the moment of intervention as long as possible. The actor, on the other hand, feels disturbed, and argues otherwise: The girl's actions had taken too much energy from his performing, and his cooperation with the musician had not worked out as arranged. He feels that interplay with audience members should not be allowed to compromise the performance of the actors. He defends the artists' creation against random, starkly individual interference. In his opinion, the collective audience members are also disturbed by such unusually individual behaviour, since this girl's 'private theatre' is of no interest to anyone else. He recommends that children, who, for whatever reason, obviously have special individual needs, should be removed from the performance early, because otherwise whatever happens cannot be controlled.

These different assessments of the incident within the *Helios Theatre* ensemble let us plainly see a general complexity: Is a lack of focus among audience members in fact an expression and a part of collective creativity, as it is in such moments that the asymmetry of theatrical interaction breaks down? Or is it an indication of failure of collective creativity, since those present are not relating to each other sufficiently? To these questions, there is no universally valid answer. It is within the judgement of the theatre artists to determine how keenly they want to focus the attention of the audience, or what forms they might find to make space for individual responses as well. However, if they make a fundamental decision not to hermetically seal the onstage events away from the actions in the auditorium and yet, they also decide against dissolution of the role division between the performers and the audience, and do not let the theatre event become a 'happening' or an interactive game, then, with every staging and every performance, the balancing act between the ground rules of fair play and the openness to play must be explored anew.

*translated by Lydia Baldwin*

## References

*16th World Congress and Performing Arts Festival for Young People*, programme, Adelaide 2008

Fischer-Lichte, Erika (2004): *Ästhetik des Performativen*, Frankfurt a. M.: Suhrkamp 2008

Klotz, Volker (1976): *Dramaturgie des Publikums. Wie Bühne und Publikum aufeinander eingehen, insbesondere bei Raimund, Büchner, Wedekind, Horvath, Gatti und im politischen Agitationstheater*, München: Hanser 1976

Pfister, Manfred (1988): *Das Drama. Theorie und Analyse*, München: Fink 1988

Schumacher, Max (2008): Expect Expectation – Gestaltung der Erwartungshaltung als Teil einer „Over-All-Dramaturgy", in: Jan Deck und Angelika Sieburg (Hg.): *Paradoxien des Zuschauens. Die Rolle des Publikums im zeitgenössischen Theater*, Bielefeld: transcript 2008

Wartemann, Geesche (2005): Interaktionsraum Kindertheater, in: David Roesner/Geesche Wartemann/Vollker Wortmann (Hg.): *Szenische Orte – Mediale Räume. Medien und Theater*, Neue Folge Bd. 1, Hildesheim, Zürich, New York: Olms 2005

Wartemann, Geesche (2009): Spielen und Regeln. Die Exposition als Bedingung kollektiver Kreativität im Theater für Kinder, in: Hajo Kurzenberger/Hans Joseph Ortheil/Matthias Rebstock (Hg.) (2009): *Kollektive in den Künsten. Medien und Theater*, Neue Folge Bd. 10, Hildesheim, Zürich, New York: Olms 2009

Wekwerth, Manfred (1974): *Theater und Wissenschaft. Überlegungen für das Theater von heute und morgen*, München: Hanser 1974

# Starting all over again?
## Changing ways of perception through theatre – not only for young children

*by Ute Pinkert*

Theatre for the very young appears to me to be an extremely heterogeneous and open field. Although many organisations have been experimenting in it, across Germany and elsewhere, its mention to date has been sadly absent from the reflections of theatre practitioners, and from educational theory discourse. This neglect may happily become a thing of the past, due to a national project initiated by the *Federal Republic of Germany's Centre for Children and Youth*: "Theatre from the very beginning!"

When one asks, "What actually *is* theatre for the very young?" the only authoritative answer thus far is defined by the specifics of the audience. Theatre for the very young is theatre for children (and by children) under the age of five. If one wants to investigate the structures and educational effects of this form of theatre, it follows that one must adopt the point of view of this particular audience. More precisely, one must take on the perspective of small children, their ways and means of perceiving, experiencing, and constructing their realities. If we overlook for a moment the fact that *'the* small children', in the sense of an abstract target group, don't exist, there are various viewpoints from which to examine states of perception among children under five. The most fundamental perspective, to which "Theatre from the very start!" is committed, is that of the empirical study of theatrical practice. The initiative's study has been conducted since fall 2006 at four project sites. As a complement to that research, this article aims to bring a perspective from the scholarship of theatre studies and cultural sciences into play. What interests me is the question: What do small children make of theatre?

From the vantage point of theatre studies, the following questions are interlinked: What are the general needs that small children bring to the organisation of perception in theatre? In what ways are their requirements, which relate to current issues, being discussed within theatre studies? And how can these considerations be potentially productive for a 'theatre from the very start'?

## How small children encounter the world in the realms of everyday life and art

The very youngest audience, as it is commonly called, comes into contact with reality less on a linguistic-discourse basis, than on a bodily-sensory basis. This way of encountering the world is connected to the subjective experience of processes, and thus, to the direct interplay of physical movement and sensory input. "The objects and events that they [small children, U.P.] perceive are imbedded in their bodily activities and interactions, just as much as they are scenically determined by the situations in which children find themselves." (Schäfer 2001: 109)

In theatre, the very young are perceptibly physically present and, with their bodily-based perceptions, geared towards the theatre experience as a whole. They are reacting *in equal measure*, more or less, to the atmosphere, as to the configuration of the room; *at the same time*, in varying degrees, they are taking in the theatre plot via the linguistic, physical, and affective communication of their closest parental figure; and they are *also*, to a greater or lesser extent, in direct contact with the children in their surroundings. – As I remember visits to the theatre with my two small daughters, it occurs to me how much was in motion there, and how much seemed to be happening all at once.

In our society, small children's economy of attention – I suspect – can hardly be distinguished from that of 'big' people any more. Because it's no longer considered current, in our times, to 'shield' children away from the world, they are now present with us, right in the midst of our aesthetically-formed reality, within our 'experience-driven' culture. Early on, they create strategies – some healthy, some less so – to deal with the constant alertness that this orientation requires. As so-called digital natives, they grow up with digital media, and develop early into specialists in the area of audiovisual (television) symbols and formats. Very young children may not yet be able to read and write, but they are definitely not 'semiotic illiterates'.

In contrast to older children and adults, however, young children experience and use these signifiers exclusively in the pragmatic context of daily life. For them, for whom "the origin of all experience of self and the world is esthetical experience" (ibid: 87), there is not yet any separation between everyday spaces and artistic spaces. They integrate their experiments with aesthetically-dominated forms of expression (babbling, singing, doodling, scribbling, colouring, dancing, playing) into the activities of everyday life, as a matter of course. And within this context, it's constantly fascinating to experience how quickly and effortlessly small children can switch back and forth between two ways of perceiving and formulating. On the one hand, they can be deep in "pathic", autonomic absorption, almost lost in concrete events, in the material nature of things and phenomena; on the other hand, they are practising mimetic, self-generating "gnostic" habits, corresponding to these material objects in their everyday functionality (Buytendijk 1933: 30 et seqq.). For example, the movement of a spoon, while eating, seamlessly becomes the motion of the spoon as a paintbrush, creating images with the food splotches (S. Peez 2006). On the way to kindergarten, a rhythmic singsong patter of nonsense words may be broken off and resumed interchangeably with prosaic remarks upon the weather, hunger, or the passing scenery. It seems as if the realities of young children are like a Möbius strip; the inner and the outer, the world of absent-minded, fully absorbed play, and the world of the cultural everyday, are twisted together, influencing children from their first days of life.

These conditions of perception in young children, as sketched only briefly here, are a great challenge to the theatre in its historically developed artistic form. The essential questions are: What factors and dimensions determine theatrical forms of communication, and how are those being handled in accordance with the concrete parameters of young children's perception and communication? Here are some specific questions in this context, by way of example:

- How can theatre be conceived as more physically based, and situation-based?
- What is the relationship between theatrical situations, on the one hand, and everyday situations on the other? How can one develop out of the other, and/or how can one transform the other?
- Since we can recognise different varieties of attentiveness, which of these can engender particular spaces of perception for young children, in theatre? Which form of concentration is appropriate for them; what kind of attention stimulates them?

## Discussion of traditional systems of organisation in theatre, in regards to perception, the body, and language

It goes without saying that theatre for the very young, while investigating such questions, does not mean to merely reduce the historically developed form of bourgeois dramatic literature to meet 'children's needs'. Fundamentally, it is more a matter of creating (children's) theatre anew (i.e., the programme of the theatre workshop "Pilkentafel", in Flensburg; see Schneider 2005: 141).

In claiming such a task, theatre for young children faces challenges it shares in common with contemporary avant-garde theatre. And I would venture the theory that it is precisely within the field of theatre for the very young that questions are being raised, and issues explored, which presently play a large role in contemporary theatre. For instance, the theme of different realities, convoluted within each other and affecting one another, has been the subject of theatrical research for some time (for example, via game instructions which push against boundaries, in the work of *Forced Entertainment*; or in the densely atmospheric simulations of reality by Meg Stuart). Other subjects of recent inquiry have been experiments with more commonplace ways of performing and presenting, and alternative possibilities for structures of authority. In the course of the "performative evolution", theatre as a whole has come to be understood as a shared *situation*, a shared "performance" between the physically present actors and audience members. This understanding, together with the discovery of the "autopoetic feedback loop" (Fischer-Lichte 2004: 61f.), has directed the main focus of interest toward the audience's processes of perception. In this context, an inquiry into forms of attentiveness takes on a special role. This examination starts with the recognition that attentiveness is not an anthropological constant, in the sense of a human quality that remains stable, but rather, a many-faceted "in-between occurrence" (Fischer-Lichte 2006: 116). This acknowledgement leads to further questions: how can attentiveness be generated and directed in the theatre, and what forms of perception are related to this activity?

A fundamental motif, throughout all of these considerations and practical experiments, is the engagement with issues of traditional hierarchical organisation, as related to perception, body, and language. As stated within current theatre studies literature, the theatre of the avant-garde "[breaks apart] the techniques of focusing and organizing attention within hierarchies, with which the dramatic theatre used to confront its audience." (Fischer-Lichte 2006: 10). It remains to be verified, to what degree this assertion can be made productive for "Theatre from the very start!" as well, and how this might lead to the creation of other perceptions and forms of attentiveness.

It is a matter of artistic praxis to experiment with new forms and their corresponding effects. Having said this, the following reflections on the hierarchy of the senses in theatre are to be understood as an incentive, for all of those practitioners who have committed themselves to the 're-invention' of theatre for the very young.

## The hierarchy of the senses in theatre, past and present

We now return to the question posed earlier, of how the theatre might be conceived in closer relation to the body and to situations, according to young children's states of perception. In following this line of thinking, it is useful to leave behind a certain viewpoint that generalises the theatre, as a physical and sensory art form, as 'eternally beautiful'. The definitions of the senses and their relationships to each other aren't cultural universals. The organisation of attentiveness in theatre, as a specific relationship between symbols and appeals to the senses, has been just as varied historically. Corresponding to audiences' changing habits of perception, this particular relationship has found expression throughout theatre history in very divergent forms.

In the Middle Ages, by way of historical example, theatre was an affair of the open market. Presentations of historical or fantastical characters and their stories appeared alongside magic shows, music, acts of the healing arts, bawdy comedy, and ribald entertainments. The spectators were not yet strictly separated from the stage; some were seated upon it, some even involved themselves into the action. A play was a direct kind of communication; the actors were close enough to smell and touch. The public ate and drank throughout the performance, talked and quarrelled with each other, and expected to be entertained. A contemplative reception of theatre by audience members who understood themselves to be autonomous, independent individuals, did not exist in those times.

That feature emerged only with the rise of the bourgeois theatre, and it originated from the need to organise perception according to the rules of written language. A basic characteristic of this perceptual organisation is the linear ordering of symbols, structured according to space and time; one sign appears after the other, and there is no effect without a cause. Perception organised according to the written word strongly supports a distinction between materially-embodied symbols on the one hand, and the ideas, their significance, on the other. Along with this comes an implicit devaluation of the material symbol-bearers, compared to the significance of the ideal, and the question of the truth of representation. Thus could Diderot, one of the most significant theorists of the bourgeois theatre of illusion, proclaim: "What, then, is truth on the stage? It is the conformance of the action, the speech, the figure, the voice, the movement, the gestures, to an ideal model as conceived by the playwright." (Diderot, as quoted in Schramm 1994: 105)

This hierarchical organisation of theatrical symbols began to be shaken apart by the historical avant-garde at the beginning of the last century. Since the launch of the performance-art movement in the nineteen-sixties, this deconstruction has become a driving force in very recent theatre history. It called into question the dominance of the so-called distant senses, sight and hearing, over the nearer senses of smell, taste, and touch, leading to experiments with enhancing the nearer senses in theatre. Following are two aspects of this work, which may be singled out and outlined with an eye toward a theatre for the very young.

## The revaluation of the sense of touch in theatre

A structural separation between the performers and the spectators is constitutive to theatre today. Yet an orientation toward historical forms of theatre, and toward other forms of art, reveals other possibilities, in which this structural separation must not unconditionally be conceived as a spatial divide as well. There now exists a diversity of forms, in which physical contact between the actors and the audience is no longer prevented, or it is even made necessary: I am thinking, for instance, of the creation of new performance constellations – such as the use of everyday spaces as a common stage, shared by the performers and the audience, in which small children are also included as a matter of course (S. Heise/Pinkert 2007, Seitz 2007). Another example is the structuring of performances upon a foundation of ritual acts and everyday rituals, familiar to small children, which they can grasp and mimetically reproduce; such as in the performance "Under the table" by Agnès Desfosses (S. Seitz 2007).

Coming from an aesthetical perspective, the sense of touch is like a patina. Literally, a patina is a coating that builds up over precious metal surfaces through oxidation – a refined kind of rust. In a broader sense, a patina is a sedimentary layering that accumulates through time and through contact with objects. The patina metaphorically and literally records an object's history, which develops as the object is handled. As opposed to a video screen, the 'skin' of an object has depth. The story of objects is explored as one dimension within the theatre of objects; in the modern art form of 'found objects', the theme of an object's story may be framed as a 'search for clues'. Located at the point of intersection between these two artistic concepts is the *theatrical installation*. This form has a great attraction for small children, since it assigns the sense of touch a dominant role within esthetical experience (See i.e. „Le jardin du possible", by Benoît Sicat).

**Staging atmospheres**

The sense of smell is the only sense that mediates between the 'near' and 'distant' senses. Since "our own personal odour [creates] just one knot in a network of fragrant signatures" (Diaconu 2005: 210), we can truly never remain outside the reality of smell; we are always surrounded by it too.

The aesthetical category related to the sense of smell is that of atmosphere. Atmosphere is that 'something more' that goes beyond the real and factual, which we can only sense when we find ourselves fully, bodily 'there' in the midst of it. Atmospheres denote those moods radiating from objects and persons. However, they belong neither to persons nor to things; nor are they our subjective projections. Rather, they must take up residence somewhere between the perceivers and the perceived. "Generally ... atmospheres rule like some mighty power, and human beings are *seized, struck, and overcome* by them" (Diaconu 2005: 445).

For theatre for the very young, atmospheres play a decisive role. They can engender trust and safety, but also expectation, strangeness, and, naturally, fear. Atmospheres set the tone for the perceptive qualities of a theatrical performance, even before the first actor appears onstage. There is no formula for the planning of atmosphere, yet it is something that can be produced, which occurs within the interplay of the 'vibrations' among the playing space, the materials used, and the bodies of the actors and the audience. If, as described by Sabine Schouten, the atmospheric also makes empathy possible (S. Schouten 2006), this might be a crucial question for theatre for small children (and beyond): Can atmospheres have an educational effect? Potentially, can theatre for the very young also allow young children to experience how atmospheres can be changeable, since they are always created by people?

**Education in theatre begins with an education in perception**

First and foremost, theatre for the very young is an exercise in ways of perceiving within the art form of theatre – it is 'theatre training'. In this article, my intent has been to direct awareness toward the fact that 'theatre' does not always equal 'theatre', and that historically developed theatre forms always occur within a context of certain underlying conditions for perception. As a doubling of the culture in which it occurs (Fischer-Lichte 1997), theatre can offer different ways of constructing reality through perception, as no other art form can. Even more than the stories and images themselves, it is the ways and means of presenting them that organise and influence perception. So education in the theatre begins with both the concrete situation, and the relationships, that arise between the actors and the audience.

Within aspects of education, the next steps for an educator would be to decide, accordingly, which ways of perception are relevant, and how those ways can be considered and devised. One essential condition of this activity would be that 'the children' are actively involved. Another prerequisite would be to clarify, for oneself, the educational goals and possibilities in a theatre for and with young children.

This is the mission of the project "Theatre from the very start!", and we may look forward to its findings with excitement.

*translated by Lydia Baldwin*

**References**

Buytendijk, Frederik Jacobus Johannes (1933): *Wesen und Sinn des Spiels. Das Spielen des Menschen und der Tiere als Erscheinungsform der Lebenstriebe*, Berlin 1933

Diaconu, Madalina (2005): *Tasten Riechen Schmecken. Eine Ästhetik der anästhetisierten Sinne*, Würzburg 2005

Fischer-Lichte, Erika (1997): Theater, in: Wulf,Christoph (Hrsg.):*Vom Menschen. Handbuch Historische Anthropologie*, Weinheim 1997

Fischer-Lichte, Erika (2004): *Ästhetik des Performativen*, Frankfurt Main 2004

Fischer-Lichte, Erika (2006): *Wege der Wahrnehmung. Authentizität, Reflexivität und Aufmerksamkeit im zeitgenössischen Theater*, Berlin 2006

Heise, Juliane / Pinkert, Ute (2007): *GastMahlZeit*, Katalog, Oldenburg 2007

Peez, Georg (2006): Phänomenologisch orientierte Fotoanalyse – "Schmieren", der weitgehend unerforschte Beginn der Kinderzeichnung, in: Peez, Georg: *Fotografien in pädagogischen Fallstudien. Sieben unterschiedliche qualitativ empirische Analyseverfahren zur ästhetischen Bildung – Theorie und Forschungspraxis*, München 2006 [www.georgpeez.de/texte/schmieren.htm]

Schäfer, Gerd E. (2001): *Prozesse frühkindlicher Bildung*, Online Resource: www.uni-koeln.de/ew-fak/Allg_paeda/fkf/texte/pfb_1side.pdf, 1/18/2009

Schneider, Wolfgang (2005): *Theater für Kinder und Jugendliche. Beiträge zu Theorie und Praxis*, Hildesheim Zürich New York 2005

Schouten, Sabine (2006): Was die Tasse zum Fliegen brachte. Zur wirklichkeitsgenerierenden Funktion atmosphärischer Einfühlung, in: Fischer-Lichte et al. (2006): *Wege der Wahrnehmung. Authentizität, Reflexivität und Aufmerksamkeit im zeitgenössischen Theater*, Berlin 2006

Schramm, Helmar (1996): *Karneval des Denkens. Theatralität im Spiegel philosophischer Texte des 16. und 17. Jahrhunderts*, Berlin 1996

Seitz, Hanne (2007): Leiblichkeit, Spiel, Ritual – ästhetische Erfahrung auf performativen Wegen. In: Gerd Taube (Hg.): *Kinder spielen Theater. Spielweisen und Strukturmodelle des Theaters mit Kindern*, Berlin Milow, Strasburg 2007

# The joy of re-discovering the world
## 'Communitas' and streaming in the performances made for babies

*by János Novák*

Following the thousand machinations of 'black' or 'toxic' pedagogy we successfully wean our children from the habit of following their inner commands dictated by their emotions. If we succeed in discouraging them from all individual initiatives, we can get after school lessons started. All that they might have learned happily and effectively following the impulse of their own senses will be learned without happiness and with little effectiveness under constraint. It would surely be better for our children if we could give up the everyday use of the poisonous traditions of 'black' pedagogy, but why would it be attractive to us as well? What would we, poor present day adults gain from this, while we are worried about our own importance, suffering the educational aggression once used against us – now trembling in our guts to be passed on?

The answer in short is happiness! If we exploit the special possibility which being together with little children provides us, if we give space for discovering the wonders of the world together with them, we will also be enriched. With their help we can get back the ability the joy of recognition supplies against the usual, against routine. We might try, even if for a short time, putting subordination and power aside to consider babies our equals. If we start to believe in the possibility of two-way communication well before the little ones would gain the arsenal of verbalism, we will take part in a wonderful experience. Anyone can ascertain this in moving performances for children and also here and now, when it will be really *the smallest* sitting (standing, toddling, marvelling and wondering, laughing or shouting) *with us* in the auditorium.

**Are you comfortable in your seats? Let's start!**

The embarrassing scene of an indignant, embarrassed parent leaving the auditorium with a frightened crying baby – often making whole rows stand up – is every theatre-maker's nightmare when doing theatre for children. In these cases all action on the stage is overwritten by the 'action' in the stalls. It is difficult to start again, to continue playing with credible intensity. The box-office personal and ushers are on the defensive in anticipation – they told them but the mother could not leave the little one at home while taking the brothers and sisters to the theatre. And anyway, she said that she had been to the theatre wit the baby before and the baby did watch that performance all the way through without problems, and what's more the baby enjoyed it. – Hm…, sure! We get the hint!

No, we won't negotiate any longer! – We can already feel that we've just overreacted – but we say in defence of our productions, ourselves and our audience will not let children under five into the auditorium! This is a pledge we can only keep feeling guilty and even then, only inconsistently.

We have expected our audience with a many-day non-stop family theatre program every autumn called the *Kolibri festival* right in front of out theatre building on Jókai square for the past fourteen years. Generation differences (conflicts) dissolve at such times. While the bigger children are watching performances, mothers with prams can freely move about with the smaller ones between the playground and the seats. There is no scandal, there is general contentment. Everyone can enjoy the program according to his/her own requirements, but still dissolving in the joyful feeling of being together. Our organizers are often plied with question by mothers of small children even during the season whether there are any performances they could take their children to? Let's not get into for whom this theatre-going is more important, for the mother or the offspring. It is also good for us if there is demand, and it's bad for us if we cannot fulfil it. We would like everyone to have a good time in our theatre. While guessing the child's age we contemplate what we can responsibly suggest, which performance of our repertory is the most suitable not to cause disappointment or an embarrassing situation, it being the first encounter with theatre.

## Why have no productions been made for babies before?

I'll just give you one artistic – and one financial – reason. One is Obrascov's axiom that children's theatre is harmful under the age of six! The other, that the smallest and their mothers can only watch the performance in a small auditorium and in smaller numbers, and the playing time can be less than average, maximum thirty minutes. Well, this also makes lucrativness difficult to achieve. Okay, okay! These are excuses! If we believe that this new theatrical medium can be inspirational also for us, than we can rightly expect our maintainers and the politicians to be convincible that (also) the productions made for babies are worth support and subsidy!

Still, from what should we gather our strength, if not even public demand and continuous interest could convince us that is was worth making productions for this age-group as well?

Today in Hungary if somebody regularly plays for a child audience – but desires greater professional esteem – he makes a production for adults. Look, we represent such a high quality that we also do performances for adults! – The artists of children and puppet theatre longing for more recognition thus protest to themselves, to their bosses, and to their small audiences. In the meanwhile they forget that they can meet a quite big adult audience also in the auditoriums of performances for children. They are an integral part of our audience, bearing different functions (parent, grandparent, relative or the friend of the family, teacher accompanying children, fellow artist, theatre expert, school psychologist, etc.) and it depends solely on us, artists, to have them overwhelmed by the happenings on stage. Their integration is all the more easier because the adults who come to a performance with children are emotionally motivated to worriedly see how the performance effects the children and if they are satisfied, they themselves also relax and accept the collectiveness in becoming an equal member of the audience and an integral part of the performance. If they are not stressed by some retrograde pedagogical preconception, the success of the performance is just as much important for them as for the adult actors. Their presence makes it possible to talk about real rituals and is case of children's theatre as well, and what's more, it seems that in this day and age besides all liminoid theatre forms, only children's theatre would give them a real liminal ritual experience, where adults form a community with children, the actors with the audience.

A professor of the *Freie Universität* of Berlin, Sabine Schouten called my attention to the fact that the theatre staging done for babies often meets the requirement of *performativity*, a new notion widespread among philosophers in the nineties. She mentioned those performances as examples where the stage-setting does not produce the illusion of something, but the stage is transformed into something else by the collaboration of the participants/players. In these cases it does not make sense to ask why and for what aim these events occur. The artists don't want you to recognize anything; the materials, the movements mean themselves, they are true in their own reality. The events are also references of themselves, thus the stage plot looks like a series of not repeatable, unique events. The performance cannot be played in the same manner twice due to the feedback between players and audience.

The performativity observed in children's theatre also makes it possible for adults to sense the stunning novelties of the world waiting to be discovered, since if the events on stage are not illustrations but create an independent self-identical world – where we can share the joy of discovery too (!) – the adult and baby can cast a glance into the world constructed by theatre.

Can we except that in the name of artistic exploration and the search for the root of theatrical effect-mechanisms the new stratum of audience will be made up of babies and their mothers, supposedly inspiring the birth of interesting new theatrical forms? This thought seemed nonsense to us until now. And I cannot boast about having thought of the idea first, but luck still played into my hands this time.

When the Norwegian organizers first called me to say they were planning this co-operation in the framework of the EU project for the ages up to three, it thought I wasn't hearing right. After meeting them in person and seeing the finished Norwegian performances I began to comprehend how important this baby-theatre co-operation must be for them. I succeeded in getting the creative team of *Kolibri Theatre* –Zoltán Bodnár, Bea Tisza, Károly Szívós and Ágnes Török - involved in the common work, as well as Yvette Bozsik, Attila Rácz and their artist companions. And as it usually happens, even here in Hungary there are more and more people interested in what the results of our project will be. When we were looking for partners for the tour preceding the Budapest Meeting, we were welcomed with interest and joy by the directors of theatres and puppet theatres in the country. They were happy that we would also show the already finished productions to the audience of our city. Is it possible that toddler's theatre is 'in the air'? The interest, the several months of working together, the revelation-like experiences of audience-reaction during the rehearsals in theatres and day-nurseries urge us to re-think some basic questions concerning general characteristics of theatre, of theatre for babies and children. We've also asked professionals for help, but have put the question to ourselves as well: what is happening in the auditorium during performances? What aspects determine the reception of our work?

## The change of physical traits of humans

The typical changes of form that occur during the growth of a human have inspired a significant literature of biology, writes Stephen Jay Gould, a professor at *Harvard University*, specialist in science in his article entitled "Biological respect to Mickey Mouse". As it is the embryo's head that develops first and grows faster than the leg part (technically speaking this is called antero-posterior gradient), the relatively big head of an infant is connected to a medium size body and small feet. Later in the process of growth this gradient changes to the contrary when the leg part gets ahead of the head in terms of growth. The head continues growing but a lot slower than other parts of the body, thus the relative size of the head diminishes. In the course of the growth of a human, a number of changes occur on the head itself. The skulls of our embryos hardly differ from that of a chimpanzee. And the change in shape follows the same route during the growth: the fornix of the skull grows relatively smaller, as after birth the brain grows a lot slower than the body, while our jaws also grow more or less continuously. But while these changes are quite explicit in the case of chimpanzees and can result in a significantly different adult considering the form of the infant, we proceed a lot slower on this road and don't even approach the amount of change they undergo. Still, we change enough for there to be a significant difference between infants and adults, even though the change in us is a lot less than what we can observe in the case of chimps and other primates.

After the age of three the brain grows very slowly and the small child's round skull gives over to the more stretched form of adult skulls with a lower forehead. The eyes hardly grow at all, and their relative size diminishes abruptly. The jaw, however, gets bigger and bigger. Children, compared to adults, have bigger heads and eyes, smaller and thicker lower limbs and feet. All in all, the adult skull is more monkey-like.

In one of his most famous articles Konrad Lorenz proves that characteristic differences between small children and adults are used by humans as important warnings for behaviour. He believes that the characteristic traits of youth start the "hereditary mechanism" of caring in adult people. *If we see a baby-formed living creature, we are flooded by an involuntary wave of disarming tenderness.* The adaptive value of this answer cannot be doubted, as we have to nourish our infants. Our deduction, that we consider the tender reaction of adults to the outward form of small children generally characteristic of mankind, is independent of whether we had *inherited* this inclination directly from our primate ancestors – as Konrad Lorenz thinks –, or it can be simply *derived from firsthand experience* with our infants and correlates to our evolutional ability of connecting *emotional threads to certain learned signs*. Our statement is also supported by the main thesis of Lorenz's article, according to which we do not react to the whole or the form (Gestalt), but the reasons are elicited from us by a series of characteristic traits. This reasoning supports the evolutional identity between the behaviour of humans and other vertebral animals. We can learn from Lorenz's article "Ganzheit und Teil in der tierischen und menschlichen Gemeinschaft" (1950) that many birds often react to abstract forms rather than shape and figure.

The way Disney changed the proportion and look of the figure of Mickey Mouse film by film in the span of fifty years, thus changing its character traits as well, can be interpreted in this context.

National symbols – and Mickey Mouse represents the USA all over the world – are not usually changed on a whim. Market researchers (especially in the doll business) have spent significant amount of time and energy to find out what figures seem nice and friendly to people.

Biologists have also spent a lot of time examining similar questions among a series of animals. The have observed that a lot of animals – for reasons absolutely irrelevant to the induction of human emotions – have common traits with human babies that cannot be found in human adults. Namely, the big eyes, the bulging forehead, and the retracting chin. We are attracted to these animals; we coddle them as pets and admire them in the wild. But we reject their small-eyed, long muzzled relatives, even though those may be even more loving companions and could claim our admiration with more reason. To put it short: the answer we formulated for our own infants deceives us when we transfer our reactions to the same traits even when they are embodied by a different animal.

These observations may answer the metamorphosis Mickey Mouse's figure had gone through along the years. Its adult proportions were more and more substituted for infant proportions. The aim at popularity turned the ontogenetic route around and developed the character from an adult into an infant.

Disney's character followed Mickey Mouse in their struggle for love and sympathy. Donald Duck also put on a more youthful shape, while the wicked figures of the cartoons put on more and more adult traits.

**The development of the 'hydrocephalic' attitude**

The moral of Mickey Mouse's slow transformation met conscious and – a lot of – instinctive followers all over the world. Figures having a hydrocephalic look invaded the illustrated storybooks as well as cartoons, the creators of which didn't shrink back from the uncritical copying of Disney, envying his international success. It was the same kind of fad as the streamlined kitsch-wave of the sixties when everything from toilet paper holder to corkscrew was shaped to the same drop form by the designers hoping for greater financial success. They are the ones who would use or abuse the infant proportions in favour of consumption-results if they thought it was needed.

Recently an international company which produces female dress-up dolls with adult shapes has turned to the hydrocephalic trick, as they realized that interest towards their dolls was diminishing. They started producing their classic dolls with bigger heads. Success was inevitable as the little girls practicing adult female roles on the dolls also had the opportunity of pampering and loving their big-headed dolls in a motherly way while dressing them up as grown women. It is not by chance that these dolls are most popular among teenagers, as they are the ones who perceive themselves as big girls in one instance and a little girl in need of pampering in the next.

Infant-projection unleashes its 'beneficial' effects in different areas through our unconscious. This condescending hydrocephalic attitude which abuses our reflexes is what impedes the acceptance and spreading of modern views concerning infant behaviour and the possibilities of communication with them. The trick which helps marketing personal and designers get round us so easily seems too simple and it is degrading to everyone who wants to seriously rethink the notions concerning infants. Incidentally, even the wave of love that overflows us at the sight of an infant, as if a "button had been pushed", that is, the very strength of our feelings can prevent us from really perceiving the infants' personality, their unique characteristics, and from sensing how important interpersonal communication is from the very first moment on, in the way it is most acceptable for children. Of course the mothers have always been in possession of this knowledge, but they too are isolated from a bigger group of society in this period, together with their infants, thus remaining alone with their realizations. Theatre also contributes to this isolation when it banns mothers with small children from its performances! For this view to change we have to reinterpret our requirement for the theatre for children radically and as soon as possible!

## The comparative symbology as regards children's theatre

In this phrase 'symbology' means the study and interpretation of symbols, while 'comparative' only suggest that this science also uses the method of comparison.

In Victor Turner's 1969 work entitled "The Ritual Process" we read of observations based on the analysis of the habits of the Ndembu tribe in Zambia, which help everyone in the deeper understanding of the rituals of theatre. During the analysis of the habits connected to the cyclic change of nature or to the change in the status of certain people, he observed the liminal (threshold) situation prevalent in tribal societies in which the three phases of the ritual of transition can be clearly defined. These are: separation, transition and integration. In the theatrical behaviour – i.e. liminoid (threshold) rituals – of industrial and post-industrial societies these three phases can be well grasped, in performances for adults as well as for children. We can also come to fruitful conclusions researching the parallels of children's theatre with the above mentioned phases; still, out of the notions of cultural anthropologist Victor Turner my curiosity was most aroused by the description of the rite of status-inversion mostly characteristic of the liminal phase. It wasn't until I read it that I felt that the notions of cultural anthropology give us a new point of view, possibilities for new approaches for all of us in the better understanding and explanation of the phenomena experienced during performances for children.

During the *apo* celebrations of the North Ashant ethnic group in Ghana, which take place during the eight days directly preceding tekiman New Year starting on 18th April (first described by the Dutch historian Bosman in 1705), everyone can talk about the faults, wickedness and cheating of their superiors with impunity. In the Zulu nomkubulwana celebration analyzed by Max Gluckman in 1954, which is held when the crops start growing, women get the dominant role, while the men behave as if subjugated. During the *holí* rituals in India, an analysis of which was published by Professor McKim Marriott in 1966, in a celebration connected to a Krisna ritual, the women beat the shins of the wealthiest Brahman and Djat/Ghat farmers if they find them on the streets. Often the most ferocious beater are the wives of lower caste workers, craftsmen and servants who are at the same time lovers or housekeepers of the victims.

What is common in these rituals? The inversion of status during the celebrations frees the people of their own status and also causes a temporary equilibration of social differences. Those above have to bow in the face of humiliation; while the submissive ones are raised by direct speech, a privilege freely exercised as a way of getting rid of accumulated aggression. If the ritual is connected to a yearly cycle, this makes it possible for the participants to get rid of all their bad feelings that were accumulated in structural relations in the previous year. They ensure that the bad deeds – by which usually high ranking people do wrong to lower ranking ones – come out into the open. And the perpetrators of these deeds refrain from taking revenge on the ones who had just reproached them for their bad deeds. Professor Marriott writes about the *holi* ritual:

> "Here the village population's interpersonal relations based on love, but being very different, often waning ... all suddenly step out of their narrow channels due to the sudden and simultaneous increasing of intensity. The usual separation and indifference of the isolated families and castes is flooded by a one-sided feeling of love without boundaries. This liberated libido overflows all hierarchical order of age, sex, caste, wealth and power ... Under Krisna's charitable supervision every person plays and experiences, if only for a moment, the role of his opponent; the obliging wife that of the overbearing husband, and the other way around, the rapist that of the raped, the servant that of the master, the enemy that of the friend, the youth kept well in hand the role of the leaders of the community. The anthropologist undertaking the observation was given the role of a dumb farmer. Every participant takes on the roles of the other people who are in relation to them, thus everyone can learn to play their own role in a different way, having a better understanding of it, maybe having more good will, maybe mutual love."

The blissful experience of temporary equality is a trait of the state called 'communitas' by Turner. The anti-structure experienced in liminality, by the end of the process, in the phase of integration results in the strengthening of the original structure. The rituals of status-inversion in the tribal and farming societies ensure the constancy of the structure by getting rid of the accumulated tension.

**The ritual of status inversion in a performance for children**

The moment we cross the threshold of the theatre, the child under our supervision turns from a subjugated being into a spectator, a person all adult actors, stagehands, auditorium and box office staff, parents and teachers – the people who in all other circumstances are 'superiors' of the child just by the very nature of them being adults – want to please. When the lights go down the child has the same status as the adults, because the taboos of theatre defend him – e.g. the accompanying adult cannot rebuke him without consequence –, if he accepts one or two rules; not to shout when you're not allowed to, or to shout when the performance urges you to. Not even the adult spectator can make a decision about which attitude to choose now: will the self-restriction of 'peeping' theatre or the rules of interactive theatre be valid? The rules of theatre apply to the adults just as they do to the children. This can be especially uncomfortable for the adults with interaction, but this discomfort can nowadays find the spectator also in performances for adults. Adults, for the duration of the performance, have to give up the role of being omnipotent and infallible. The performance's elements of effect are a challenge to them also; they can experience unexpected surprises during the play. They can only voice their opinion as any other audience member. The taboos of theatre apply to them, too. This isn't bad; what's more, it can be a pleasant and liberating experience for a normal adult. By giving up their status of power, the parents can also experience the floating, blissful state of 'communitas', the joy of streaming overflowing the auditorium. The 'degraded' adult and the 'raised' child are also enriched by a lot of new realizations about each other in this 'adjunct' situation. They get to know a new personality of the other one, which is enchanted by playing, something they didn't or hardly had a chance to see, thus after the performance the habitual child-parent or child-teacher relationship is deepened and enriched.

Through the reactions of the infants to a theatrical production made especially for them, we, the adults, can become part of a kind of ritual process only the members of tribal societies had possibility to experience. In our day and age, in the centuries following industrial revolution, playing and celebrations have clearly been restricted to within the boundaries of free-time as opposed to working, which by the very juxtaposition of the two things suggests the useless frivolity of the former. In farming societies on average 150 holidays were celebrated. These celebrations all served the interest of the community, reflected the values of the community. The games and rituals also followed higher aims. The games infants play, are also part of the work through which the world becomes understandable for us. These games are very serious! In the theatre, in celebration-like conditions we can also become part of this ritual, we can make such discoveries together that would draw us into a circuit of happy levitation both as artists and people sitting among the audience.

**Crumbs and experiences: The first fruits of common work**

The smallest ones know nothing of theatrical conventions. Of course it can work without making them conscious of it, as the mothers with their infants on their lap are all turning towards the stage, being full of expectation. This behaviour influences the children. We can also decide to only let the little ones into the auditorium at the very last moment, so boredom and expectation would not break their attention too soon. However conventional the space, – be it even the least suitable guckkasten-theatre –, the free movement between stage and audience has to be ensured. Nothing may impede to safe return of the little toddlers, – for example too strong a light or a dark auditorium. If what they see is attractive, they go closer, imitate what they see there, and if they are frightened, they run back to their mothers. The events on stage are perceived by the children as real happenings. Events as the mere illustration of things already known are uninteresting. What they see has to gather some importance as something that is interesting in itself *during* the performance. The dynamics of the succession of stage events gives the material, the arch and the culminating points of the performance.

The theatre for infants also shows similar ambitions to repetitive compositions, as the repeated elements at this age are almost indispensable. Repetition makes the performance more friendly and familiar, thus making the production – and life through it – comprehendible and accessible as an experience.

It is important to know that at the infant stage children cannot yet be separated from their mother or caretaker. Adult and child are inseparable in the theatre as well. Their being together makes it possible for us to view this kind of performance as a special form of theatrical ritual. The events on stage have to have an effect on the adults as well. Besides, I have not seen as many happy mothers in theatre auditoriums as during these productions. The realization that theatre actually had a good influence on the little ones spread among them. While the mothers list the ways the playing affected their children, what they perceived, when and how the little ones reacted, these recognitions become their own experiences. Their empathy is transformed into their own feelings, and the child's happiness liberates the mother too. Theatre gives them a chance of being together happily in a period when they are usually characterized by the syndrome called post-partum blues caused by their isolation and the growing number of duties.

The children pay attention to each other as well. The sounds of excitement, of fear or laughter pass through them as it usually happens with 'real' audiences. Norwegian performers have said that they had been to a lot of places all over the world and they usually had success because their performances were understood everywhere.[1] The actors can play with the best efficiency if the children in the auditorium are more or less the same age. In this period even one or two months can make a difference, not to mention differences that amount to years. A child that reacts differently or at a different time from the others can break the attention span of the others, and draws them away from the performance. This feeling can be familiar to adult theatre-goers as well. If we happen to sit next to a well-informed audience member or a relative who reacts to the performance with loud sensations, we have a good chance of being left out of the enjoyment of the play. This is why we usually ask that children older than four are not brought among the younger ones, because the older ones, with their faster reactions do not make it possible for the younger ones to contemplate and receive things undisturbed. Of course we still have to strive not to create stupid rules that are impossible to implement and which suggest the separation of families!

The three-year collaboration and rehearsal process insured by the program "Glitterbird – art for the very young" is a refreshing opportunity for all Hungarian participants. In the last year we had three open rehearsals asking for the opinion of a specialist of day-nursery education, a psychologist, a brain researcher and a music therapist about their impressions. The Budapest Meeting creates the possibility of incorporating the experience of the artists of partner

---

1 Attention! Here understanding is not connected to verbal means; we can rather define it as the active experiencing of stage events. Now we are really down to the roots of theatrical effect-mechanisms!

countries into our own work in the remaining time. We hope the present meeting helps their work too and that we can give an account of what we learned to each other and to the French public at our closing program in Paris. Maybe it is not an immodest hope either, that through this collaboration we might gain the right and opportunity of theatre-going for infants and their mothers, and that our example may inspire more talented artists to further experiment with the theatre for children and infants. To do some work of discovery!

# The category of simplicity and the complexity of the theatre
Art education requirements, neurobiological justification and cultural policy considerations for the dramatic arts beginning with earliest childhood

*by Wolfgang Schneider*

Hanne Trolle from Denmark is absolutely essential in any discussion of theatre for the very youngest children. Her artistic work is valued in Germany as well. Her *Teatret Mänegogl* in Grenaa is doing a production for one and a half to four year olds. 'Elverklokken' means 'fairy bells', but sounds much prettier in Danish. So it's about fairies and bells, about a magic forest and a magic cave, a child and some animals. There are finger figures and hand puppets, puppets on sticks and dangling from threads, and they perform in front of, behind and on the stage. And that surprised me. I always thought things should be as simple as possible when performing for this fidgety audience in diapers. Not at all! Everything is so colourful that you can't perceive colours anymore; everything is so complex that I myself have problems keeping up with the arsenal of figures. And do one and a half year-olds need theatre in the first place? "No, they don't," says Hanne Trolle, "but they still enjoy it!"

Agnès Desfosses' infant theatre in France takes psychomotoric developments into account just as it does the short attention spans of children under three or above four years old. Their mobility plays a role and the importance of all forms of their perception. So her play, "Sous la table", is a play for climbing, nibbling and touching things, for listening, looking and dancing. To tame the feelings of the children so they aren't so wild, the youngest spectators get to watch while the actors change their clothes and put on makeup. For actors, this kind of theatre is often a baptism by fire. A lyrical singer finds it hard to accept that some babies fall asleep under the charm of their singing, and it's not easy for a dancer to watch as some of the youngest in the audience imitate him during the choreography, and it's not easy for anyone to be touched during the performance.

Roberto Frabetti from Italy writes and performs imaginative stories for one to three-year-olds. One of them is called "Dinosaurs" and begins with a cabinet. The little ones and their teachers sit on mats; Frabetti greets each of them and this way creates a small circle of spectators. Then he tells about a trip to a big tree in the forest and his little birds and other animals, a simple story about big things, small things and changes. The cabinet contains the secrets of the imagined forest which the storyteller gradually discloses. Again and again, Frabetti folds out a section of the cabinet and allows us to see his arsenal of figures. When finally everything is uncovered, he turns the cabinet around and lo and behold; and there it is, big and powerful, that animal from primeval times.

Thirty-five minutes later, Frabetti packs everything up and bids farewell. During the performance he never withdraws from the children. He is often among them – because they are the theatre. The key to success is to gain their attention. The theatre gives something, the audience takes it. That demands enormous charisma on the part of the storyteller. Frabetti responds to the smallest movements of the children. Among them are those who are very active, the lazy ones, the shy ones or those who are easy to distract. The pitch of voice is important, just as is his friendly but determined look. I never would have believed that theatre like this works if I hadn't seen it with my own two eyes. And I don't know if theatre means anything to the youngest children. But the way they are treated, what is shown to them, and the intensity with which a person pays attention to them must have a positive impact on their lives.

## Simple is not easy

Simplicity as a category seems to be fairly straightforward. How is theatre for children different from theatre for adults? Most people who think about this question for the first time would say that in order to be accepted by its target audience, children's theatre must keep things simple compared with other forms of theatre. In terms of language, manner of representation and subject matter, it cannot exceed a certain level of complexity. A subset of theatre – children's theatre – is thus judged to be 'simple' based on the relatively low level of decoding ability that is required of its audience.

Simplicity is a negative characteristic in the correlation between the child spectators and their limited ability to anticipate art. The implication is that as part of the overall system of theatre, children's theatre is on a lower level because the little spectator can only be reached by means of 'simple' theatre. It is assumed that accessibility for children, which is indispensable for children's theatre, is necessarily created in an artistically uncomplicated way.

But it is necessary to investigate whether plays that accommodate a child's field of interest and comprehension require less sophisticated, so to speak undeveloped theatrical patterns, or whether regard for the child's ability to comprehend makes it necessary to provide not very complicated forms of presentation. If we consider the many issues raised by the relationship to the child spectator and the variety of approaches taken for their solution, as well as the various levels and functions of children's theatre in the social reference field, classifying all children's theatre as 'simple' would seem to be a dubious undertaking indeed. Simplicity, as a defining characteristic that distinguishes it from other theatre, is thus likely not suitable to the extent it designates a lower level of theatre.

On the other hand, the fact cannot be overlooked that the notion of 'simplicity' is significant in the context of children's theatre. This is already evident on a practical level, in the area of children's theatre criticism. Widespread children's theatre criticism has a pragmatic interest in the level of 'simplicity' that arises out of its task as facilitator and consultant. By helping adult facilitators of children's theatre – parents and professional educators – make selections and review the offerings, it at the same time classifies them by quality and degree of difficulty, thus meeting the need adults have for expert orientation when they search for 'simple', 'not too simple' etc. plays for children. In this practical-journalistic usage, the term 'simple' is being applied in the generally accepted sense, i.e. synonymously with 'easy'.

The conflation of simplicity and accessibility in terms of reception presents its own set of issues, however. Speaking of a simple performance as easy receivable only makes sense, of course, with reference to a reception standard on which it is based. The notion of this reception capability, regardless what its nature might be – average, ideal or childlike? – implies at the same time an objective meaning that is comprehended or not by the spectator. What goes unnoticed here is that meaning in theatre is created in the emergence of a *new* theatre – namely, theatre in the minds of its spectators. Compared with the theatre experienced on stage, this can be of more or less complexity. Inexperienced spectators e.g. can elude the cumbersome process of creating meaning with complex staging by quickly grasping, understanding and enjoying them in simpler ways. On the other hand, it is known that children e.g. also use so-called trivial children's books as 'musical scores' for complex creations of their own.

**Simplification as art**

The provisional character that theatrically simple things assume in connection with children's theatre represents a constriction of sorts. We learn this from a look at history. With the beginning of the middle-class culture and way of life that also gave rise to children's theatre, the theory of poetry of the eighteenth century, in particular, attributed to the 'simple' a variety of meanings under the name of innocence, simplicity and naivety that can encourage a grasp of the conceptual complex that is so significant for children's theatre in ways that do justice to its wide variety of features and that are more sophisticated and of greater theoretical clarity.

1. Simplicity was for a long time the ideal of writing in the early Enlightenment period, a response to the Baroque courtly standard of linguistic adornment. Things in Germany, clear and comprehensible were viewed more favourably.
2. In his theoretical efforts to achieve unity of dramatic form, Lessing arrived at the concept of simplicity; he attributed it to the dramatists of antiquity who knew how to "simplify the plot itself, to remove everything dispensable so carefully that, reduced to its essential elements, it became nothing other than

an ideal of this plot." Simplification, accordingly, is the poetic procedure of focusing on the essential elements of a subject.
3. Herder's appraisal of common people's poetry as poetry of the highest order is based on Rousseau's discovery of the naturalness of primitive peoples. Naive 'folk style' or 'children's style' that is not fractured by art convention is superior to established art. The character of art is always attributed to simple things. From the variations of meaning sketched here we can say that simplicity in various poetological contexts can refer both to the complexity of linguistic and artistic forms and the complexity of the world that is being depicted. It is not necessarily connected with the concept of comprehensibility, but at times is its opposite if e.g. it departs as an expression of immediacy, spontaneity and 'child-likeness' from the forms of orderly communication. The ways of understanding the simple mentioned here would also be described in a theory of children's theatre. When speaking of the child's need for uncomplicated actions that focus on individual, essential moments, the simple is being addressed as the organizing principle of the dramatic subject.

How, therefore, should we proceed to make the category of simplicity useful for the complexity of theatre? Our starting point is the basic conviction that children and adults live in the same world. A premise could be derived from this, namely, that theatre can be a place of understanding and communication between children and adults, that children's theatre should be an introduction to the complexity of the theatre and that spectators – no matter whether old or young – therefore must be introduced to the complexity of reality.

A second premise is that children have a need for information and that this need is directed not only to the conditions that surround the children but also to those that are inaccessible to them. We would have to address the situation of today's children with the media offerings, and consequently also the utilization of their informational needs by the entertainment industry that – in contrast with children's theatre – reaches all children. Commodities that make an appeal to children in this area are a response to the need for an explanation of reality, supplied in the form of dream products. For children's theatre the question arises here if children being catered to in this way are already or even at all in a position to look for something else in theatre or if, equipped with a finished world view provided by tapes, television and comic books, they expect only for it to be confirmed; at issue here is thus the leeway remaining for their need for information. Under these circumstances, the explanation of the world provided by children's theatre is hardly an answer to open demand; it answers questions that possibly might not even arise and asks questions which the children have no more time to think about. Such doubts must accompany our reflections on children's theatre today.

A third and final premise is our society's demand for education. If theatre for children thus can be a dialogue of the generations and seeks to satisfy the need to acquire the world, it will require a culture-pedagogical conceptual design that on the one hand appreciates children as target group in the respective state of development and on the other hand provides them with offerings that take them seriously in both content and aesthetics as partners in cultural communication.

The role of Art education should be redefined in this connection. It can be meaningful in the context of a theatre for the very youngest children and can be of special significance particularly in an artistically designed programme for the first years of life – the kind of significance that unfortunately is not yet adequately appreciated in the political realm.

**Art education is a challenge for society**

As part of all social and individual educational processes it reflects the changing demands placed on general education. It is a response to the trends that mould the future of our society: the growing diversification of circumstances and lifestyles brought about by Europeanization and globalization, the transformation into a society of knowledge and the mediatisation of all circumstances. Art education is indispensable because it makes it possible to experience, understand and endure the permanent change taking place in society. It defines education as process and permanent change.

Art education is necessary because living and learning in our society have changed. For a long time now, family and school have not been able to cope alone with the tasks of socialization that are necessary for society. Rather, they are part of a greater context of learning and socialization. The educational processes themselves have thus become different. In addition to formal opportunities for learning, informal learning processes are becoming increasingly important.

Art education can contribute to more equal opportunities because it begins its approach with the subjects of the new educational processes and taps their potential and creativity. It must become a part of all educational processes and will change them – in pre-school education in nurseries, kindergartens and all other school types, in vocational training, at colleges and universities, and in adult and continuing education.

Especially in the context of pre-school educational facilities, the creative abilities of the children – in a compensatory sense as well – can be fostered and developed. The basis for Art education is not the teaching of knowledge, but the unfolding of sensory experiences and the experience of creating something alone and with others. Other points of view and forms of expression can be encountered directly, especially with children of pre-school age. Individual aptitude, cultural background and social origin are not hard-and-fast distinctive characteristics. Art education in nursery school, kindergartens and elementary schools thus has the important task of promotion and integration.

Educating children and young people about culture can allow them to become creatively involved in art, culture and everyday life. It can promote their artistic-aesthetic activity, develop powers of perception, strengthen their faculty of judgment and encourage them to become active members of society. No one will argue with me when I say that "Children need art". When I state it as a question "Do children need art?" again, no one will disagree. First of all, of course, children need food and drink, a roof over their heads, health care and social services. These are essential, but even so not always implicit in our world. The recognition is also not self-evident that art and culture play a critical role in changing our society because they have always interacted with economic and technological developments. The *Commission for Future Studies of the Free States of Bavaria and Saxony* (*Kommission für Zukunftsfragen der Freistaaten Bayern und Sachsen*) writes:

> "In the end, supporting art and culture is of central importance for the transition to the entrepreneurial knowledge-based society. Art and culture tap the creativity of a population. By no means are they mere decorative elements. For this reason, expenditures that support them are not frivolous but rather indispensable investments in the development of a society."

Official support is necessary for cultural institutions so that art and culture can be accorded the significance that e.g. the authors of the *Commission for Future Studies* attach to them. While information, raw materials, transport and labour costs are still crucial industrial resources in an age of globalisation of world markets, it has long been recognized in terms of innovation and quality of new products – they can be very critical for the economic success of industries – that in the twenty-first century a company's product-oriented creativity and people skills are also essential resources that are becoming increasingly significant.

## Nothing is in the mind that was not previously in the senses

Brain research has shown how important it is to accompany human beings from their first year of life and to help them integrate themselves into the world in which they are born. Today there is no doubt that the development of the human brain continues until the end of puberty. The newborn comes equipped with a brain in which all nerve cells are already created, but they are largely unconnected. The neural networks that must be created for the brain to function are only in rudimentary form and many centres, in particular the cerebral cortex, are still unable to function. With the exception of structures in the brain that are responsible for maintaining vital functions, most regions of the brain undergo a tumultuous development process that culminates during the first years of life and then again just before puberty.

A dramatic example for the eminent role played by the interaction between brain and environment in developing brain functions is the development of basal cognitive capacities. If the visual centres in the brain are prevented from receiving visual information through the eyes – for example, if the lenses of both eyes are clouded – the necessary connecting architectures cannot be developed. Already created connections are destroyed because their function cannot be acknowledged, and the result is that the child remains blind even if the optical media of the eyes can be corrected later in an operation. The eye then supplies the brain with normal signals from the environment again, but the visual centres are unable to process these signals in a meaningful way. Even just a few months of visual deprivation are sufficient to cause irreversible damage. This applies in similar fashion to the development of centres that are responsible for understanding and producing speech. Here, too, the corresponding neural structures must be formed during critical developmental phases. This would also pertain to the development of social skills, sensitivity for artistic forms of communication, development of aesthetic criteria and much more.

In viewing our current system of education, it is striking that it emphasises very unilaterally certain competencies and neglects others. Of the many possibilities for expression and communication that people use, we predominantly train the use of the mother tongue. "Much of what human beings must communicate and actually do communicate to each other in order to build stable social structures cannot be contained in rational languages alone," maintains the director of the *Max Planck Institute* in Frankfurt am Main, Wolf Singer. This would apply in particular "for affects, unconscious action motifs and contradictory moods". From this he derives the necessity to provide optimum development of non-linguistic communication capabilities, and they also require practice and refinement. Surely, however, current educational and school structures fall short here. The ability to understand and transport the contents that must be encoded in non-linguistic form is precisely what is important for acquiring social competencies and becoming integrated into the cultural world.

How old, actually, is the demand for holistic learning? In any case it is nothing new. Early on, educators, philosophers and psychologists recognised that holistic learning and a large variety of sensory experiences are significant for a child's development: John Amos Comenius (1592-1670) was one of the first educators to point out that knowledge is based on sensory perception. Philosopher John Locke (1632-1704) declared: "Nothing is in the mind that was not previously in the senses" But he was still basing this on a dichotomy, that people have both sensory and intellectual powers. In his famous educational novel "Emile" the philosopher Jean-Jacques Rousseau (1712-1778) devoted a chapter to the "Use of Organs and Senses". And we owe the saying "Learning with head, heart and hand" to the educator Johann Heinrich Pestalozzi (1746-1827). These early theoretical approaches took serious sensory training to be a sharpening of the individual sensory organs. They still did not know that concerted use of all senses is able to improve our thinking and learning performance. The Italian physician Maria Montessori (1870-1952) was the first to postulate that the child in its development follows a biological blueprint that should be nurtured by education. Based on the idea of "Help me to do it by myself" she developed sensory-stimulating learning aids that are now known to all educators as Montessori materials.

This brief historical excursion is supposed to show that holistic learning is not something invented by contemporary educational theorists. 'Learning with all the senses' is a demand that has been rediscovered. Today, however, we can substantiate it with data provided by brain, intelligence and learning research. At one time a conjecture that head, heart and hand could form a learning unit; this is now scientifically based certainty.

Not only new data provided by brain and learning research, however, but also the increasing behavioural abnormalities (movement, perception and concentration disorders) require that we rethink the learning process. A kind of thinking that respects children in their entirety. After all, they come as small children to kindergarten and school full of curiosity. They do not hang up their feelings on the coat rack like they do their parkas, and they don't wait around with empty heads waiting to be filled with knowledge.

Children need more than ever for their own thought, feeling, experiencing and actions to be challenged. That is because the artificial pictures from the media are increasingly displacing the concrete, 'real' encounter of child and world. Children need a wide variety of personal experiences because the grasping of the physical world (German: 'greifen') that precedes all understanding (German: 'begreifen') of it cannot be replaced by either the media or the computer. Children need learning processes that begin with experiencing, discovering and exploring. They need learning processes that successfully combine motion, perception and realisation.

"A child has 100 languages", observed the Italian philosopher Loris Malaguzzi, "but we have stolen 99 from him". Theatre can – in my opinion – return these through listening, seeing, singing, understanding, feeling, speaking, playing and much more. "Theatre for Early Years" does not separate head and stomach; it can be an emotional experience, an intelligent imagination, a cultural investment.

# Reports

# Big drama for small spectators
*Unga Klara's* **Swedish experiment**

*by Dan Höjer*

– Theatre about fertilization, about life in the womb and the meaning of life, a performance for babies between six and twelve months and adults who accompany the children. There were many who smiled at director Suzanne Osten before the performance "Babydrama" was set up at *Unga Klara* in Stockholm.

Never before had anyone ever produced 'serious theatre' for such small children: nobody in the whole world. But its success has been total. After more than seventy performances, the play reopened on the 27th of April 2007. And the audience's rush continued. Only a few days on, most shows were already sold out.

The critics tried to surpass each other with superlatives. Enthusiastically, they described how an audience of twelve babies and their parents was sitting there, spellbound. The newspaper "Göteborgs-Posten" commented: "There is a level of concentration and on-the-edge attentiveness in the auditorium which every theatre ensemble dreams of." And *Swedish Radio P 5* broadcast the ultimate praise: "I think this play is a reason for having children."

And, like the onion on top of a slice of salmon, the ensemble of "Babydrama" was nominated for the "Swedish Award of Drama Critique for Children's and Young People's Theatre" 2006.

And the world became curious about this Swedish theatre experiment. Suzanne Osten and Ann-Sofie Bárány, author of "Babydrama" travelled to Paris where they presented the project and were met with great interest. Psychoanalyst Ann-Sofie Bárány considers it vital that children are allowed to explore their fantasy and creativity in order to develop their ability for empathy. She is tough with those who question the very idea of theatre for babies; those critics who call "Babydrama" superfluous, those arguing that babies lack the necessary understanding. She said in an interview:

> "Babies understand much more spoken language than they can produce themselves. One cannot generalise. We are dealing with a kind of 'baby-apartheid'; we push them all into one category. Babies' individualities differ just as much as adults' personalities do."

But how is it really to perform for a completely inexperienced audience? "Opsis Kalopsis" has met actor Claire Wikholm and theatre musician Torbjörn Svedberg who act in "Babydrama".

## Like a small miracle

Claire Wikholm's answer is lyrical when she describes the meeting with the audience. "I detest all kinds of new age or fuzziness," she says.

"But in this performance we often encountered situations which are impossible to explain, incidents which you just have to experience. People who watched us during the rehearsals saw a gang of actors who were so content; we just walked around and smiled. There have been times of complete magic between stage and auditorium. Times when the children experienced that we were 100 percent concentrated and they, in turn, answered us with all of their attentiveness. It feels almost as if you have experienced a miracle.
And it was fantastic to see that the performance worked so well for adults as well. Many parents told us that it was so intense that they started to cry. And this happened although we did not address the adult audience at all."

Torbjörn Svedberg has had the same experience. "It was magic," he says.

"Here you can really talk about an honest audience. When it was too boring, they slept. And vice versa: When they liked it a lot they just started to roar with laughter. Their laughter could come at any point of the performance and it was very contagious."

Both, Claire and Torbjörn, were sceptical about the idea of baby theatre when they got the offer to participate in the performance. "I thought that was a joke," says Claire.

"I had never worked with Suzanne Osten or in children's theatre before. First, I thought it was to be a play for adults. And this, I thought, sounded very interesting. But when I understood that this was to be a theatre performance for babies I thought: This will never work, we won't get anywhere with this."

Torbjörn's first feeling was "Mmh..."

"I didn't really know what was going on, just curious. I hadn't had any problems with doing concerts for small children. This became clear to me. But theatre, and dialogue – And what should it be about? It's safe to say that my reaction was a sceptical one."

At *Unga Klara*, it is part of the normal work processes that the whole ensemble does in-depth research regarding the subject matter of a play they develop. For the production of "Babydrama" this process lasted several months which is quite unusual compared to other theatres.

The actors had a thorough introduction into the life of newborn children. They met a midwife and a child psychologist; they talked to a gynaecologist and met premature babies. They studied babies' development, needs, language, concepts of time and much, much more.

Psycho-analyst Ann-Sofie Bárány, who wrote the script, interviewed the ensemble about their memory of their own birth. In case they did not have any, they created their own stories about how it might have been. Claire Wikholm had never been part of this kind of research and thought it was extremely interesting to learn so much.

> "But I can't remember a thing about how it felt in my mother's womb. So I just had to start to fantasize and remember what my mother had told me. I decided for myself that I enjoyed being in there. It was wonderful and I didn't want to come out."

## For god's sake – they understand!

The close cooperation with the scriptwriter is also something special in Swedish theatre. In the majority of cases the actors receive the script and start working with it directly. Claire Wikholm had never been involved in anything similar.

> "First I was surprised that we should work so much with Ann-Sofie Bárány. Besides, psychologists are the worst I know. I have big difficulties with all kinds of things they talk about. But I changed my mind. I learned a lot from her. From only groaning over Ann-Sofie's ideas in the beginning we became friends in the end. And I realized that it was me who had been inflexible and prejudiced; and that you don't have to be so extremely negative all the time."

When the group had got quite far regarding research and rehearsals, they performed some scenes for a reference group as a test. The small audience consisted of four or five babies and their mothers or fathers. "I remember the first time so well," says Claire.

> "We sat under a piece of fabric and we were supposed to look up after a while. I became totally confused when I saw the babies sitting there in the row. I don't know what I expected. But I was completely overwhelmed when I saw them sitting there, absolutely concentrated and attentive. Then I realized: For god's sake, they really do understand what we are doing here!"

The ensemble noticed that the reference group knew their way around the theatre after several visits. They recognized the actors and they knew the order of the different scenes in the performance.

Many parents reported how their children were hard to please and whiny when they were on the way to the theatre, but when they came to Sergels torg, where the *City Theatre* and *Unga Klara* are situated, they became happy. And at home, the children cheered up every time they played the music from the performance. The performance lasts approximately one hour, which is a long time for a baby. Still, most of them sat there the whole time as if they had been fixed to their seats.

"I have met parents who told me that their children normally can't sit still for more than five minutes, but now, during the performance, they were completely caught up in it the whole time," says Claire. "Some children are exhausted afterwards. I particularly remember one child who slept like a log in its mother's arms already when the mother came to thank us right after the show."

## An elegant starting point in the foyer

"I had thought that the children would react somewhat differently," says Torbjörn. "How, I don't know, but differently. But they sat there and listened and reacted exactly like an adult audience. Here and now, that's where they were". He remembers that, almost every time, they were very interested for about 25 minutes.

> "After that, they often lost their focus. But they were welcome to go to the sofa and play for a while when the performance became uninteresting or they did not feel like watching anymore. Everything was ok for us. We absolutely didn't want the children's first experience of theatre to feel challenging, either for parents or children."

The performance began already outside the theatre, in the foyer, where the actors welcomed the audience. They played games, wrote name badges for the children and introduced themselves. "I talked quite a bit out there in the foyer," says Torbjörn.

> "And sometimes I switched to speaking Chinese which I speak fluently. This was very interesting, because the children realized that they didn't understand. And the parents experienced how it feels, when you do not understand what is being said."

"Many parents tell us that they learned a lot about their children," says Claire. They learned to respect them as individuals. Because parents and children live so close to each other when the children are so small, for many this was the first time when the children encountered reality. "Those children who got to see the performance are enormously privileged," she says. "I think it may have effects for their whole lives."

Claire points out that it was important that "Babydrama" should be real theatre. Even if the audience was little, the stage was huge and the scenography gigantic, she says. "Just because we performed for babies it didn't need to be a cheap production. It should be serious. For example, I myself wore an evening dress and could easily have gone to the "Nobel Prize"-ceremony after every performance."

Torbjörn remembers that they were fairly nervous because the acting should happen so close to the spectators and because they did not know how it would feel to perform for such a small audience. "We were forced to play more directly," he says.

"And you had to really mean what you said, you had to face and address the audience. You had to be more present in the room; and feel feelings more intently than you usually would. It was a bit like playing theatre for a child at home, in a small private space. The pace of our acting could vary more than it could when playing for a different audience. Usually you determine which level suits the performance and you stick to it throughout, but here this didn't work at all."

Claire adds some comments on what the work means to her personally: "I have tremendous respect for small children's intelligence and receptiveness," she says. "Also, they are a wonderful audience, because they don't have any preconceived opinions. I am determined, that I shall never again talk to children in a childlike manner. And that I shall respect them as individuals."

The work with the play also reminded her of how she herself behaved as a young mother.

"I never thought about equality when my son was little. Of course, he was a wonderful gift of love, but never was the question of equality and respect between us even asked. During the research process, I remembered how I had made decisions for him all the time, disregarding his wishes, and how I thought that it was enough if you just loved your child.

Now, I always start with saying my name when I meet a baby and, generally, I behave more like you do with adults."

*translated by Claudia Mayer and Meike Fechner*

# Babies and theatre
## Notes about the imagination on stage

*by Charlotte Fallon and Michel van Loo*

The idea of introducing theatre in Belgian crèches was first initiated by the *Théâtre de la Guimbarde*.

In the course of those first years, six creations were produced: "Shadows and Lights", "Earth", "Duo des Voiles", "In the Garden", "Bach... in the sand" and "Bramborry". Those creations have sparked numerous wishes, new ideas and questions. If the initial philosophy of the project – i.e. to awaken babies to culture through shows created for them – remained the same, the methodology was progressively refined.

We do not wish for shows for toddlers to become another consumption product aimed at a new public. Rather, we aim for them to become a first cultural approach for toddlers and a new possibility for them to awaken to senses and emotions. This proximity to the sensory world of toddlers and the questions it raises, bring us to work more and more closely with the professionals who accompany them.

Theatre is a tool enabling to awaken children and adults' desire for culture. As artists, we see art for toddlers as a movement, an approach which is built in collaboration with all early childhood professionals.

We choose to create for toddlers because we think that theatre – and art in general – can nourish their imagination and help them grow.

Our wish is to share with them the imaginary universe of performing arts, to amaze them, dazzle them, make them dream, contemplate, exult, be scared – only just a little.

This exchange exists because we work in partnership with early childhood professionals. The nursery nurses are the ones who know the children, who give them security, and without always knowing it, who allow them to enjoy the show or not.

If the crèche' staff is in agreement with the arrival of the theatre company, if they have been told of the meaning, form and running of the show, chances are that this experience will be a pleasure for everyone.

"This association surprises and raises questions. Before wishing to create something for this particular public, I asked myself whether it wasn't important to let babies live quietly. But when I saw at the *Théâtre Athénor* a show called 'Cuddles' performed by Brigitte Maisonneuve, I discovered the moving and fascinating exchange which can exist between an actor and toddlers.

Toddlers fill me with wonder. The contrast between their strength and their fragility touches me. Their strength comes from their capacity to be there, entirely available to the present time, with an endless curiosity. Their fragility comes from their natural openness to the world, their lack of boundaries regarding their emotions."[1]

Early childhood is the age of the blank page, when everything can still be written. The ground is still virgin. It is the time of first experiences, the age where everything is possible. It seems important to us to nurture the toddlers' real-life and imagination with elements of quality. In order to live, to acknowledge themselves, children need to be nurtured with imaginary.

> "Because they are at the beginning of their lives, babies often discover things for the first time in an attitude of curiosity and with an exhilarating feeling of discovery. As I see it, in their desire to discover the world, toddlers are at the source of all artistic expressions. While looking to find balance to walk, they dance. When playing with sounds, they are into music. When exploring a material, they are in the mobility and sensory world."

## What are the objectives?

The *Théâtre de la Guimbarde's* objectives are threefold: to create shows, to work with children and to work with the adults who accompany those children.

> "There is nothing more beautiful than to watch a baby be, to follow the path of his curiosity in a place for a day. More and more, I felt the urge to meet them, play with them, watch them be, listen to them, suggest music, songs, stories, situations and characters, slip into theatre. Arise surprise and be surprised in return. Experience the pleasure of being together, learn to communicate without being intrusive ..."

Curious about life, toddlers need to be loved, supported and protected. You cannot enter a crèche like you would a work place; you need to leave your hyperactivity, productivity, desire for result at the door. Being there is almost enough.

However, when we offer toddlers a universe in which they can exercise their curiosity, we witness them having long moments of intense concentration. A child builds its imagination from his first sensations and the emotions that come with them.

"Through my shows, I wish to contribute to this development by sharing with them my favourite images, music, paintings and dances, in a sensory and organic form."

Toddlers also question us as human beings. They go against the current of what is being asked of us: efficiency, profitability. To observe them leads us to reflect on our society, on people, on frailty, on the pace of our lives. They make room (again) for intimacy, listening, pleasure and sharing.

---

1 Original quotations by Charlotte Fallon.

## How do you create for toddlers?

Here again, there are no pre-established rules, except that of listening and sharing pleasure.

> "Inspiration comes to me any time. It can be sparked by an emotion, a painting, a piece of music, an idea, a discussion, an exchange, a meeting ... It comes from life. If I feel inspired by a theme, I check whether that theme also affects the children. Being small does not mean having small emotions. We are all concerned by emotions such as joyfulness, confidence, the happiness to meet, the need to love and be loved, fear, neglect, loneliness, anger, insecurity ... Then, this theme finds a form of expression, whether theatrical, plastic or geared towards dance ..."

Although a real public, toddlers from one to three years old do watch shows differently than us adults: they watch it with their bodies, their senses, their heart. They intensely take in images, sounds, songs, movements.

> "As their perceive life in a sensory and emotional way, I try to give my work a sensory and organic form. For the scenography, we try to create a décor which can fit a crèche. It is often minimal but it transforms the ordinary space of the crèche into a theatre space."

## The personal investment of actors

During the creation process, the Guimbarde always visits crèches to experiment the various steps of the creation, to see how children react and to share impressions with the nursery nurses who know them well.

Once a show has been created, we test it a dozen times before its final form is defined.

These experiments help actors get used to the public of toddlers. To play in front of toddlers can be daunting at first: they don't function according to pre-established codes. A child can get up, want to walk around the playground, start talking, laughing and sometimes crying. As they play two meters away from them, actors can straightaway feel the children's emotions and don't always know how to react, especially when they cry. Little by little, actors learn to relax, loosen, to not be afraid of the children's emotions. A non-verbal communication is established. And once they start exchanging glances with each other, the game becomes full of softness and pleasure.

Actors often say that they acquire a lot more honesty in their acting quality when working with toddlers. Children make them face themselves; they force them to 'be' instead of to do.

A psychologist is called in on several occasions during the creation process. The idea is to check that the proposed show is in line with the child's development. How does the show help the child to evolve?

"They explain to us the psychological evolution of children in relation with the theme that we want to explore. She answers our questions and worries. To one actor who was afraid and felt guilty every time a child would cry, she said: 'It is not a problem to cry as long as our emotions are received and recognised. A crèche is not meant to be a closed and protected cocoon but a place to grow up.' "

Our work is also done with the support and help from the city of Charleroi's psychomotor specialists.

## Observations on the progress of a show

Toddlers are born-spectators because they discover life. They are not only theatre spectators, they are spectators of the life that surrounds them; they are a dream public! But it is a public that can also easily be disturbed.

"For this reason, I prefer for the children to be present and participate when we transform the space of their crèche for a show. I like them to get used to the décor, to approach the actors, to watch them warm up ..."

During the show, it is normal if children express themselves, talk, sing, move around, provided they don't enter the actors' space. If a child cries, it is often enough for a nursery nurse or the mother to hold him or take a few steps away from the scene to give him a securing distance space.

If we sense a child is terrorised, we think it best to take him outside. A show should not be a traumatising experience.

Our shows for toddlers don't tell a story with a beginning or an end. They represent moments linked by a thread. It is better if adults don't guide the children in the way they perceive and understand the show. Often adults are tempted to comment and explain the show to children. It is best not to interfere and let them be with what they feel and let them live the show in their own way.

Before a performance, we like to meet the adults who will participate to the show, to explain to them the aim of this artistic work for toddlers. It is important that the performance takes place in the most harmonious way possible for both children and adults.

Our crèche work is above all a partnership work. If the adult feels secure and involved in the arrival of the show in the crèche, if he is aware of the practical development of the performance, he will then be able to secure the child whom he knows better than we do. He can also surrender to his own pleasure. The more the child feels the pleasure of the nursery nurse, the more he will be able to indulge in his own pleasure.

Ideally, we also like to exchange with the adults after the performance, to receive their emotions and their questions regarding the attitudes of the children and the theatrical form they may not be familiar with.

At the end of the show, we like to plan time for sharing and exchanging with the children. And if the technical conditions allow, they are invited to venture on stage, to explore this universe that they so far have only observed, and experiment with the various materials.

## The training of nursery nurses and students in childcare

The *Guimbarde* intends to get more and more involved in the artistic training of the nursery nurses and the students in childcare.

We offer training on movement, work with earth, sculpture, music, video, object theatre, the transformation of the daily universe of the crèche, painting, drawing and playing.

During those trainings, we insist on the experiences of pleasure, confidence, and acceptance of everyone' own expression.

> "I work with adults in order to make them reconnect the pleasure associated with the spontaneity of playing with the child and the state of discovery in a non-judgemental pleasure. Together, we go over the sensorial path of discovery of expression materials."

The nursery nurses involved in this artistic work tell us that this work changes the way they see their professional practice. In doing so, they leave aside the daily character and routine of the crèche to do a more personal job. They are in contact with the expression of their emotions and can share them with other adults, outside the work environment. In the crèche, they tell us they are rediscovering the emotions of the children.

Provided we have the opportunity and the means to continue these trainings, it would be interesting to give them the chance to go and see shows, exhibitions, concerts made for adults to extend the approach of cultural opening.

# Little ones and adults, alive and aware
## Theatre brings together

*by Agnès Desfosses*

The very small child feels things before understanding them. A live performance gives young spectators an opportunity to refine their capacity for perception, to pass through different emotional states and to feed their imagination. Each different artistic language (design, acting, text, movement, sounds and music) has its own important role within the performance. Theatre brings together, and provokes an exchange, between children and the adults accompanying them. But when children cannot yet speak, how can we share their feelings and perceptions?

To talk about the role of perceptions in theatre aimed at a very young audience, I am going to draw on my professional experience in the shows made over the last dozen years with my theatre company, *ACTA*.

My first shows for babies and children under three or four years old were in 1994: "Ah! Vos rondeurs..." ("Oh, so round...") and in 1996: "Sous la table" ("Under the table"). These shows were commissioned by two festivals. This was of key importance to me, because it meant being in a partnership, having moral and financial support, promotion of the show for touring and a chance to meet people.

"Under the Table" has toured in France but also across Europe and this has made it possible to meet and have debates around this field of experience with people engaged in the same practice in the four corners of Europe. So in 2004 I too wanted to create a festival: "First Encounters, early childhood, artistic awakening and live performance" – a European biennial festival in the Val d'Oise, an administrative area near Paris. The aims were: to promote knowledge of shows specially made for the very young, to encourage their production and to share ideas and experience with presenters, parents, people working with the very young and with artists in a forum and training workshops. We have made a new show for babies and very young children at the end of 2005 called: "renaissances" ("rebirths") and presented the third festival in 2008.

We are now working on the fourth edition of the festival from 27 March to 15 April 2010. We are also making a new show for the very young called: "Me Alone" directed by Laurent Dupont in collaboration with *ACTA*, to be premiered in March 2009.

First of all I am going to talk about two aspects of theatre which particularly interest me when I am making something in this art form.

We find ourselves between live actors and a live audience; a double human presence. Theatre is therefore a 'house of the emotions' because it engages all our senses at once. Certainly, just like a book, there is a beginning, middle and end, but here we arrive, we enter and we leave – physically. That changes everything.

I choose the relationships I set up between actors and audience just as I choose the arrangement of the space which either encompasses the audience or does not.

You could do it all without being there and pass the ideas in CDs, DVDs or even books. But that's not the point.

A story to illustrate this idea: Two small boys leave a show all red faced and stirred up by the performance and they ask me: "How can we get to see this show again?" To which my reply is: "Close your eyes and you will see behind your eyelids all the pictures and the moments you enjoyed in the show; it's all in your memory!" "Ooh!" And they go away happy.

Theatre, even if it is ephemeral, gives value to absence and the capacity for memory and imagination in everyone.

**Sharing my world, my passions, my questions**

I consider a human being, adult or child, as 'continually being born'; the child being a little closer to their origins with a little less experience than us adults. So I create shows which do not make age the first consideration. Yves Nilly has said, "Creating something for the very young is to create for the child in ourselves and the children we have been."

I have confidence in their ability to perceive, receive, and in their curiosity and desire to discover things. I love the quality of their presence as spectators, which provokes a positive response from the actors on stage. They give me a profound desire to share something from my world, my passions, my questions and my views. I know they will keep traces of all that in their memory even before they can express it in words.

Anne Francoise Cabanis has said: "In theatre, not to respect children is to offer them something sickly-sweet without artistic commitment and real meaning." All artistic languages can reach them. Of course, we need to develop and enrich their perception too.

They experience theatre as otherness, something different. Joelle Rouland has said: "A theatre production is a coming together of several imagined states and these clashes should create sparks."

I also know that if for them play is a necessity, for me play is a choice. They can see very well the difference between playing by themselves or with others and watching actors perform.

As this is a matter of 'First Times', first experiences, I take particular care to welcome them to my shows like people invited to undertake an extraordinary journey and to embark them gently into unfamiliar kinds of perception. They are not those of everyday life, but poetic perceptions in a completely fabricated, symbolic world. For the very young, theatre can have a place in their life: the extraordinary in the ordinary.

**Composing scenography, words and music**

Starting with an already well developed concept, I bring together a team of artists (designer, writer and composer) to make the show: I create the production and direct the actors.

I spoke before about the importance of being among live people during a live performance, which might seem an obvious and inconsequential fact. However, as the audience, all our senses are wide awake because our physical presence is total! My first task is with the designer, Patricia Lacoulonche:

- In relation to the chosen theme, what space do we envisage for the audience and the actors?
- Are they in the same space?
- Will there be a journey, a movement of the audience during the performance?
- What physical sense of the space do we want to give the audience?
- What does the space tell us by the way it changes, the material it is made of and the way it is lit?
- Will the details matter?
- Will we emphasise the physical differences between the view each audience member will have of the performance?
- How are the actors going to inhabit and fill out this space? How will their bodies tell us in a recognisable manner about feelings, emotions and perceptions?

You can well imagine that such a practice implies a great deal of rehearsal with audiences during the making of the show before it is finalised.

In some of my work, the distance afforded to the audience by an end-on, frontal relationship between stage and auditorium (the invisible fourth wall) does not exist. However the illusion still works if the audience uses its imagination. The proximity of the two presences, of actors and spectators, is encouraged. This theatre form appears in some kinds of street theatre. In this practice, the impact of movement is enhanced and is perceived by everyone.

Some examples from "Under the Table": the bodily presence of adults and children is taken into account: Being seated successively around the table where the tablecloth becomes an immense ocean on which tiny boats are sailing about, then lying down or being squashed together under the table on a thick, soft carpet the colour of sand and to see two Mermaids very close up: these are strong sensations!

All these perceptions will feed the memory, young children and adults will put words to these sensations, revealing meanings. Sometimes these words will come out during the performance and in any case afterwards.

If a lot is expressed by the performing space and the acting, words also have a big part to play. However, we are not into linear narrative. The words do not communicate the whole unfolding of the action; which does not mean that there is no meaning!

"Words and their meanings go straight to the heart of adult spectators but very young children are little by little being born into language through the music of the words." (Francoise Gerbaulet)

I particularly like poetic language. Yves Nilly, the writer with whom I worked on "Under the Table" has written several haikus which touch children very directly. There are also some very technical but beautiful words to name the imaginary sails on our 'boat-table'. Even the adults do not know all of them. But the words become beautiful in themselves, sound material, rhythm, power, song in the mouths of the performers.

The vibration of a lyrical song, of a trumpet, an accordion, touches us to the very bottom of our being. There is no age at which this starts!

## One audience of adults and children at one play for the very young and the others

It is a fact: the younger the children are, the more adults there will be with them. To whom are these shows addressed? – To adults as much as to very young children. And perceptions, sensations, emotions are not just for the children. "Pleasure communicates. Happiness is transmitted. Happiness in one produces happiness in others." (Joelle Rouland)

"The adult knows he has entered a theatre, first of all because, as an adult, he has chosen *not* to feed himself exclusively on reality." (Pascale Mignon)

The adult has to accept that an artist can reach the inner world of the child without his mediation. This tells the adult implicitly that the child can look elsewhere and experience something intensely, still by his side but apart from him.

> "By appropriating the words and images of another, the child finds outside himself what he perceives, without words, inside himself. It's a determinant of the emergence of a desire of his own, which gives him a taste for others." (Pascale Mignon)

The adult helps in this and surrounds the child with his own spirit of discovery. It is a moment when adults and children become peaceably aware of their different reactions. Not being alert to the same moments in a show, not being interested in the same way becomes something rich to be experienced during the performance and shared afterwards.

## Before, during and after the play

*Before*: It is important that the child knows what he is going to see. Theatre is not cinema, nor is it like a book or a DVD. Inside the doors of a theatre something different will always take place. The clown or the dancer that the child saw in the previous show will not be seen this time. If you say nothing, the child may be waiting for them throughout the performance and be heavily disappointed on leaving!

Theatre is ephemeral. Yes, there should be surprises. But surprises that have been prepared for: everyone will benefit that much more.

*During*: The adult is doubly a spectator – both of the play and of the child, or children, watching the play. It is a triangular relationship between the adults, the show and the children.

As well as being a spectator, the adult is no less a companion and a guide. "Sometimes children need the adult's knees and sometimes they are even stuck in the adult's embrace in 'that extreme fear which is tied to an irresistible curiosity'" says Laurent Dupont. Some children go to sit on the cushions right on the edge of the playing area and only turn round to the adults from time to time to see if they are still there or to say out loud what they have recognised or felt.

Others again will need to put a lot of distance between themselves and the stage and to watch the show right up close to the doors of the auditorium, ready to go out, – Oh Yes! You can close a book, you can turn off the TV, but in the theatre our bodies are totally present. To escape the strong sensations produced by a show means leaving the theatre.

However leaving the theatre is rarely a good solution, except in those extreme cases where the child is absolutely not ready for that kind of situation. It is always preferable for the child to watch the show to the very end, so that the child knows that the theatre, this house of words, emotions, imagination and perceptions is not dangerous even if it makes your heart beat very fast; and then to know that the end of a show always brings an untangling of the story, a resolution, a conclusion.

The adult retains frames and gives life to the children's perceptions, emotions and words. If the adult is frightened of the child's fear, afraid he will not please the child. If he is afraid of being bored during the show, then it is better if the adult does not go: he will be a poor companion for the child. Will the child allow itself to like something which bothers, annoys or produces indifference in the accompanying adult?

*After the show*: Take time to leave the place of performance and return gently to everyday reality – coats, pushchairs. Let the extraordinary become part of the ordinary rhythm of our lives.

Much later – elsewhere, create a climate of confidence so that there can be an exchange between the adults and children who have language about what has been experienced during the show.

But who should speak about what they have felt? – Only the children? What about the adults? Have they nothing to say about the emotions and perceptions excited during the show? Should they not begin this dialogue?

Everyone's emotions, perceptions and imagination are different. One person will laugh and another cry in the same situation. To recognise and know that everyone is different allows and enriches the dialogue and reinforces each one's individuality and personality.

With children who do not speak, to give names, to put words to things is to give recognition to the child's emotions and perceptions: the infant will feel comforted by the adult's concern.

A great many will express themselves through their body, often replaying scenes from the show long after leaving the theatre, without warning: they have recorded the experience in their body.

Then again, the adult can revive a child's memory with mention of a sound, a word, an object used during the show.

In this way, the extraordinary in a show will not be an exceptional moment closed in upon itself within a bubble, but will long-lastingly enrich the personality of everyone in their 'ordinary', everyday life.

*translated by Paul Harman*

# Surprise
## Creating "Theatre for Early Years" between everything and nothing

*by Stephan Rabl*

The entire room smells of roses and mandarin oranges. The music is still sounding in our ears; the children smile and twirl themselves around, the parents and the students of the *DSCHUNGEL-Academy* remain in their seats, watching the video and letting the event's effects linger.

It is just after five p.m. on a gorgeous winter Sunday in Vienna. Actually, this performance should have been the premiere of our newest theatre piece for 'the very youngest', as this genre is so fondly known. Unfortunately, an illness within our team prevented this. So we made a presentation of almost all of the parts of the piece, and I myself stood onstage again for the first time in seven years.

– How so? I'm really just the director. But I filled in, and played the parts of our sick technician, who not only designed the lighting and ran all of the onstage technical cues, but also filmed with a live camera, kept an eye out for the video edits, operated the scent machine, and would have been an actor, as well.

"Duftträume" ("Scent Dreams") is the title of our production about Malika, a girl who can sense every scent. Only her favourite children's book has no odour. Together with the composer Mathias, who also performs the live music, and our stage technician, Stefan, she dances and acts for 40 minutes onstage through seven worlds of smell.

The idea to work with scents and sounds came about during the production work on "Überraschung" ("Surprise"). In the fall of 2006, for the first time, I wanted to create a production for very small children. In our festival *DSCHUNGEL WIEN MODERN (VIENNA JUNGLE MODERN)*, which focuses on contemporary music theatre for young audiences, there had always been music theatre plays for children aged one-and-a-half or two and up. But why not produce and design one, ourselves?

## The quotient of animation, pedagogy and esoteric auras

My first play with the very young as an audience was in a classroom in Denmark in 1991, and had something to do with a rainbow. To be honest, at that time I was more concerned with whether theatre could even function for this age group, than with artistic craft.

Later, at all of the various theatre festivals, I observed this active scene coming from Italy and France, and then slowly, its growth in both in Belgium and Germany.

The past few years have seen a boom, and now there is hardly a festival that doesn't offer something for babies, scarcely a country without its own hit play for "the very youngest"; and multiple *EU*-projects are touring theatre venues at once.

And I must admit, I'm playing right along with them. In *DSCHUNGEL WIEN*, there are productions for the very young every month, partly self-produced, partly with Austrian and international guest artists. The *SCHÄXPIR* Festival offers six productions for this audience, and in *DSCHUNGEL WIEN MODERN* there are always two such productions as well.

At first, I was sceptical about this scene as well. Not that I believed it wouldn't work, but in all honesty, the quotient of animation, pedagogy, and esoteric auras onstage was a bit too much for me.

It was difficult to find any piece for my *SZENE BUNTE WÄHNE (SCENE OF COLOURFUL ILLUSIONS)* Festival in the nineteen-nineties, of which I could truly say, "Yes! –That is a creative process taking place on stage, – that's theatre being conveyed there, – that is about art, not just about nice moments."

In Austria at that time (1992-1997) the theatre scene rejected those productions; I can still remember how everyone said that such pieces couldn't have anything to do with theatre. And yet, over ten years later, I took an artistic leap of faith with this age group.

And this succeeded, even though it was only my second directorial effort in the field of children's theatre. At the beginning, the title "Überraschung" ("Surprise") was a short program note, and music was the central object of focus. So I searched for and found an excellent fiddler, in Mathias Jakisic, who brought a diversity of music into the rehearsal space daily along with the willingness to play a character, as well. Dance had to play an important role, because movement is not only the most appropriate means of expression for this age group, but is also my own most direct access to humanness. I recalled the very natural and childlike aura of the dancer Adriana Cubides, whom I knew from participation in seminars in *Bruckner-Konservatorium* (*Anton Bruckner Privatuniversität*) in Linz. She understands, in a breathtaking way, how to bring her 'inner child' onto the stage with powerful dancer impulses and authenticity. Through her, I also came to Raul Maia, a Portuguese dancer who had been very active in Belgium and the Netherlands (*Hans Hof Ensemble*, *Ultima Vez*, ...). Along with his inexhaustible dance and movement resources, Raul brought a strong male component of the child to the stage, which created a contrast to Mathias' very feminine style. All three artists had never performed for children before, and certainly had no experience with an audience of 'babies'.

## The perception of impulses, emotions and relevance

The fear that one could not create any such thing as art for this age group was very great. Just as great was our confusion, since the title and the theme of "Surprise" proved to be meaningless in the early days of rehearsals. What can possibly surprise a person at the age of two? Between everything and nothing, there's not much room to play when expectations are already set up 'to be surprised'. Otherwise these become discoveries, rather than surprises.

The improvisational tasks I gave to the three artists were very wide-ranging. Memories of first surprises were told; we searched for the surprises in the body, in children's games, in the act of eating, in nature; we experimented with objects, with lighting and costumes. Each time, we began with sensitive blindfolded exercises, in order to come into the origins of childlikeness and the perception of impulses and emotions. I wanted to see the childlikeness of these three onstage, to explore their very earliest childhood between one and three years.

Anything to do with pedagogy or childish cavorting was to be avoided. All threatening fears such as, "one cannot and should not show such things to the very young", had to be simply shut out. I knew: Whatever we find in the process of our work must also be important to the three artists and to me; it must have relevance to us if we are to bring it to the stage, and it should have relevance for everyone, for adults as well.

We were often in deep doubt, because we could no longer tell whether the piece was meant for children at all any more, nor whether it had any artistic significance whatsoever.

So we invited small children to rehearsals, or simply sat together in the *DSCHUNGEL*-Café, which is filled with mothers and very young children daily.

Until the end, we were very unclear about the stage set design process. We needed space for the dance sequences, we needed objects with which to surprise, we wanted to make it possible to experience water and sand and, in the very opening, to bring even more elements from nature onstage. And all of that must always disappear very quickly, to make room for the choreography.

As we moved from the white rehearsal studio into the classic black of the theatre stage, we were clobbered by the strictness of the laws of colour against the sanctity of our piece. And so everything was rearranged shortly before the premiere, in order for it to be played against a light white backdrop on a white dance floor.

The first preview performances were deep plunges on an emotional roller coaster. The audience proved to be very positively affected, assuring us of the appropriateness for the specific age group. Yet the great euphoria that we encountered, throughout 100 performances in many countries, could be reached only after the first fifteen interactions with the audience.

## The yearnings that never lose their power

It took experience and time for the performers to find the 'same breath' as the children, and it took time to develop the stability to bring their own childlikeness into play with full authenticity. In the early performances, one could sense the great difference in whether Raul and Adriana were being children or adults onstage. All at once, the 'lion' would become too aggressive, the stories around love too grown-up, and the physical games with water too erotic. And some small changes were needed to make Adriana stronger in her girl's role, since the men together were often too dominant. If Raul throws Adriana out of the chest and then, grinning, starts making music with Mathias, it can seem like the most brutal macho posturing; but it remains at a lightly childlike playful level, if she turns around and self-confidently steals the object back instead, and the two boys chase after her.

At first we performed for 65 minutes; this was too long, of course, but important for our experience. Since then it has become a 50-minute piece dealing with animals, balloons, packaging, and children's games. At the close of the piece, the stage is under water, and the audience is filled with yearnings that never lose their power.

Now, with experiences from Colombia to Australia, and through half of Europe, I am myself fascinated by what we have discovered in our work. I have forgotten all of the early doubts again, to devote myself to the 'scents' of the next piece.

*translated by Lydia Baldwin*

# "Dance and movement is a natural choice of language"
## The art of making theatre art for small children

*by Ivica Šimić*

In the fall of 2007, the artistic director of *Theatre Mala Scena* was interviewed by Meghan Henry, a Master of Fine Arts student at the *University of Central Florida* in Orlando, USA for the need of her thesis on how dramaturgy influences the storytelling in devised movement based theatre for children ages three to eight. The basis for the thesis were three different performances of three different theatres, including „The Parachutists, or on the art of falling". Here are the parts of the interview that were used in the final paper entitled "Devising dramaturgy".

*M.H.*: Why have you chosen to create work for very young audiences?

I like the idea that art can still have an important role in the life of humans. When working for children, especially for children that have never before experienced theatre, we implant in them our sense of beauty, messages, ethics etcetera, and our work is becoming important and our responsibility for the aesthetic development of children so big. Children believe that the scenic reality is just another reality. Children believe and they trust us! Adults don't believe, they are indoctrinated, and they are afraid of emotions of any kind; they want to understand rather than feel. In theatre for young audiences, especially for very small children, we can deal with theatre art, and thanks to the emotional connection with the audience we can even talk about cathartic function of theatre.

Creative freedom that theatre for young audiences offers to the artists, possibilities of research, imagination employed in the process, is unique and so different in theatre for adults. Working for very small children opens new doors of creativity for the artists in closest connection with the audience.

*M.H.*: What draws you to produce movement based work for very young children under the age of five?

Dance and movement for small children is, I guess, natural choice of language through which we can communicate with them since we can't understand each other using spoken language. Children themselves communicate more with movements, gestures, emotions, rather then through spoken language. They don't have problems in expressing feelings, and they can understand the language of movements. The common grounds for our communication with children are emotions, and that is the shortest way to approach them. A major influence in the dramaturgy of „The Parachutists" revolves around reaching children on an emotional level and as a result helping them to develop an aesthetic sense based on their emotional reactions. I believe that emotions are the only connecting fabric between children and adults, and this influences all the artistic choices I make.

Also, children don't have problems with abstracts. Everything is abstract to them, only emotions are real. They don't know what theatre is and they don't know what theatre conventions are. They accept theatre reality as any other reality and they believe that the message they get is real. This fact allows us to communicate with them directly through emotions and movement. Spoken language is preventing us to have that direct communication with children. When speaking we describe our emotions, and very rarely succeed in being honest. Children feel and recognize that.

Dance and movement are the language of children games, and they are experts in understanding that language. They feel the intentions of the performers and they understand them. They don't have intellectual background, nor the experiences that the memories are made of, and they can't contemplate upon the descriptions. Theatre time in theatre is always present, and they are living it.

So, I am always searching for the shortest way to children's emotion, and that is the way why I work very often with movement and dance for very small children.

*M.H.*: "The parachutists, or on the art of falling", the performance that became known all around the globe, was made on those premises? How did you devise the performance?

At the beginning of the process of creating "The Parachutists", there was an idea that I wanted to explore: the gravity, the biggest physical force on earth that has decisive impact on the physical life. We don't even think of it. Every thing that we throw in the air falls down and it is normal for us. Gravity has the impact on our psychical life as well. Our desire for flying is the attempt to win over the gravity, with the predictable result – falling! How to fall down and not to suffer serious consequences, how to stand up and continue after the fall, that is the art of falling. However, very soon, through a series of brain storming we (the dancers Larisa Lipovac and Damir Klemenić and I) made clear that our performance will not be about the physical force but about people, mutual attraction, about the bodies that are decisively connected with the earth and the souls that want to reach the sky, about the different 'falls' that accompany every and each life. That way the metaphor of falling became a story of living and learning how to stand up after the fall and how to 'fly'.

Next step was the exploration of movements. Dance and movement is a language of children's games, and they are experts in understanding that language. They don't have intellectual background, nor the experiences that memories are made of, and they can not contemplate upon the descriptions. Theatre time is always present, and they are living it together with the performance.

The dancers invented lots of different movements and games in which they were exploring the relationship between two bodies in attraction and the relationship of the body that wants to go in the air with the inevitable fall that follows. In some movements and dance sequences dancers needed a hard wall to lean on, in some they needed a cross bar to hang on. That is how we invented the cube of cross bars that turned around on wheels, two times two times two meter with one hard wall at the back.

We knew that we have to start our show warily, with the knowledge that for small children everything that is presented to them is a reality and that most of the time they are afraid of that reality. Also, since they have no experience in watching theatre, we wanted to draw their attention naturally. So, we started with small things like sounds and balloons. A balloon begins to inflate, until suddenly it blows away, deflating wildly. The audience is thrown into an uproar, but their attention proves quickly regained by more balloons. After a while, when the sensation of flying balloons is consumed, the children are ready to receive more sensations and are focused on the stage. We continue with building up the images of the parts of the body that are shown through the holes in the wall put together in a strange way. Bodies that are looking to the world with the same curiosity and fear the children are looking to them. After a while, different objects start falling down from the sky (the rear wall is painted like the sky with the clouds), introducing the theme and bringing the metaphor of creation, birth, beginning until a human with a suitcase falls from the sky as well. Now the introduction is made, the theme is posed, the characters are born, and the performance can go on.

The above opening sequence was devised as a result of my belief that most children are experiencing theatre for the first time when they attend "The parachutists". The performance has to begin slowly in order to ease the audience into being in the theatre and to prepare them for the new experience. I believe it is crucial to ease young audiences getting into the theatrical experience and I believe artists should forego speeches before performances or beginning with a blackout.

*M.H.*: What about the dramaturgy?

I believe that dramaturgically the performance text for very young children must consist of small segments due to two to five year olds' limited attention span. Therefore, we devised segments which could essentially stand on their own, with a mini beginning, middle, and end. Dramaturgically the segments of the performance text for "The parachutists" move in and out of realism and metaphor through the devising of scenes based in the realistic presentation of friendship, hurting a friend's feelings, and making amends alongside more metaphorical moments of sheer movement that explore the body in space as well as the action of falling, which leaves the exact interpretation to the viewer. The movement between metaphor and realism keeps the very young guessing about what might happen next creating 'a performance with a secret'. We accomplish this goal by gently guiding the young children in a general direction and allowing them to fill in the specifics of the story through using their imaginations: When creating abstract movement you still have to have some lighthouses along the way that will help children swim in the sea of abstract thinking. Children don't have troubles with abstract thinking, but the lighthouses are there to help them understand where they are going. That is why sometimes in "The parachutists" you come back from pure dance into a joke or a literal movement that we can recognize, so the audience can travel together with the actors through the sea of the story.

I hope that the movement between metaphor and realism presents the audiences with a 'big story', a very strong story hidden behind the movement, which is not an explicit story, but a big story inside. And it is left to the audience to discover and build up their own story. Dramaturgically we present the 'big story' through small everyday moments, which occur in "The parachutist" when the characters fall down and express physically their pain through dance. The appeal of the story for adults and the very young prove different. The falling down and getting back up, can be interpreted by adults as a metaphor for the larger story of the trials and tribulations of life, and yet the same sequence might resonate with a three or four year old because falling down and getting up are important moments in their everyday existence that they can identify, and understand emotionally.

*M.H.*: The performance is very well received worldwide. Is it also successful in your country?

In three years we did more the 150 performances out of which we did more then 100 abroad. In Croatia we perform very little. The performances do not always reflect the expectations of teachers and pedagogues what should theatre for very young be, and what function in the process of growing up it should have. It is a long way to tune the expectations of adults with the needs of the children and the artists that are working in theatre for young audiences. Nevertheless, and besides all the problems that we encounter in everyday life, our duty and responsibility towards the children is to continue insisting on the artistic approach when making theatre for the very young and embarks on each new project as an adventure to see how far we can push the boundaries of the art forms.

# Installation theatre
## Creating a performance space for babies and toddlers

*by Cate Fowler*

Performing for the very young child is one of the more difficult theatrical practices, and the subject of much debate. I have long been interested in the creation of work for babies and toddlers. Often very young children are taken to a theatre performance with older siblings which is not a positive experience for them. I was interested in exploring and creating a meaningful introduction to the performing arts for a very small child. At this young age, children's development involves becoming literate about their world. Inhabiting their world are sounds, movements, words and images. There are specific bodies of knowledge focussing on the disciplines of early childhood: dance, music, visual arts and literacy. All these disciplines are drawn upon to create an early childhood performance experience. In addition, when very young children participate in a performance experience, they become part of a space in which they interact with others. This interaction constitutes the beginning of their first audience relationship. With these observations, I decided that *Windmill Performing Arts* would embark on an exploration of what I would define as 'performance' literacy.

During a visit to London in 2002, I experienced the work of *theatre-rites*, a company specializing in work for five years and under. I found their work particularly inspiring and relevant and realized that inherent to their work were many of the ideas I wished to explore. With assistance from Professor Wendy Schiller (Director, *de Lissa Research Institute, University of South Australia*) Jeff Meiners (Senior Lecturer, *School of Early Childhood, University of South Australia*) and Julie Orchard (Arts Project Manager, on secondment from the *South Australian Department of Education and Children's Services* to *Windmill Performing Arts*) a project titled "In the beginning" was set up.

## Knowing the audience

I started with the question "what would make a meaningful 'first' performance for a very young child?" For many children this experience can be alienating or even frightening as the performance is created for older children. Often a young child's first theatre experience is pre-empted by a black out in a huge auditorium. They become terrified of the dark and don't have the faintest clue what's going to happen to them. Many performers do not know this audience sector (children aged 1-3 years), so they tend to overact in a patronizing and clichéd manner. So, it was important that the artists, who were to be involved in performances for very young children, learnt to experience and know their audience. I decided that if the project was going to have meaningful outcomes, then it was important for those involved to visit the children's space and world.

In order to learn about these very young children, three artists (musician, dancer and visual artist) undertook residencies in three childcare centres. Basically the artists were asked to play with the children and allow the children to observe them practising their particular discipline. The children's responses to these artists were documented by undergraduate students from the *School of Early Childhood, University of South Australia*. The observations informed and provided practical examples of how children at this young age respond to external stimuli.

Following a conversation with internationally acclaimed Mem Fox, well known children's author and literacy expert and advocate, I chose her book "Where is the green sheep?" as a text to underpin a performance experience for very young children. As the book deals with concepts and concrete objects (and uses rhyme and repetition), it was the perfect vehicle to explore with artists and young children and translate to a theatrical performance. In addition, like many examples of great literature, it dealt with a quest!

The second stage of "In the beginning" involved three artists (musician, dancer and visual artist) spending further time in childcare centres. This time the artists explored specific words and concepts using sound, movement and images e.g. *thin* and *wide*, *near* and *far*, *up* and *down*, *moon* and *star* (all part of Mem's text). Again, the *Early Childhood* students documented the children's response. Towards the end of this second artists' residency in the childcare centres, the artists combined and offered a more multi-level approach to the words and concepts i.e the dancer and the musician worked together, the visual artist and the dancer etc. It was a chance to explore how children and the artists used sound, movement and images to make sense of text, interaction with others and the world around them.

**Creating the space**

The students' observations over this two year period were collated and provided a basis for the development of the performance experience. It was at this point the expression 'installation theatre' became part of the project's vocabulary, as it became increasingly apparent that small children are more comfortable in a flexible space rather than being regimented into formal theatre seating. A decision was made to use a visual artist rather than a theatre designer to create the space in which the children were to experience the performance. The illustrator of "Where is the green sheep?" Judy Horacek, gave permission for her wonderful illustrations to be utilized as part of the design of the production.

The "In the beginning" project informed the development of the performance experience "The green sheep". Prior to formal rehearsals commencing, the performers spent a two week residency in an inner city early childcare centre, along with the director (Cate Fowler), designer (Roy Ananda) and composer (Fleur Green).

Wendy Schiller provided a strong insight and knowledge into the various stages of development of children from twelve months to three years (the production's targeted audience). This gave the performers a background in what to expect from their very young audiences. Schiller debriefed with the students following each session and affirmed or suggested alternative ways to communicate with young audiences.

It was important the audience felt safe in the environment. The babies and toddlers respond to an intimate space and need to be contained in a clearly defined but flexible area. The sheep pen provided this intimate but flexible space. Should a child become distressed, there were easy exit points. The research, the student's observations, the choice of the text, the need to contextualize the work, and knowledge of the audience and the space, were all integral to the success of *Windmill Performing Arts'* first piece of 'Installation Theatre', "The green sheep".

*Windmill's* second piece of 'Installation Theatre', "Cat", by Mike Dumbleton and Craig Smith was created and had its initial season in July, 2007. This production is part of a three year initiative, in partnership with *South Australia's Little Big Book Club*, whereby a picture book is chosen on an annual basis. This picture book is translated to a performance experience for very young children by *Windmill Performing Arts*. The young children (as readers and audience members) had access to a picture book, an e-book and a performance as part of the "Cat" experience. Both "The green sheep" and "Cat" were presented as part of the "2008 *ASSITEJ* World Congress and Festival".

*Windmill's* founding director, Cate Fowler (who also directed "The green sheep" and "Cat") sought to identify, understand and interpret the key arts elements that had been used in these theatrical experiences for very young children. The use of simple literal words, easily communicable concepts, music and sounds, gesture and movement and simple rhyme and repetition all contributed to the works. All elements were integrated and reinforced meaning making. E.g. in "The green sheep", the sheep were variously defined by their shape; star and moon, or colour; blue and red whilst in "Cat" the children were introduced to a tall tree and a high fence by a number of easily identifiable characters; a cat, a dog, a mouse and a bird. Each production had a refrain "where is the green sheep?" and "thank goodness for that!" which the children echoed. In partnership with colleagues from *Flinders University* in South Australia, a project was developed that aimed to identify the immediate responses of children aged between twelve months and three years to live performances of "Cat" as part of a process of identifying the essential elements of theatre utilized for this age group.

## Observing the performance[1]

During performances of "Cat" we observed and documented the young audience's responses to; the use of props and costumes, the story and script, the way the space was used, the movement of the characters, and the sounds and music. Performances were also videoed so that we could refer to them after the event. What we found was that the story seemed less important to the young audience than the music and sound and movement. We noted strong physical responses to the performance. For example:

> "... some of the bodily, physical reactions and responses, I saw them moving, standing, kneeling up at particular points, or raised eyebrows, eyes following sometimes sound, sometimes characters, the responses to the different props and characters was fascinating; so with the mouse, they were trying to touch it; the fish – they were trying to grab it; the bird – they're trying to reach it, and, you know, that really rapid head movement when there was a sudden sound; the smiles – peering around others to see, pointing."

We noticed particularly, how important the parents and care givers were in supporting the children and helping them to be involved in the experience of the performance. Some young children were overwhelmed with the noise and movement and new venue and needed to stay close to someone they trusted but others:

> "... once I started looking. ... I didn't see many examples of children initiating the contact with adults. They were more engrossed in what was happening. The adults were often whispering, or pointing, or doing the actions but it wasn't the children turning to the adults for their interpretation."

Another interesting aspect, and probably the most powerful evidence was the response from adults who personally knew the children when they looked at the video of the performance at a later date:

> "... by looking at the video, they could say: 'that child never leaves his mother'. There was a parent there who has two twins – a boy and a girl. And they were surprised to see him sitting amongst the other group. He doesn't usually step out of his own zone, particularly when mother's there. So they learnt a lot about their children by watching that tape there. Another child went home and for a whole week was playing the dog, being the dog. Another child saw "Cat" being read on Playschool and said 'That's the show we went to'. So there were a lot of conversations, between parent and child, when they went home, an obvious sharing of an experience."

In the two pieces *Windmill* has developed to date, the audiences (babies, toddlers, parents and carers) are placed in a flexible setting (a sheep pen and a backyard).

---

[1] The following observations and comments were collated by *Flinders University* staff (working with Assoc. Professor Heather Smigiel, Dr. Susan Krieg and Dr. Barbara Nielsen) who observed live performances and analysed video documentation of young audiences attending performances of "Cat" (July, 2008).

These are environments where young audiences are able to move around, respond to the story and follow the journey to find the elusive green sheep or experience a day in the life of a cat. Sound, movement and images are used to reinforce the text and provide an association with the written word. It is crucial the performers understand their audience and that they develop skills in directing the young audience's focus of attention without being overly prescriptive with directions. Throughout the performances, the young audiences are encouraged to observe at some points and participate at others – they gradually learn how to be an audience.

*Windmill* has made a significant commitment to the development of work for very young children. The work is accorded the same production values as other *Windmill* productions. The audience capacity per performance is limited and the productions are age specific to ensure that it is a memorable and engaging 'first' performance experience. 'Installation Theatre' is also an important part of *Windmill's* overall audience development strategy and the company is very keen to ensure the young audiences are not compromised in any way.

Theatre, which blends music, movement, visual art and text, provides a wonderful context where children are able to learn. All of us who have watched young children at a theatre performance can attest to the delight and absorption which is obvious in their expression and movement. However, theatre can also provide a unique opportunity for very young children to learn about new situations that they may not have faced in real life. It can provide a very powerful and important learning environment. Not all theatre achieves this outcome however, and this article describes a research project which sought to identify the essential theatrical elements that could provide the most powerful learning experiences for children twelve months to three years. It observed how children developed performance literacy (language, visual, sound, movement and audience literacy) by attending a performance specially created for them.

These performances frequently provide rite-of-passage experiences for very small children. We have many anecdotal examples of the impact the performance has had. One of my favourites is of the child who always slept with his parents. Following a visit to "The green sheep", he moved out of his parents' bed and made himself an installation from pillows and chairs. He slept in this installation for a couple of weeks and then made the transition into his own bed. Another child painted the family's white poodle blue after seeing the performance. Unfortunately the paint was of the house variety and the poodle had to be shaved by the vet to have his vibrant colour removed. I believe the engagement and the long term impact a performance has on babies and toddlers is the true indication of how successfully it has communicated with its young audiences. I have witnessed a number of productions which purport to target one to three years, but in reality they resonate more strongly with children four years and over. I always gauge the effectiveness of a performance by the engagement of the babies and toddlers.

**Passionate the art**

During my time at *Windmill Performing Arts*, the work I created for the early childhood area drew its inspiration from picture books. Picture books are an obvious source for translation to a theatrical presentation. However I believe that one can draw on many sources. Whatever the production is about, it will be most effective if it allows the young audience; to make sense of what is happening; to be engaged; to experience and respond to a range of performance genres; to respond emotionally and to be exposed to a variety of stimuli.

*Windmill Performing Art's* exploration of 'Installation Theatre' and 'Performance Literacy' has been a commitment to creating what constitutes a memorable and engaging 'first' performance experience for babies and toddlers. *Windmill* has recognized and respected this age group as an audience in its own right and created a performance form that honours the age and developmental stages inherent to this group. Children may be noisy, messy and the income generated by their attendance small – but I believe that if their engagement with the arts is positive, then this will ensure that they embrace the arts with a passion that will contribute to them being part of a healthy society as they evolve through the various stages of their growth to adulthood.

# Visionaries wanted!
## Theatre for *very* young audiences in the United States

*by Megan Alrutz*

I stood at the entrance to a small, white tent, simply decorated with white fabric stars. The toddler in front of me took off his shoes, and crawled inside the tent. I did the same. A single performer, dressed in white, welcomed us in the tent with gentle eye contact and carefully guided us past white, three-dimensional, star-shaped boxes that lined the front half of the floor and walls of the circular tented space. The toddler in front of me crawled onto a white cushion resting on the floor, close to the back wall of the tent. I did the same. Everyone around us sat low to the ground, shoulder to shoulder and faced the winter-wonderland of star-shaped boxes that surrounded the lady in white.

We were embarking on an adventure. And as I took in the tented space, I remembered how I used to play for hours beneath blankets draped across chairs in my living room.

And for the next thirty minutes, I experienced my first piece of 'Theatre for the Very Young' (TVY), or 'Early Years Theatre' (EYT): *Teater My's* "Songs from Above", a Danish production written and directed for children ages two to four years old. As the performer unveiled a series of interactive dioramas within each box, choreographed to a gentle musical score, I relived some of the most poignant moments in my life: splashing in puddles, flying kites, running barefoot through the grass, and blowing paper boats across a pond. And the toddler next to me rarely took his eyes off the performer.

The piece included very little language and no plot per se, but the low-context performance contained bits of story and emotion in images, objects, and movement. It felt like a three-dimensional stream of consciousness – a series of moments perfectly strung together. There were many surprises; boxes opened revealing rain, light, music-but nothing was jarring or startling. Nothing felt big, bright, fast, rowdy, or over-the-top. It felt like a poem, a whisper. I had not seen anything like it in the United States (US) where much of the theatre for young children is full of colour, spectacle, energizing music, and scripted audience participation.

## A need for visionaries

Admittedly, 'Theatre for Young Audiences' (TYA) in the US varies greatly in style, aesthetic and quality, and targets a broad age-range (typically five to eighteen years old). While some companies offer one or two productions a year that target youth as young as four and five years old, more often than not, theatres recommend minimum age limits to discourage caregivers from bringing babies and very young children to the theatre, rather than to distinguish a clear target audience for a particular performance. Very few theatres are presenting or producing work that is appropriate for children under four years old.

While TYA in the US has made great strides over the last fifty years with an increase in professional artists and theatres targeting young audiences, practitioners recognize that much TYA (specifically for youth under five) still lacks artistic credibility, remaining behind the curve in terms of production values and substance.

> "For some unfortunate reason, things that are becoming taboo in the world of TYA (acting down to children, sugar-coated or meaningless plots, gratuitous audience participation and ridiculous animal characters) are still ok for children under four,"

says Rozz Grigsby, education director of *Oklahoma Children's Theatre*. Grigsby believes that TVY in the US needs some visionaries. And although some of our counterparts in Europe, Australia, and Canada are developing a specific approach to, and aesthetic for, theatre aimed at very young audiences, only a handful of practitioners are beginning to explore this territory in the US.

## The space in-between

In the US, TYA has a long history of being tied to education. For children under five years old, theatres tend to offer process-centred drama experiences in classroom settings, rather than more formal theatrical productions. These drama classes focus on imagination, creative expression, and multi-sensory, guided play, but rarely address art or aesthetics with very young children.

"The thing that captures kids at this age is active involvement," says Kate Bryer, the associate artistic director of *Imagination Stage* in Bethesda, Maryland. "They may be young, but they have a lot of opinions and they want to participate. The classroom setting allows a teaching artist to tell the same story twelve times, to improvise to get deeper and deeper with the kids."

Prior to her role with *Imagination Stage*, Bryer spent years as a teaching-artist with the *Wolf Trap Institute for Early Learning Through the Arts* (Vienna, Virginia), an organization committed to arts-in-education services for children ages three to five, as well as their teachers and families. Like many US organizations devoted to both children and the arts, *Wolf Trap* emphasizes the educational value of the performing arts, focusing on child development and core curriculum content.

"We worked quite a bit with teachers," Bryer says, when recalling her years with *Wolf Trap*. "We used story, song, and creative movement to engage the kids in all kinds of curriculum, everything from colors to counting and sequencing."

"As the storyteller," Bryer says, "I structured opportunities for the kids to make up dialogue, to express how they felt." Using a technique called 'Coffee Can Theatre', where tiny toy figures come out of a coffee can and a story evolves with the students' help, Bryer encouraged kids to get on their feet and give voice to the characters. "That was how they got to know the world," she says.

In addition to drama classes aimed at youth, many TYA companies have started offering drama programs for children (as young as one year old) and their caregivers to enjoy together. "These classes focus on imagination, social skills, and motor skills," says Grigsby, who develops curriculum for adult/child drama programs. "For example, by warming-up with animal-themed yoga stretches, the kids build balance and muscle control while the grownups get a chance to breathe and stretch sore muscles. Beyond the typical play-date, "these classes offer unique situations for parents to supervise and enjoy the social development of their children in a mixed-age group setting".

Creative drama classes for very young children are most often designed as a tool for social and cognitive development, focusing more on the educational experience than the artistry. Bryer and *Imagination Stage's* artistic director, Janet Stanford, are inspired by the idea of achieving both ends. "We know that workshops and classroom settings work well for very young children," says Bryer. "Physical involvement captures kids at that age, so I am fascinated to figure out how that engagement translates to a performance on the stage."

This season, Stanford – who gained inspiration from several English and Canadian performances for the early years – began offering interactive storytelling shows for pre-school children, ages three to five. She was nervous about competing with libraries, many of which offer free storytelling. "But," she says, "people seem drawn to a more theatrical experience that comes with lighting and other elements of a production."

The shows in Stanford's "*StoryTheatre* Series" at *Imagination Stage* are outlined, but not strictly scripted, and the performers remain highly attuned to the audience's engagement. Solo artists use music, movement, song, and audience interaction to engage pre-school children in fairytales, international stories, and children's books.

"A fully realized performance can be difficult for our youngest audiences to take in," Stanford says. "It is easier to follow a single storyteller who continually improvises to re-engage the audience as needed." Stanford suggests that their "*StoryTheatre* Series" serves as a stepping-stone, helping prepare their youngest audience members to appreciate a more formal theatrical experience in a darkened theatre with multiple characters and a detailed plot.

As in the drama classes, audiences for *StoryTheatre* are invited to physically and vocally participate in the story, and the performer, much like a teaching artist, is able to negotiate the needs of the audience, helping the youngest audience members process the story through repetition, participation, and collaborative story-building, albeit from their seats in the theatre.

Moses Goldberg, an early pioneer in TVY in the US and the former producing director of *Stage One: The Louisville Children's Theatre* (Louisville, Kentucky), believes that the theatre helps young people move from experiencing the "actual" to experiencing the "aesthetic." He describes it as "Young audiences' transition from physical to mental participation". "Their natural inclination is to physicalize the character of the dog. Then we help them delegate that responsibility to the artist and that experience begins to become more mental." These theatrically produced, classroom-like experiences, such as the *StoryTheatre*, are staged or produced to some extent and attempt to bridge process-centred, dramatic play and a formal theatre production.

Goldberg's comments further foreground the spectrum of classroom and theatre experiences we offer to very young children, raising questions about the over-arching goals of TVY and how we move toward aesthetically/artistically sound theatre that also remains engaging and developmentally appropriate for youth less than five years old. How do artists negotiate the close-knit relationship between arts and education in the US as they develop theatre for the early years?

Kate Bryer is not exactly sure, but says she is willing to experiment with theatre for the very young – even if it does not always translate. "At two to four years old, children are taking in the physical, rather than following the story, the language," Bryer says. "I am not sure how much form they can pick up, but I want them to see the best theatre now. That means the best playwrights, the best language, and the best content or story."

**Toward an aesthetic**

Building on their "*StoryTheatre* Series", Stanford and Bryer have plans to further experiment next season with a fully realized script for three to five year olds. "Parents and children have responded really well to our storytelling series. Next, I want to start with one play, test the waters with a production that has two to three actors, and see how it goes," says Stanford, who is currently considering scripts such as "The Nightingale", "Bear Stories", and "My Mother is a Pirate". She believes that they have room to play with less-known titles for this age group. "If we deepen our relationship with this audience, we can produce more unusual, creative work," she says.

Stanford, who speaks about aesthetically rich theatre experiences for their pre-school audiences, wants to mirror the aesthetic of the international TVY that she has seen at festivals. "I hope our productions for the very young will have a European feel," Stanford says. "It's playful, exploratory, not plot driven.

[It is] like a doll's house that's come to life, as if the actors are at play, too. Music and movement are very important and it is distinctly gentle and humorous."

"I don't want to do it unless it is visually sophisticated and beautifully done," Stanford asserts. And while TVY in the US continues to include productions with exaggerated caricatures of young people and/or low production values, a handful of artists are aiming to create a different aesthetic for children under five.

Like Stanford and *Imagination Stage*, a few of the most established TYA companies in the US, such as *Children's Theatre Company* (*CTC*) in Minneapolis, Minnesota, and *Seattle Children's Theatre* (*SCT*) in Washington, have begun to adopt the practices of international companies engaged in TVY – such as *Windmill Performing Arts* and *Patch Theatre Company* in South Australia and *Teater My* in Denmark. Many of the new trends shaping the face of TVY in the US come from increased exposure to international performances that philosophically, aesthetically, and literally connect with babies and very young children on their eye level.

## Theatre of intimacy

Theatre in the US is largely unsubsidized and tends to be created through a short-term (two to five weeks) rehearsal process. This financial and cultural reality shapes many of the logistical, as well as the philosophical and creative approaches to TYA in this country. While some of our international counterparts are honing developmentally specific theatre for small and distinct age ranges, such as zero to two, or two to four years old, the trend in the US veers toward serving a wider audience base with theatre that garners mass appeal. While this practice can be logistically and financially profitable, and invites families to enjoy the theatre together, it often means that children under four years old are discouraged from attending the theatre at all, and seemingly assumes that children, whether five or ten years old, will appreciate the same theatre experience.

In addition, US theatre companies are hard-pressed to provide the intimate performance spaces and experiences more common in countries with greater support for the arts. Theatre spaces in the US are rarely designed to accommodate less than a 150 people, while a 300-seat house is more common for professional companies producing for family audiences. While limiting audiences to 30-50 people at a time, and creating intimate theatre spaces (such as tents and small theatres with close-up, floor seating) remains appealing to many US artists, the financial reality of this 'boutique' approach to theatre proves challenging on many levels and requires new models for marketing and producing theatre.

The few US companies that have begun to pursue work specifically for very young audiences remain acutely aware of the need for creating intimate theatre for our youngest audiences. Elissa Adams, director of new play development for *CTC* stresses the importance of creating an environment for preschoolers that is specifically sized for small bodies. "We present work for preschoolers in a tent made out of blue silk panels that sits within the larger black box space, so the space which they watch the play is small and intimate," says Adams.

> "The children enter and can sit either on benches with their parents or on very low benches and pillows close to the stage. This allows them close proximity to the actors and also embraces their natural impulse to wiggle and move as they watch a performance."

In 2005, *CTC* built a new, flexible black box theatre with the specific intent of expanding their programming to include shows for preschoolers ages two to five, as well as teens ages 13 to 20, marking a clear recognition of the unique needs of specific age groups. "Our interest in, and vision for work for two to five year olds was deeply inspired by European companies," says Adams, "We were drawn to the theatre they were creating for the very young – work that felt inherently different than the work we were creating on our main stage for the five and ups." That difference, says Adams, lies in the performance style of the work. "It is a fluid, participatory, gentle, interactive presentation of theatre that welcomes the very young into the experience of theatre-going and storytelling," she says.

For the last three years, *CTC* has presented one production a year for very young audiences, working closely with international companies already immersed in creating theatre for babies and toddlers. In the first season, *CTC* presented "The Cat's Journey," an extant work by the Swedish company *Dockteatern Tittut*, which was followed by *Windmill Performing Arts*' production of "The Green Sheep." In 2007, *CTC* partnered with *Tittut* again to commission and co-produce "A Special Trade," which marked *CTC's* first efforts to produce plays for two to five years olds.

For Adams, this meant re-thinking the theatre experience for very young children, including the details of a child's pre-show experience, as well as their relationship to the actors. In the US, theatre for youth often mirrors the theatre structure for adults, and children are expected to sit quietly in theatre seats for up to thirty minutes prior to the start of the show. During "A Special Trade," the three-member cast entered the lobby and directly addressed the children, providing a brief introduction to the story, singing a song, and inviting the children into the performance space.

With a similar goal of connecting to their very young audiences, *SCT* started their show prior to the audience entering the stage space. Members of *SCT's* cast and crew of "The Green Sheep" entered their lobby playing various instruments and engaging youngsters around the where a bouts of the green sheep. The audience, hooked by one-on-one interactions with the musicians and actors, then followed the cast into the sheep's pen where they sat on a patch of grass while the interactive performance surrounded them on all sides.

This pre-show interaction, coupled with up-close interactions throughout the show, foregrounds an emphasis on the child's connection to the performers and the intimacy of the theatre experience as a whole, elements not always focused on in TYA in the US. Moses Goldberg believes that the relationship between the actor and the audiences is one of the most important aspects of creating an intimate theatre experience for youth. "But," says Goldberg, "not every actor can be intimate with their audience. This kind of improvisational interaction does not fit with most of the actor training in this country, and some actors find it threatening, making casting choices challenging in TYA." This reality points to why some of the recent TVY shows produced by *CTC* and *SCT* present notable developments in our country's TYA.

Reviews of *SCT's* production of "The Green Sheep" and *CTC's* "A Special Trade," make special mention of the unique actor/audience relationship specifically supported by the performers. "When the pint-size patrons talk to the characters or shout out questions, the cast members respond in character and then move on. And instead of high-pitched, breathy-voiced, elaborately enunciated sort of acting [...] the cast accommodates but is never cloying and never talks down to the audience," writes theatre critic Dominic P. Papatola (*St. Paul Pioneer Press*) of the performers in "A Special Trade."

According to Adams, the exchange between the actors and the audience in their TVY shows is different from that in their shows for older audiences. "Our pre-school work is created specifically to encourage and embrace and respond to the audience's participation and involvement," Adams says. "The children interact with the actors constantly. They ask their own questions, they occasionally wander into the playing area, they sometimes offer their teddy bear to an actor whose character is sad." This fluid and improvisational interaction moves away from strictly scripted and often predictable actor/audience relationships common to many TYA productions in the US. The developmental needs of our youngest audience members further complicate the role of theatre artists creating and performing for children under four years old, pushing us to further evaluate the relationship between the actor and very young audiences.

**Building theatre for very young audiences**

As US artists take cues from international companies on producing work for very young audiences, we are beginning to see the birth of a quieter, more intimate theatre aesthetic for the early years – one that may require artists in the field to re-think theatre spaces, actor training, and the ways and reasons that we invite the very young to engage in theatre. We may begin to re-consider the role of child development specialists in our creative process, examine our somewhat rigid and financially driven creative processes, and think less about realism and narrative text, and more about the role of movement, music, objects, puppets, and ensemble-based devising. And if we truly want to achieve a theatre of intimacy, we may begin to re-imagine a theatre where marketing and profits are measured not only by ticket sales, but by the cultural and aesthetic development of our next generation.

For artistic directors such as Stanford, the opportunity to re-imagine theatre-making is a dream. "The most exciting thing about creating work for very young audiences is the opportunity for artistic experimentation," she says. "This largely untapped audience is often less bound to popular titles and cultural and social norms, leaving more room to play with new forms and content for the stage." In turn, she says, this relationship helps to grow an aesthetically critical audience base for the future.

With an increase in professional training programs and gains in artistic legitimacy, the number of professional theatres, playwrights, and artists targeting young audiences is on the rise. However, theatre for our youngest audiences is only beginning to appear on the map, and aesthetically sophisticated work for this age group has yet to gain a foothold on a national scale. But as we develop and hone theatre for the early years in this country, I look forward to seeing more little ones in and around the playing space and more artists re-imagining the face of theatre in the US.

# Distinguished theatre for young children
## About the European network *Small Size*

*Gabi dan Droste*

Theatre for the very young is emerging on an international scale. Festivals are currently being organised throughout Europe: in 2008, "Premières Rencontres" took place in Val d'Oise, as well as "Visioni di futuro, visioni di teatro" in Bologna, and "L'art et les tout-petits" in Charleroi. Theatre conferences in Bucharest and Madrid have established their own chapters for the very young, which will convene again in the fall of this year. Great numbers of the artists participating in these festivals are involved not only for the stimulus of interpersonal exchange, but also due to their active engagement in networks.

## The network

The most significant pan-European network of Theatre for the very young is *Small Size*, organized by actor, director and playwright Roberto Frabetti in September 2006. According to Frabetti, this network exists to "promote the idea that theatre for the very young is possible."

Roberto Frabetti (of the *La Barraca* theatre, Italy) formulated the idea of a network, in cooperation with the *Théatre de la Guimbarde* (Belgium), the theatre *GOML* (Slovenia) and the *Accion Educativa* (Spain). Thanks to funding from the *European Union's* Programme "Culture 2000", their proposal could be brought to life. The *HELIOS Theatre* (Germany), the *Polka Theatre* (Great Britain) and the *Theatrul Ion Creangâ* (Romania) signed on to the project. The network is now widening its circle of influence; with the sponsorship of its *Small Size Seeding Fund*, it has supported eight projects from six countries. Protégé projects include the *Toihaus* and the *Dachtheater* of Austria, and Melanie Florschütz of Germany, among others.

## The players

The European network *Small Size* primarily brings together individual protagonists from different countries, thereby mapping the current landscape of distinguished theatre for young children in central and south-eastern Europe. The structural, cultural, and educational-political conditions, as well as the paces of development, are extremely different in each country.

Daniela Miscov, who is responsible for literary assistance and PR at Romania's *Teatrul Ion Creangâ*, started out two years ago after seeing one of Frabetti's live productions, "with nothing more than a DVD of the performance, and literature about children". Today, she's already planning her third production. This lone warrior is integrating her staging into her self-produced festival, which is Romania's first international festival for children. She also wants to send her production on tour, and would like to encourage other artists in her country to create theatre for the very young. Her hope is that theatre contributes to a shift in the audience's thinking. She wants to use theatre to clearly show that nursery- and preschool-level caretaking is an opportunity, not only to provide supervisory care to small children, but also to educate them.

By contrast, the Belgian playwright and director Charlotte Fallon, of *Théâtre de la Guimbarde*, has been arranging stage productions for the very young in Belgium for eight years now. Her recently created programme "L'art à la crèche" gained momentum at the level of politics. The political support opened nursery school doors to the artists. Fallon grounds her artistic work within a social web of meetings and conversations, especially with the child-care educators. The subject of human and social competence development stimulates Fallon artistically and impacts her work; she is just as convinced that theatre has completely changed life in the nurseries. Within this framework, she has presented five productions with over hundred performances for children under three, and has implemented multiple new standards for the professional development of educators.

Jo Belloli of London's *Polka Theatre* reports on a growing number of companies and organisations in Great Britain. She names *Oily Cart* as the first theatre to begin, five years ago, producing works for the zero- to three-year-old set. After just two such productions, the *Polka Theatre* experienced a huge demand for theatre for children aged two and up. In the meantime, a network has developed between Wales, Scotland, Northern Ireland, and England; artists such as Paul Harman and Sarah Argent, and organisations such as *Starcatchers* and *Sticky Fingers*, have become involved. Jo Belloli hopes that there will be a way to support these initiatives financially. She wants to demonstrate that high-quality art for small children has social and cultural value.

## The research

The members of the *Small Size* network consider their collaboration to be a functional tool. They advance their projects from within their own countries, while also exploring the opportunities of international networking. "We are building this project from day to day", Frabetti says of the network.

For a broader exchange of expertise, they are developing a system to share data, to offer further professional training, and to do cultural research. An unusual example of a direct exchange of experience is the artistic research created among three directors: Charlotte Fallon, Barbara Kölling (*HELIOS Theatre*, Germany) and Valeria Frabetti (*La Baracca*, Italy). After a phase of investigating their various artistic approaches, they are spending a period of one year, coming together on site at three different locations, to offer three workshops to interested artists. Each of the directors in turn leads the day-long workshop at each different site, while the other two directors observe. At the end of the day, the entire group reflects on their artistic process. They are recording a chronicle of their working process as research findings, for a book series to be published by *Small Size*.

For Barbara Kölling, this artistic research is exciting because it is so very unlikely:

> "We three directors, from three different countries, with three different languages, are struggling for a common understanding. That's our main problem. On top of that, we work very differently artistically. Yet in this situation, we treat each other with the greatest respect, because that's the only way we have any chance. Together, we go to these countries where theatre for the very young is just beginning to develop, and share our experience and vision with the interested artists there. Very practical; it's wonderful".

## The discussion

The struggle for communication and the search for a common language are remarkable within this international association. But these are also essential, since many questions and issues within this new art form for the very young are just beginning to be raised.

For example, basic conditions in theatre for the very young are significantly determined by the fact that small children have an unprotected access to their emotions. Their unfiltered experiences and their unguarded reactions directly impact what happens between the performers and the audience. So it's no wonder that the artists debate the issue of emotions.

Charlotte Fallon frames the question as follows: "What does the actor do with the emotions of the audience?" Based upon her observations, this is the greatest discovery for the actors, when they begin to perform for small children. For babies, simply being in a theatre is already highly charged with emotion. It is important to leave the audience enough room for their feelings. The desired goal in her company's theatre productions is to allow the audience the freedom to think and feel. On this note, director Fallon expresses her personal viewpoint: "If a theatre piece is well-made, then emotion is the content of the production; the production is the image of that which I feel within me, and of what I would like to show." In her opinion, actors should visit preschools often, to become familiar with making contact with young children.

Roberto Frabetti emphasises: "We are not trying to instruct during a performance." The aim is not to put forth a feeling for the audience to receive. His company's productions aim to create an empathic situation, in which an interchange of emotional levels is possible. For him, this could be a theatre of emotions. He sees eye contact as one way to reach out and connect with the children. However, that is not intended as a concrete acting direction, guaranteed to assure the actors' success. Ultimately, the actors' own motivation is fundamental, both for engaging in situations with young children, and for being willing to work on themselves in the process. While acting, they must find the balance between "letting themselves go completely", and "never losing control".

This possibility of making contact leaves many esthetical forms open to the imagination.

## The diversity

There is an enormous esthetical diversity across the European map of theatre for the very young, as confirmed by a look at the French festival "Premières Rencontres", organised by the *Compagnie ACTA*. Theatre with objects and with puppets, and works of performance and installation art, could be seen here along with acting. Productions such as "Lait" (*Cie A. M. K.*, France) and "Ets-beest" (Katarina Brown, Netherlands), for example, offered unusual and surprising approaches.

The dancer Katarina Brown directs her performance toward children aged two and up. At the opening of the 25-minute piece, the audience is seated on a large white piece of paper on the floor. During the piece, the dancer combines her choreography with drawings which she creates on this surface. Her actions are accompanied by the body percussion of musician Hans Buhrs. Gradually, the children also join into the action; they begin to move, and take hold of the crayons to draw on the floor themselves. The dancer, the musician, and the children are all in motion, interacting with each other, and at some point it is no longer possible to tell who is giving the impulses and who is following them. In closing, the action calms down and fades away.

For the half-hour production "Lait", Cécile Frayasse / *Cie A. M. K.* built an interior space, reminiscent of a cage, constructed completely of white fur and plastic shapes. The children in the audience, aged 18 months and up, sit on white furry mats in front of this installation, surrounded by a sound collage emitting from all four walls. The performer, within the interior space, wears a white, furry, full-body mask covered with bulges and dangling appendages. She is lying down at first, and gradually comes to a standing position; she continuously pulls bits out of her own insides or from the fluff surrounding her. Lipsmacking, swallowing, sucking and moaning can be heard within the bizarre sound collage, as a constant background underlying the occurrences on stage. A cartoon film flickers briefly in the interior space, showing the birth of a baby in swift flashes. A very odd event for the adults present; all the more so, since the children clap along to the clapping playing in the soundscape, babble in communication with the babble from the speakers, and comment upon the performer's actions with such remarks as, "It's going poop!"

This production generated particularly vehement discussions, conducted among the international audience of professionals, about artistic parameters for theatre for the very young.

The topical discussion within an international context demonstrates, in a refreshing way, that theatre for the very young can always go in unexpected directions, and can bring upon itself some fundamental questions of theatre and art. As Frabetti says, "It is a great opportunity for us to work with very small children, as we have for over twenty years now. It's an unlimited path..."

These international incentives could lead to ripe international encounters in Germany. Within this country, as well, the first national festival has come to life: "Theatre from the very start! The Festival of Theatre for the Very Young" had its premiere in November 2008, in the *Theater Junge Generation* Dresden.

*translated by Lydia Baldwin*

# Experiences

# Does theatre for children exist?
## An unlikely model

*by Roberto Frabetti*

Does theatre for children exist? Maybe it does, maybe it doesn't. But asking this question again today, while I start writing this article, is not an academic exercise. I have been asked this question many times. I have also been asked other questions, and they were all similar to this one. Questions like "But is theatre for children real theatre?" or "Why divide an audience of children into age groups, isn't theatre always theatre?" or "When a show is good, it should not be for a particular age group, can't it be good both for children and adults at the same time?" Now then, though I always to respect the others' different opinions, I like going in a "stubborn and contrary" direction.[1]

Not only do I think that theatre for children exists, but I also think that it has got its own dimension, that it is an exciting subset (in its mathematical meaning) of that wonderful set represented by theatre. I also believe that theatre for children is a set itself, formed by many subsets, each of them different from the other. Specificity is separation, but no necessarily contrast. Different units coexist and create a great big unit. These are the basis of set theory.

*But* if we don't see the subsets, the particles; if we don't see that each of them has its own particular balance; if we don't observe the fragility of that balance, sometimes so similar to a cobweb, then we refuse to see the wonders of creation.

Back to the first question, not only do I think that theatre for children does exist, but I also think that every age group has its own specific features. The teenagers, the children from eight to ten, those who are six or seven years old, the kindergarten children and the young, the very young, those who are one up to three years old or even younger, those who are often called 'babies', using a word that I do not like, because it does not represent their complexity.

If I had ever believed that theatre for children did not exist, then I would not have been working with them for more than twenty years. And I have been doing it without frustration, intensely living a kind of theatre that many will never consider as real theatre. In fact, I have always been doing it stubbornly, because we always move in a contrary direction.

Now I am not supposed to demonstrate this to myself. Because it is a pleasure for me to stand in front of that uncatchable audience of children, and to challenge myself time after time, for if at the end I feel surprised and astonished, it is because they have trusted you once again, and I can say "I made it". And they

---

1 As suggested by the title of a very good collection dedicated to one of the greatest Italian poets of the twentieth century, Fabrizio De André.

have listened with their sensitive ears; they have listened to me and my stories that come from an imagery that the children themselves keep on to nourish.

So I will wait before telling you my story about how good it is to do theatre for the very young and how lucky I have been to live it, because I would like to tell you first the reason why I think that theatre for children exists. Or, better said, the reason why I think there are many theatres for children, different for every age group, and different for each and every social and cultural context. I will try to make it as clear as possible, and to find an apparently plausible explanation – a possible model, a proto-scientific explanation.

I have been working in the field of theatre for children for thirty years, and I have always heard many actors justifying themselves and saying no, that there is no theatre for children, and no, there is no difference, theatre is theatre and if a show is good, everybody is going to like it. And this may be true. Rather, it is certainly true. A good show for children may sometimes reach the adults' hearts. But it cannot be the other way round, that is, that a show for children is good for children only when it reaches the adults' hearts. In my opinion, a show for children can be very good for the particular age group it addresses, and at the same time leave adults completely indifferent.

Why? – Because it is a matter of time and space. Time and space are imperfect reference units. A time unit is contiguous to other fragments of time. The same can be said for space, its measurement being relative and conventional.

In their frenzy, men try to measure everything, but sometimes they forget that each measurement is strictly relative and possible. Let us imagine that there are several time spheres and several spatial dimensions, and that, along with the physical models of space and time, there are also personal dimensions, perceived space/time fragments. If we are able to conceive this, then we can assume that each and every one of us has a different perception of space and time. – It is almost obvious.

Taking one step further, we can also assume, however, that the different space/time perceptions can get nearer when there are similar conditions, driven by culture or age. Let us add an element. The basis of artistic creation, whatever the kind of art may be, is the 'art' of knowing how to master the foundations of composition. The golden number of the ancient Greeks and Phidias's art immediately make us reflect upon how the work of art, created more or less consciously, always responds to a particular and well-devised 'composition'. And composition rests upon the relationship among the elements of space, those of time and the possible relationship between space and time.

This being said, and going back to the assumption that space and time are the basic elements of composition; we can also state that the children have their own vision of space and time, which is not an adult vision.

The adults who want to relate to children through art have to face the children's space and time, and they have to make them share and co-exist with their own adult space/time. The particularity of a work of art made by an adult for the children derives from this concept. A work of art created by someone who tries to sail in other times and spaces, a bit adventurous, a bit reckless.

It is not a matter of looking for our own inner children. As a matter of fact, it has nothing to do with this. It is instead a matter of crossing territories not known anymore, knowing that we are something else, aware that we are an elephant or a bear walking in a forget-me-not meadow.

In search for an impossible delicacy that may become possible thanks to the physically unlikely ability of a forget-me-not to hug a bear, or of the children to welcome the adults, their stories unexpectedly opening and breathing new spaces and other fragments of time. Doing theatre for children is to go towards the simplicity of time and space units. It is to go towards the complexity of composition and its need to be simple in order to be effective.

A 'simple complexity' is an oxymoron, a figure of speech that tells the alchemy of contrast which does not divide, but identifies. It tells the alchemy of the possible meeting of opposites, of their co-existence and mutual exaltation.

After all, the meeting of a child and an adult could also be represented by an oxymoron. After all, the fact of having tried to combine crèche and theatre is also an oxymoron.

## The reasons of an experience

"Theatre and crèche" is a project that has involved and continues to involve the crèches of Bologna. It is a piece of research developed by *La Baracca-Testoni Ragazzi of Bologna*, in collaboration with the *Municipality of Bologna (Department for Education, 0-6 years Services)* in order to investigate the opportunities theatre can offer, to give children, even the youngest, and adults a chance to meet.

The relationship with the children who attend our crèches is one of the many adventures that Italian theatre for young people has lived in its short history; a history that, in its best moments, has been characterised by a strong need for a contact with children, teenagers, with the 'other-than-oneself'. Where the search for amazement, and the search for being amazed have guided apparently unlikely projects, like the ones for children up to three years. A history made of a thousand bell towers, long distances, differences, but also sudden convergences and/or parallel paths.

One of these is the one that, from the mid-eighties, has led some Italian companies to undertake a piece of research on theatre for early childhood and to produce shows specially devised for children attending crèches.

Although only few companies are involved, it is important to underline the fact that in France and Northern Europe there has not been any movement of this kind with the same dimensions or quality of proposals.

If today more and more companies of theatre for young people in several European countries have started to produce shows for children under three, it is thanks to those few Italian companies that have tried to open this fascinating track of research: from *Tam* in Padua to *Giallo Mare Minimal Teatro* in Empoli, from *Stilema* in Turin to *Drammatico Vegetale* in Ravenna, from *Baracca* in Monza to *Kismet* in Bari, from *Teatro Mangiafuoco* in Milan to *Il Melarancio di Bernezzo*, from *Teatro dell'Angolo* in Turin to us, *La Baracca-Testoni Ragazzi* in Bologna.

In their diversity, the shows produced are a 'small fortune', a collection of thoughts, artistic intuitions and pedagogical visions passionately dedicated to early childhood.

If Italy has been one of the vanguard countries in the domain of research on theatre for the very young, this has been possible thanks both to the companies of theatre for young people and to the Italian educational institutions for the early years. We can certainly find many imperfections in our country, but it is just as certain that it is difficult to find a public network of services for the early years similar to ours, both in terms of quality and quantity.

Except some countries in Northern Europe, where maternity legislation offers more favourable conditions and children enter the educational system with the age of two years, we have to acknowledge the fact that in most European countries the institutions for children under three have the features of social services, not of educational ones, in which mainly paediatricians work, and not educators.

Moreover, in Italy the pedagogic research on children up to six years has been largely developed, both in universities and through fieldwork, the latter involving mainly pedagogues from local authorities. Besides, particular attention was paid to the structural, prescriptive and legislative aspects.

Finally, in this framework, 'arts' played a major role; 'arts' at the plural form, and not simply 'art'. In the educational area, particular attention is also being paid to plastic and pictorial arts, in Europe and beyond its borders. I think it is interesting that, in Italy, research in fields like music, dance and theatre was often taken into great consideration.

Starting from the Reggio Emilia model, the Italian experience has touched and influenced the sensibility of many European professionals, and I have been able to verify it myself during all these years of exchange with operators from other countries. At the same time, among its many artistic and communicative focuses, Italian theatre for young people has always been concerned in producing shows for kindergarten children, often resulting in high standard research quality.

Among its merits, Italian theatre for young people has certainly the one of always having taken into great consideration children and youngsters, both as subjects and as audience. This led many companies to produce shows with a particular focus on the special features of each age group, always avoiding simplifications. Moreover, either because of what we have just said, or because of our never ending ego, in Italy we were able to create a very rich contemporary dramaturgy made of new and original productions, using the classical repertoire only marginally.

This made it possible for some shows by Italian authors to be performed, for example, in Germany by German theatre companies, in particular for the very young. Thanks to the liveliness of Italian theatre for young people, we were given the opportunity to go on tour around Europe several times, which allowed us to gain credibility abroad. In this way, the Italian theatre proposals for the very young were not viewed and dismissed as unrealistic, but observed first with curiosity and then with amazement.

From this starting point, the research carried out in Italy by theatre companies and educational institutions fostered, from the late nineties on, a new European production in the field of theatre for the very young. New companies from other countries became in a short time new engines for the research process. The experience of *Théâtre de la Guimbarde* in Charleroi, for example, is particularly important, for since it began to produce shows for the very young in the year 2000, it has become one of the main reference points in Europe in the field, creating a new interest and occasions for new productions.

Today, theatre for the very young, though remaining a niche phenomenon, is finding its own raison d'être in many European countries. This is the reason why, in 2005, with the support of the *European Commission* and the *Culture 2000* Programme, *Small Size* was founded, the *European Network for the diffusion of Performative Arts for Early Years*.

## Traces of a theatre project

"You cannot build a house from the roof, children need theatre".

– This is a sentence we wanted to write on a wall at the entrance of our theatre, the *Testoni Ragazzi* in Bologna, a theatre in which the productions are exclusively for children and young people. We 'stole' the second part of the sentence from the *Children's and Young people's Theatre Centre in the Federal Republic of Germany*, whereas the first part is ours.

We do not know if it is effective, but we wanted to make clear what is obvious for us: That the contact with art should begin as soon as possible, to make sure the 'house/human being' is built on strong foundations.

That is one reason why we started, in 1986, the "Theatre and Crèche" piece of research. It is a very particular piece of research and describing some of its aspects is a way to describe also an idea of relationship between children and artistic languages.

In Italy, the crèches are called 'nido'. The 'nidi' are those educational institutions for children up to three years. The term 'crèche' – reminding of the manger and the nativity scene – that the French give to these institutions and the similar German word 'Krippe', in Europe is much more used than our 'nido' to refer to these institutions. But I think the Italian term 'nido' (nest) is really beautiful, maybe for its lay connotations, or maybe because if it carries the concept of care and 'weaning', it also reminds of the place from which to fly off, from which to begin an autonomous path that, for a kid, means to begin to relate with the others, with a collective culture through social relations. In Italy the nido is a place of culture for children up to three years.

For adult people, the 'inhabitants' of the nidi are usually far away. When we think about a little baby, we rarely manage to see a baby of this age, if we do not live together with them our everyday life. – Let's try. It is more likely that the little baby we see has a newborn child's face and a four years old one's language. The thirty-six months between zero and three years are characterised by continuous changes.

Every time I meet nursery children, I get so astonished. This astonishment makes me feel the strong desire to be in contact with them. To be in contact with a little baby means for an actor to find a balance between talking and listening, trying to privilege the latter. We should look for the pleasure to listen inside of us, listen with all our senses and communicate this pleasure to the children.

Listening is complex. It means paying attention to what is not said, to the hidden, the evoked. It is the attention to the originality of every sign. And babies talk with their eyes and silences. Sometimes the children's silent eyes open doors to hidden worlds. Most of the times we are not able to see them, and we lose a good chance to get astonished.

Silences, curious and amazed eyes, I saw those eyes in nursery children so many times. They are the eyes of Teresa, who, at 13 months, watched the whole show standing, leaning against the leg of her teacher, in a crèche in Ferrara. Teresa and I made immediately eye contact, and with her few, fair hair and her big eyes, she seemed to ask me: "What do you want from me? Why are you here?" – silently.

With their 'tininess', nursery children offer you their stately presence and make you drown in a river of emotions. Emotions just like the ones Riccardo felt. We used to call him 'the kisser'. At that time, we had just begun working at *Testoni Ragazzi*, and we were preparing and producing three performances for nursery children. I was going to perform in all of them.

Riccardo did not reach one metre of height, and he listened very carefully. He sat on the carpet in the middle of the first row of children, with attentive and serious eyes, almost glaring at me.

During the performance, he suddenly turned to one of his mates and, without saying a word, he hugged him, pulled him closer and kissed him. Then, he turned his eyes back to the scene and did not make a move until the end of the show.

Two weeks later, we performed again in the same nursery, and Riccardo was again sitting in the first row of children. In the middle of the show, 'the kisser' performed once again. He changed his target but all the rest was just the same: hug and 'Rhett-Butler-style' kiss, like in "Gone with the wind". I do not remember whether the kissed were boys or girls. It did not matter to him: whoever was sitting beside him was sooner or later bound to share his emotions.

The third time I went there, I impatiently waited for him to perform his kiss again, and he did not deceive my expectations: hug, kiss and back to his position. I thought that the kiss was his manner to express his deep emotion. Maybe it is true and maybe it is not. I'll have to be satisfied with the image of the kisser.

Very young Children react unpredictably, and, above all, they are *uncatchable*, and this happens mostly because we cannot use verbal communication with them. This is the phase in which children absorb billions of pieces of information. They begin to understand what language is, and to understand that it is necessary. At the same time, they are trying to understand the surrounding world, to distinguish between right or wrong, to tell what is good and what is bad, true or false. Maybe they do not understand, or maybe they do. How, what and how much a baby can 'understand' is another amazing mystery.

My son's name is Bruno. He was twenty months old when he experienced a theatrical performance at his crèche. I felt cross-eyed that day, because an eye would look at all the children, but the other was always looking at him, who sat in his teacher's lap. It was March and the performance dealt with the "Journey of a cloud".

Once home, Bruno did not say a word about the performance, but, on the other hand, we did not ask him any question. Maybe he had not liked it, maybe he had not 'understood'. Three months later, during a car trip in Tuscany, under the pouring rain, Bruno began to tell us the whole story of the cloud. Who knows why he had decided it was time to do it and why he had kept it inside for three months. Early childhood is a faraway place and theatre can be one of the many ways to try and reach it, because it is a 'human' language.

In theatre often happens what *should* happen in human relationships. That is to say, grow up together and keep on learning. Individuals who meet and influence each other, sharing experiences, memories, projects, with no defence of power or privilege. It should be so for an educational relationship, as well as for a theatrical one.

Perhaps an actor playing for children should consider his role, his 'job' as a continuous chance to meet children and influence himself. Every single day I spent with nursery children was characterised by great influences and returns, by new emotions and discoveries. In my opinion, theatre for nursery children is a beautiful experience for the adults involved. These twenty years of 'contacts' make me think that nursery of children like a theatrical relationship; I am not sure, however. On the contrary, I am sure that it is a unique experience for adults, because you must be at the children's disposal, you must be ready to continually and promptly change shape in order to establish deeper contacts.

You must be able to talk and listen, all at the same time: me and you, you and me, here and now. I'm going to tell you a story and I'd be pleased if you listened to me. You are a very good storyteller, with your silences and your pauses. Nursery children's pauses take our breath away.

I always tend to be over-talkative, especially when I am surrounded by children, because I am not able to overcome my fear of their silences and of the pauses deriving from a vocabulary that has to be completed. They are long pauses, pauses that make you consider time from a different point of view. In our everyday life, time is our enemy; in this particular case, instead, it is a companion, able to highlight the importance of such moments, like short poems that build an experience. We cannot judge them according to adult aesthetic parameters.

The children's silences belong to another culture and their richness derives from the fact of being just silences: it is a kind of 'simple' poetry.

"Yet I believe that if there was a little bit of silence, if all of us kept silent for a little while, perhaps we would understand something" (Federico Fellini, "The moon's voice")

## Are children a good audience?

Peter Brook, the famous English director, in his book "The open door", writes: "An audience of children is the best critic: children do not have any bias, they can become bored as suddenly as they become involved; they either follow the actors, or they become intolerant."

Are children a good audience? – What about the young ones, those who are three or four years old; or the even younger ones, those who are two or three? – And finally, what about the youngest ones, those who started walking yesterday or a few days ago?

Many may think that they are there because they do not choose, so they do not listen. They are not enjoying the show and they cannot understand the difference between a story and another. But it is not exactly like this and I would like to try and tell you why. I am not a pedagogue, and I am not a teacher, I am just a very lucky man, who has the luck to experience 'close encounters' with little aliens and who can collect very interesting images.

I say I am lucky because my job allows me to meet a two-year-old kid in the morning and work with an eighteen-year-old boy in the afternoon. Then, the morning after, I meet a thirteen-year-old teenager or a four-, seven-, ten-year-old kid. There are not only 'years' between the youngest and the oldest. It is clear to everyone that they are very far apart.

Every age is like a big planet with specific and unique morphological features. The one of the children from zero to 36 months is the planet where the 'it-has-just-happened' feeling is kept, the 'revolutionary', critical moment, in which something unique takes place, a turning point, a radical change.

Last spring I performed a show in a crèche in the North of Italy. The teachers decided to let take part all the children, even the babies, those who entered the school in autumn, before their first birthday. There were approximately forty children. While telling my story, I could see in front of me, in the middle of my audience, a young boy who, as often happens, was watching the show standing on his feet, hardly keeping his balance. During the tale, very slowly, he began to move forward, getting closer and closer to where I was, though never invading my space. At the end of the show, he came to me, finding support where he could and walking the last bit without help. Then he stroked me gently with the back of his hand. While he was doing this, the teacher told me: "He began to walk yesterday". Not "some time ago", not "a few days ago", he had begun "yesterday".

I experienced a very strong feeling and I felt I was witnessing something extraordinary. An 'extraordinary' that I felt over and over again during the "Theatre and Crèche" research, a project during which the production of shows for the early years, the workshops for teachers about theatrical languages and theatrical workshops for children intertwined.

It was one morning in 1986 when I saw nursery children at the theatre for the first time. In our theatre there was a performance of a show for kindergarten children (3-5 years). Before the show, I stopped to observe the children. I liked watching them sitting comfortably on the seats, but I didn't expect that they could be so small, that they were sitting 'in pairs' on the same folding seat to avoid being transformed into sandwiches, so small I couldn't help watching them. And I watched them instead of the show, at which end I went to speak to their teachers and that's how the "Theatre and crèche" journey began. A research aimed at devising a show for crèche children, those from zero to 36 months of age, in order to understand, mainly, if it was possible, if it made any sense and what it would be: If it made sense for the children-audience and for the adults-teachers-actors.

These twenty years of work make me say that presenting a show to nursery children does make sense, at least for the adults that perform it and the small nursery children that enjoy being an audience, because being an audience is not a passive attitude.

To live art does not simply mean to act, but to enjoy: our eyes and ears and, most importantly, our ability to work out and process visual and acoustic information are in action. This happens to the youngest children too, and it is a false legend the one that claims that they are involved only if they 'act'. If acting is a very useful activity, enjoying is just as useful. Acting and enjoying are complementary like communicating and listening.

The enjoyment of being an audience can be found in the smallest children, those up to 24 months of age. Normally, the children who take part in a theatrical performance are the older ones, those who are at least 24 months. Educators decide whether to bring the younger ones or not.

Years ago, I spent two days in a crèche in Genoa. It was a beautiful experience, organised by the town Municipality, during which a very curious aspect emerged. I was going to perform on the second day, while during the first I just watched, listened to and played with the children. I tried, in vane, to make them sleep, while they kept on asking me to tell them stories and then laughing at me because I was not able to tell them correctly. We felt and listened to each others.

It was the first time I performed in front of children who already knew me. I was worried because I kept asking myself if I would be able to keep play-time and performance-time separated. I thought that it would be natural for them to interact with me in the same way as the day before.

Instead, they did not stand up; they 'respected a convention' for 45 minutes and eventually came back to me, repeating my name, which they had forgotten for a while. I still ask myself why they waited until the end of the performance to start playing with me again. Perhaps the answer is, because they feel this urgent need of being an audience. A need of living theatre that comes from an unknown place.

As it happens in all audiences, in crèches audiences are different individuals, each of them with a particular taste and sensibility. They either enjoy what is shown to them or they do not. An audience of children under three years of age is a kind of audience that has, perhaps, fewer conventions, because they hardly clap their hands or laugh when they are supposed to, but they are able to surprise you with their silences, sudden laughs and many, many kisses. I can also say that there is not just one way to play theatre for children, because they can enjoy different kinds of theatre. Dance shows or shadow theatre, surreal and emotional stories, tales with few or many words, funny or romantic stories, with abstract images or toys.

Theatre for nursery children may mean, for an actor, to ideally find fundamental sounds, gestures, signs. Not just because they may be easily comprehended, but because they are more communicative. We should not need to hide behind useless cultural walls. In this kind of situation, we should instead need to enjoy the spontaneity of an audience that is there and it is not, that accepts and refuses what is shown to them through strong reactions. An audience with a particular breathing rhythm, that is frightened or it is not, that cries because of high-pitched sound or that runs to the trike when it is bored.

The very young child forces you to wait for it, to give it time to understand who you are; then, gently, you can begin to measure everything and feel at ease. It asks you total respect, because it *is*.

Working with nursery children, I started to try and understand the meaning of standing in front of an audience, in particular, of an audience of children. As a possible answer, among the thousand possible answers, to the question "What does theatre for children mean?" I once heard Valeria Moriconi, one of the greatest actresses of the twentieth century in Italy, talking about what an actor should look for: *a balance point*.

That paradoxical balance that implies the concurrence of a 'feeling-at-ease' sensation and the control of the situation, – being consciously outside and enthusiastically inside. Small children can make you understand, in a very short time, how important it is to look for that balance. Trying to be trustworthy without losing your direction and vice versa, trying not to lose your direction and still being trustworthy (trustworthiness is a mix of ideas and sensibility).

To search does not mean to find, it simply means to search. It is true for an actor, and it is true for an educator. Both have to undertake paths of liberation in order not to stop feeling like singing onto themselves.

"I confess that I cannot conceive the idea of an educator working without hope …. We must have the historical ability to carry on and create a new song." (Paulo Freire)

*translated by Letizia Olivieri*

# Theatre and children are beautiful and 'ding-dong'...
## Artistic processes in theatre work for the smallest of the small
(A letter to the editor)

*by Myrto Dimitriadou*

**You asked me to describe the artistic processes of the work, development and processing of theatre productions for small and the smallest of small children**

If you were not you, I would never speak or write about the way we – I do not work alone – work. I constantly feel as if I am doing a striptease in front of a million unknown faces. I also feel haunted by the feeling of losing something as soon as I put it into words. As I contemplate and write, I am filled, on the one hand, with the superstitions of the theatre and of the Mediterranean. On the other hand, I have in recent years been juggling constantly with the questions: "What is happening?", "When does it happen?", "How does it happen?" and above all "Why?"

Today I live in Austria, yet, as you know, I spent my childhood in a different cultural milieu in the South, in a different era. Within my theatre work with small and, in recent years, very small children, I have been grappling for more than twenty years with these differences between the Mediterranean and Middle European cultures, the different ideas and concepts of childhood, and the differences between those small – and yet so great – emotional experiences in childhood.

I was just three or four years old when I had my own greatest theatre experience, when my parents took me to see Anton Chekhov's "Uncle Vanya". In Greece at that time it was quite normal to take your children everywhere with you. I really do not know what I did or did not understand, but I was deeply moved and emotionally touched by this evening. I can remember pictures and smells and an indescribable joy. I really feel it was some kind of initiation and at the same time the most 'child-suited' theatre I have ever seen. This is why I do not trust all these discussions about theatre 'suited' to children, pedagogical contents and educational motivation in the theatre. This is why it is so important for me to recreate the atmosphere I have carried within me since I was a child.

## You are interested in what was my trigger, the catalyst for the intensive work with artistic processes

I would like to describe a short scene which I watched during a performance of "And who are you?" my first production for the smallest of the small in Bologna many years ago, which was so inspiring for me.

A small child, perhaps just one and a half years of age, sits in a theatre space with mother and closely follows what is happening on the stage. Mother and child are sitting on a dusky pink mattress, a small flat area for the audience which is shaped like a bed. The child, who is, by the way, chocolate brown, is enthralled; for forty minutes. I am professionally very involved with this theatre show but find myself caught by the rapt attention the small child is paying to the performance. I have the impression that something magical is happening: a work of art is being created in the eyes of the viewer, in the eyes of this small child. I have immersed myself in the questions: "Why a work of art?" and "Why this one at all?", "What do they get out of it?" and "What do I get out of it?"

The subjects of childhood and childhood images have fascinated and preoccupied me throughout my whole adult and artistic life, my own and that of others. "How was it", "How could it have been?", "What do I wish it to be?", "How did it feel?", "How was it for other people?" My first independent theatre production was to do with my childhood (without being designed as: 'Theatre for Children'). I would like to mention here that I find all artists who have an absorbing interest in their own childhood, make art for children; even if they do not call it this. Children like to look at, to listen to and to read such works of art.

I know people who loved to watch Carlos Sauros' "Cría Cuervos" (1976) in their childhood even though the subject is very difficult and the film not especially made for children. Yet it is about childhood and communicates a picture of childhood.

## You can imagine that childhood images and the concept of childhood are keywords for me

I believe that every artist who works for children primarily communicates a certain image of childhood beside the theme or the artistic quality of the work. The contents and forms of these childhood images are precisely what attracts or repels us, are what we find pleasing or displeasing.

My perception of childhood overlaps with that of the French analyst Caroline Eliacheff: Children – even the smallest of the small – are independent beings, who have their own wishes, long before they are able to act autonomously in the real world. Their lack of experience and their linguistic abilities cannot be compared to nothingness. I think that small children understand and experience everything in their own way and within the limits of their cognitive and emotional potential. Even when they are not able to articulate these concrete experiences verbally. Later on in childhood this becomes decreasingly possible.

This is why we not only select very carefully the themes of our productions for the smallest children but also lay great importance on the choice of aesthetic means.

## My theatrical works for children always start with questions about theme and content

My starting point is the notion that inner processes of a child's world of experience may seem small but are of great significance and have concrete consequences. We would like to win small children for art and for the theatre with every play, theme and aesthetic means we choose. For art signifies a moment of pause and through it the possibility of an inner unfolding of the soul. Thus an artwork can unfold in the eye of the viewer and the soul of the viewer unfolds in the artwork too.

In my view, this is one of the most critical processes for coping with human life. To experience and live this process seems to me to be even more critical in these times when such things seem neither considered nor respected.

## I feel close to children

This lies in having a gift or a personal disposition.

In the last twenty years, I have personally created many plays with the artists in the *Toihaus* for children aged three or four. The idea to make theatre for very small children has developed along with concerns about the receptive behaviour of children from the age of four onwards and the changes in this reception in older children due to their social situation and socialisation. My experience with theatre and art in general and also in connection to the children is that you have to learn to 'receive art'; and should do this as early as possible. Just like everything else in human life. This was the starting point for the first step towards a theatre production for the 'smallest of the small' (from the age of one).

## You know the first production I developed alone...

"And who are you?" was the very production which captivated that small child in Bologna. We had previously asked Agnès Desfosses to stage a Salzburg version of "Under the table" in our theatre. When we started working on "And who are you?" we only had my memory of the mirror, my mother's dressing-table in my parents' bedroom, their stories about me and the mirror and the feeling that something really special had happened. Our research into the psychological and theoretical aspects of the child's development showed us that recognising yourself in a mirror at an early age is a highly significant event in everyone's life. None of us can remember this moment – or perhaps we can, somehow.

At that guest performance in Bologna of "And who are you?" an Italian colleague said to me after a performance that he got goose-pimples at the moment when the image of the mirror appeared. He had also thought that he would not be able to remember this event from his own childhood. But something in him did remember it after all. And I wholly believe that. I also believe that small children have similar experiences with their own possibilities and sensory perceptions even if they have other ways of expressing and communicating them.

The development of the play heavily revolved around the personal memories of all the participating artists (in this case there were two actors and two musicians). We always work a lot with improvisation, in our plays for adults too. The difference in the quality of the improvisation when working for adults or for the smallest of the small is that the actors must trust themselves to be really authentic, without censoring what is right or wrong and without fear of exploring paradoxical or irrational aspects of consciousness in the moment. And they have to trust themselves without using the template of an existing image or device. Such memories are not rational, as those of adults usually are, but are emotional images which run throughout our bodies and are almost tactile.

Our dramatic advisor, Scotch Maier, says you have to look at things 'out of focus' to understand them. This is the same for improvisation and the development of a production for the smallest of small children.

It is crucial to create a special working atmosphere for this kind of work. To be free of fear is perhaps not the right expression, it is more an atmosphere which encourages authenticity, awakens trust and carries artists like a surfboard. Of course, this all depends on the participating players. They must feel deeply committed to and interested in childhood in general. They must be prepared to undertake the work from within to dare to stumble through the mists of childhood. Not just to 'play' the action.

We pursue this authenticity in the way we perform. Openness, honesty, direct communication with the public, warm heartedness and a special kind of intimacy must be there and must not be subordinated to the complexity and abstraction of the artistic or aesthetic means through which the particular production is expressed. This 'not acting' is very similar to the 'don't act' in Lee Strassberg's "The Method", which was developed for actors working in film.

## As an actor you walk a knife edge

And this literally means that you can cut yourself or fall off. Both can mean a serious injury for the artist, and also for the public. The prerequisites for this are of course long hours of practice and also the lack of a certain kind of ambition and/or vanity. Fear is needed to be courageous. You also need conscious communication with your own inner life, emotions, memories, pictures, imagination. The inner position of the actors in theatre for the smallest of the small is summed up precisely in a sentence by Peter Brook in "The Empty Space": "The work of an actor never happens for a public and yet always because of it."

The artists on the stage give their audience space and time and their colleagues space and time. They give space and time to support the unfolding of situations, characters, images and emotions to make it possible for the spectator to experience inner pictures. Everyone hears, sees and experiences something different, and this is true also of the smallest children.

The fourth wall of the theatre is taken down, for the actor in one sense but also in respect of the set. In our work, the space for the audience is integrated with that of the stage. The performers develop their full emotional powers which are then just brushed on and fade away, like a breath of morning air, light and exhilarating, touching the pictures of childhood in our heads, the archetypes of the body and the soul, the memories of the skin.

## I'd like to tell you more about the production "And who are you?"

The five of us (two musicians, two actors and me) created the play through improvisation in the space of ten weeks working from our own experiences, memories, perceptions, dreams, fantasies and observations from our own childhoods. We went through all the different phases: the phase of excessive focus on children, on teaching aims, art for art's sake and much more. We had ten weeks of highs and lows. The eternal questions – almost like reciting a mantra – did not leave us over an even longer period.

It became evident (during subsequent productions for the smallest of the small also) that these phases recur and are absolutely crucial. Even when they are strenuous, they throw artists into crises and spread big black clouds across the theatre skies. What is important is the position inside. Nevertheless, we did have a great deal of fun doing it, too. After all we were just doing theatre – passionately, with detailed development of the diverse forms which appeared in the play and without forgetting the 'eternal questions'.

We developed the following using this type of improvisation: You see a warm light room, a mirror, a curtain, a dolls' house with tiny furniture in it, musical instruments and four young women wearing flowery dresses, two musicians and two actor/dancers. They talk, dance, and make music around that first encounter with a mirror and the wonderment surrounding it. There is someone there! There is the dance, the joy of recognising themselves. They make images around all the things a reflection can be. They develop images in response to sound. They narrate dreams. They discover parts of the whole of a tiny cosmos, of me and you, of sky and water, animals and stars. They discover the sun and the railway, dreams of the future and emotions. And all four – dancers and musicians alike – remember where it all happened: in a bedroom, perhaps the parents' bedroom. They reconstruct the room in miniature using the dolls' house.

## The lack of an accompanying adult figure is characteristic of my work

And yet there aren't any child characters present either. You do not see either children or adults acting. The characters on the stage are the same age as the actors and go their own way through the event and its development without any outside help or instructions from another person.

In "To and Fro, my little journey through the day", there are three characters on a circular stage, a young actor/dancer, a woman, and two musicians, who also act. The musicians not only accompany the story musically but they also accompany the different aspects of the central character. They support, are critical, are a little bit afraid, are astonished, loveable and make little surprises themselves.

The journey begins from waking up and progresses through the day. The structure of daily routines: getting dressed and eating breakfast, lunch and supper in the form of rhythmical, 'musically' eaten crisp bread. In the meantime, a world of tones and noises is discovered. Snakes emerge from empty boxes and start to dance. Woods appear with the twitter of birds, a city, the sea, mountains, shops, joie de vivre. Abstract ideas such as "What do adults do when they say that they are thinking?" are simply danced.

The material for the choreographers is taken from the movement potential of the one to three year olds. For example, at one particular stage, a lot is communicated with the pointing finger, the famous 'there' and 'there'. Small children point at everything and not only enjoy their newly discovered surroundings but also their own physical side and the newly won ability to move. And they keep on using their pointing finger.

We developed the choreography for "To and Fro" using this procedure of movement. Fingers point at things, become people, go for walks, express feelings of satisfaction or dissatisfaction, excitement, harmonization. The little movements of the pointing finger turn into dance episodes flowing into the whole body. Episodes which, on the one hand, are a bit strange and, on the other, have something very mundane about them.

## Above all, dance – I don't know what you think about dance in theatre

I could never again imagine theatre without dance, whether for children or adults. By dance, I mean everything pertaining to movement, everyday movements and gestures, emotional situations manifesting themselves in facial expressions, disabilities or bad physical habits. Everything (and much more which

I don't wish to list here) reduced, enlarged, made rhythmical, bound together or split apart, develops into dance for the stage. For me, dance of this kind is an extremely suitable aesthetic form for the smallest children. I have the impression that, depending upon their physical state and capacity for imagination, they dance to the music inside themselves.

I have been lucky to have been able to work with two young dancers/choreographers Katharina Schrott and Cornelia Böhnisch, for many years. Both have a similar approach to dance and childhood is very close to them. They develop – far from any fashionable dance style – small works of art for the theatre for small children, toddlers and babies.

**Dance is very suited to children even if it is an abstract art form**

This is my opinion based on my experience of the last years. In "And who are you?" elements of modern dance and episodes of everyday movement are combined and further developed. The concrete element of language grows out of choreographic passages. Non-verbal scenes evoke concrete objects. The abstract is decoded but it still retains a hint of something secret. The mirror has what is in front of it and what is behind and sometimes a whole life inside.

Another example of dance: A small production inspired by pregnancy (young female artists do have children too) is currently being developed by Cornelia Böhnisch and Katharina Schrott in collaboration with Herbert Pascher, cellist and composer in our theatre. The title of the work is "Belly and... Inside, Outside". It is at present a 'work in progress'. The stage is empty. Three people can be seen, a cello and a cello case. All of them, including the cello have broad red bands tied around them which emphasis the stomach, bringing it to the foreground.

A female actor dances and expresses the physical and emotional sides of pregnancy using non-verbal means: her relationship to the changes in her body and to the being growing in her body. The second actor, inspired by embryo images and ultrasound pictures of babies, begins to dance a 'condition of being'. Subsequently a relationship evolves between the dancers and the musician with his instrument. The music gently accompanies the happening. Ultrasound pictures of babies in different stages of development pop up out of the cello case. They are laid out as connecting lines between the performers on the floor. This is as far as they have got now. The whole thing lasts about quarter of an hour in its present form.

When we presented it at its earliest stage (we always show productions in various phases of development) something wonderful happened. A toddler of about 18 months, started to cry, silently. Tears flowed over an open face, without a single sound or need for comfort. The artists were really concerned. In our adult world, tears often mean we are unhappy. The kindergarten teacher put us at ease: the child was simply moved.

There it was again, the magic moment. The artwork unfolds in the eyes of the viewer and the viewer in the artwork.

## Music

I could never imagine the theatre without dance again. And yet I cannot imagine the theatre without music either. Not only as an accompaniment to the story or event, not only as film music making it more exciting or just as music for dance.

Music and musicians are the partners in my work who are acoustically and theatrically equal with other elements of aesthetics and content. If you like, it is all braided together or presented in layers on top of each other to give a whole. Music and musicians develop along with it. They are given a theatrical role, a character and are a part of the whole thing.

In "To and Fro" the two musicians (violin, accordion, percussion and vocals) are two aspects of the main character. One is positive while the other is sceptical and critical. Both act tenderly, but at a distance, to leave the autonomy of the main character undisturbed. Yet all three go on a small journey together through the day, a small journey through life. In "Belly and... Outside, Inside", the cellist embodies the male side of a birth, the outside. The instrument itself portrays something very female, the music creates a closed and yet generous space. The production "And who are you?" is musically structured. The composition corresponds to the pattern of a mirror image, with some small exceptions. Sometimes a quadruple mirror image emerges: performance and music, performers and musicians alternate between a mirror image and the original.

All my work in staging a production, whether for children or adults, is heavily influenced by music. My theatre productions have an inner rhythm, a dynamic. That is one of the parameters which, conditioned by my experience in theatre for the smallest of the small, has become a special theatre rule for me. At this age, the reception of impressions involves the use of all senses and does not happen in the conventional, cognitive adult way. So, with the very smallest, all their powers of perception should be addressed equally. Rhythm and dynamic belong there too.

## As you can imagine, the central topic of my artistic work is 'simplicity'

And I do not just mean this in terms of productions for the smallest of the small. The contents are glimpses of many layers of moments, a mirror image, a day, a tummy for example. Aesthetic forms can develop from such few elements. A choreography is drawn from day to day movements, a composition from a few musical motifs, a stage design from archetypical picture symbols such as a curved playing area which radiates a hug. The audience sits in a semi-circle. A few props will be filled with life but leave a lot of room for the imagination. Sometimes they are spectacular, for example an electric model railway, and sometimes quite simple – an empty box.

My way of working requires all participants (performers, musicians, stage designers, dramaturges and lighting technicians) to be at the rehearsals from the very beginning. The specific material is further developed during these beginning phases and then flow back into the rehearsal work. We are also not afraid of using abstract, paradoxical or surreal elements, as for children at that age every thing is new and nothing is impossible; they still have not learned conventions (such as right and wrong). Such elements can be a dolls' house, a bedroom, which also contains out-sized pencils and fish next to the normal sized furniture (bed, cupboard etc) or an empty box, which goes 'Quack-Quack!' or a bedspread which turns into a mountain.

**About the standards which you no doubt know already**

In works by various European theatre groups, it is normal for all the players to be standing in some kind of physical or geometrical formation at the beginning of a play. At the end, the young audience may go on stage to look at the props or talk to the players and simply touch everything. In "And who are you?" the performers also introduce themselves verbally at the beginning. However, the audience can also see themselves in the mirror afterwards. In contrast to this, there is no introduction in "To and Fro". At the beginning, everyone is 'sleeping' on the stage. At the end, the audience is invited to have little biscuits with them. And during the play there is lots of long and enjoyable eating!

As I write this letter, I realise that it is not possible to give concrete names to inner processes. Katharina Schrott can remember how, as a child, she watched her father repairing a clock. When he had finished, she was convinced that she could do it too. She took the clock apart only to find out afterwards that she could not repair it herself after all. She remembers how astonished she was at that time. She carries this small memory, perhaps with some great significance, who knows, on to the stage. Thus, using different sized boxes, she builds a tower which can hardly stand up at all. The base is too small, the structure a complete chaos of great big objects of all different sizes. The unstable tower, which collapses at the end, recreates on stage the same astonishment as that experienced in childhood.

Another example is a scene based on a personal traumatic experience. When I was a very small child, I was in Athens with my parents and wandered off and got lost in the city. In this scene we see a little girl in the turmoil of a great big loud city. There is a kind of terror, probably accompanied by some kind of thrill. On the stage this is transformed into a euphoric choreography – which also contains some fear bristling with life, yes, a joie de vivre – to extremely melodic instrumental music (violin and accordion) based on the sounds of a megacity.

Childhood images, memories, authenticity, the special acting style, language, movement, dance, music, images and settings merge together during the development of the show. Our story is the intertwining of braids. We lay one layer on top of another, like making a cake, which is finally compressed into an emotional atmosphere. This 'into each other' is more than the sum of individual pieces of single elements. It becomes a whole, a small whole, sometimes a small work of art.

### The artists and collaborators

Collaboration and mutual inspiration is crucial to our way of working together. I prefer a long-term collaboration. The artists who worked in the last productions are: The dancers and actors Katharina Schrott and Cornelia Böhnisch, the composer/cellist Herbert Pascher (I have already mentioned them), the multi-talented and sensitive musicians Yoko Yagihara and Gudrun Raber-Plaichinger, the dramaturgical advisor Scotch Maier, the stage designer Regina Öschlberger and not to forget the theatre mediator Helga Gruber.

### By the way

The small child in Bologna, who grabbed my attention so profoundly, did not want to leave the theatre space after the performance. The mother only managed to persuade the child to leave with her by promising they would come back again.

### Theatre and children are beautiful and 'ding-dong'...

Whatever 'ding-dong' may be for you, and for every one else, – perhaps the sun, the moon and the stars.

# The discovery of the small child as a spectator
## The performer Melanie Florschütz and the director Barbara Kölling in a discussion on "Theatre for Early Years"

*Melanie Florschütz*: I shall take the title literally and ask about how we should define spectators in theatre for children and young people. If we interpret the title literally, children under the age of three in Germany were excluded from theatrical events up until a few years ago. We should think about this in all directions: how can people in Germany know for sure which age groups theatre productions are suitable for? You read: from three upwards, from five, from six, from eight, from ten, from twelve, from 16 – and then there are suddenly no demarcations any more, – just theatre for adults. Were the under-threes excluded just because we didn't know what we should recount to them or because we thought they would not understand what we wanted to recount?

To my mind, age recommendations are not simply thoughtful: they also reveal a level of ignorance. It's not that I don't believe that each phase of life has its own special features. But in the last analysis we are all Homo sapiens and can delight in, or get angry about, the same things at the age of 80 as we did at the age of eight months or eight years.

To be quite honest I often come across theatre productions for adults where I think: if this were damped down a little it would make a great show for kids. In addition I have frequently noticed that adults often feel more at home when watching productions for children than they do with a production specially put on for their own age group.

What I'm getting at is this: the problem about interpreting the world in terms of specific age groups is that it always conceals a certain didactic moment. And I think that theatre which wants to discover the under-threes as a new spectator group has to look hard at one basic question. What does it really mean to have to think about and work on a show intended for a specific phase of life? In working artistically for this age group it becomes clear that we cannot just simply bend down to these small people, but rather that we artists must be ready to ask ourselves basic questions about theatre and above all about the act of making theatre.

*Barbara Kölling*: When I think about one and a half to two year old children as theatre spectators, I always think about them in connection with adults. The audience doesn't come in school classes, groups that have long since become independent from their parents and have made up their own rules. The little ones often come along with their parents or, in our case very recently in Nordrhein-Westfalen (North Rhine-Westphalia), in small kindergarten groups accompanied by a lot of grown-ups. And in this case, in terms of numbers the audience relationship between adults and children is often one-to-one. This is the composition of spectators that I have to continually think about, when I'm sitting in a show for the very young. Of course the shows which work best are indeed those which take account of this composition and which deal with a world which is equally valid for two year olds as it is for the thirty-year-olds who accompany them. You are right. Dividing spectators into age groups is only really sensible – if it is sensible at all – when it is used as an orientation. And we cannot simply extend it downwards on the basis of the fact that we've put on shows for children from four years upwards till now, so we'll change that now and look for plays which we can present for children from two years upwards. For if, during this process of discovering theatre for two year-olds, everything remains as usual – the admission, the seating arrangement, the seats, the way we use lighting and darkness on the stage and in the auditorium et cetera – it simply won't work. What is exciting about working artistically for this age group is that I am forced to put all theatrical conventions under a microscope and be clear in my mind what basic theatrical features it is possible to mediate even to the youngest spectators.

*M.F.*: First and foremost, when we are playing to the under-threes we are dealing with spectators who, in a positive sense, are not disciplined. They react openly and directly to what they experience. We, the artists, get an immediate feedback. This is rare in theatre. Here looking at theatre and making theatre are both quite clearly forms of communication. For example, during the first few performances of our show "Hase Hase Mond Hase Nacht" (lit: "Hare Hare Moon Hare Night") the children felt uneasy because the lighting on the stage went out too quickly for them. So we turned it into a game: a small prelude dealing with how you turn out the lights and put them on again until it slowly becomes dark and we can see the moon. In this way putting out the lights and creating darkness was no longer considered by the children as a threat, and the procedure was transformed into a game. In this way we have continued to develop additional ideas and variations in presentation on an ongoing basis of children's reactions to the shows. It is one thing to deal with children where they are at, and quite another to take seriously their particular way of seeing the world. Here we are moving in a very sensitive area in which the moods of the spectators are decisive. The children bring their momentary moods and feelings into the performance and – if it's the first time that they are taking their children to the theatre – their adult companions are often unsure or even sceptical about whether it will work at all.

But the greatest charge you are confronted with when you put on theatre for very small people in Germany is based on the assumption that such small children do not need theatre.

*B.K.*: Yes, these are the kind of people who equally say that small children do not need any friends: all they need is a good mother. That is why they would be much better off at home than in a group of children in a kindergarten.

The question as to whether theatre is necessary for small children has an incredible amount to do with the way society as a whole regards children, above all small children, as people.

If I understand theatre as a place created by people to communicate feelings, thoughts, experiences to other people and where we can all experience ourselves as part of a community, then it is ridiculous to want to be able to exclude anyone. Why shouldn't two-year-olds also need such a place?

I am more and more convinced – especially in Germany – that theatre needs two-year-olds! So many interesting questions crop up when I create theatre for the very young, questions about people and about becoming people. *Will* a small child eventually turn into a person, or *is* it already a person? And this in turn means that art is faced with absolutely basic questions.

Developing these questions and working them through in shows and productions needs time and conscious artistic consideration. Everyone is involved here, the actors, the director, the designer, the musician. It is of decisive importance whether we possess sufficient artistic awareness to be able to think through and work through all these problems, or whether we capitulate in the face of all the reservations. I don't think we should let ourselves be led astray by people who say: "Oh my God, now they're crawling around on the floor and trying to discover the difference between a circle and a square". We should have the courage to face up to elementary artistic questions in our artistic communication with very young people. In this connection we must continually ask ourselves questions about the relationship between the actor and the audience. The theatre can only profit from this. And we all need the theatre, don't we?

*M.F.*: Things are changing a lot at the moment. In 2004 when we started touring our first play for children from two years upwards round Germany, we knew that we had to convince a lot of people. Most promoters were doubtful and sceptical: "What do you think you are doing, can that possibly work, can it pay?" You have to be quite clear in your heads that promoters regard putting on something for the very young as an economic luxury. And only when they have seen the results with their own eyes, that this sort of theatre not only has something to say to the children – and what seems almost more astonishing – but also to adults, are they prepared to change their attitude and start to see guest productions for the very young as an investment in the future of theatre audiences. Sometimes there was even a run on tickets for the shows, because dads and mums were delighted to be able to do something else with their children other than going down to the playground.

So, as we see, in the last four years a lot has changed. German festivals are beginning to show an interest in the shows, for now any festival worth its salt considers it obvious to include a production for children under the age of three in its programme. When, in 1999, Silvia Brendenal put on the very first symposium on theatre for the very young in Germany, in the *Schaubude* in Berlin (including productions from Italy and France), she was pretty much in a minority of one. The national initiative started by the *Children and Young People's Theatre Centre* entitled "Theatre from the Very Beginning!"[1] has surely contributed to giving the movement a shot in the arm, also in municipal theatres. Now there are more and more productions specially developed by fringe theatre groups, and the market is opening up. This is good because by no means all theatre forms have been thoroughly tried out in this area. "Theatre from the Very Beginning" can only benefit from this wide range of possibilities and approaches.

But I hope that this movement does not merely fill a gap in the market. I rely completely on the very youngest spectators whom I experience as being amongst the most critical of audiences. If something is not interesting, we artists feel the reaction full in the face very quickly. Very small people have no problem at all in occupying themselves with something else if a performance gets boring. (laughs)

*B.K.*: Yes, there's a lot going on at the moment and I think that's great. I also very much like the thoroughness and the care people are putting into their work with this sort of theatre, that is growing up from a co-operation between artists, scientists and educationalists in Germany. And I'm equally delighted that there are some very lively and opening international discussions on the subject, for example in the European *Small Size* network.

And so we have discovered the very youngest children as theatre spectators, and it remains to be seen where the current wave leads. In a few years time will there be a repertoire of plays for the very youngest, and authors writing specially for them? Or are the shows simply one-offs intimately connected with the people who created them, and not really suitable to be taken up by other companies? Will developments go in the direction of 'bouncy castles', something which is easier to market, or rather in an educational direction to develop children's synapse connections at an early age? A lot of decisions are going to be made.

I hope I shall have plenty of patience and perseverance in my observations, so that I can continue to build on this area in which small and large people alike can experience art together.

---

1 See www.theatervonanfangan.de.

# Unearthing the potential
## Exploring "Theatre for Early Years" in the UK

*by Jo Belloli*

Adults, as well as children of all ages, learn through exploration and discovery weaving what emerges into our previously acquired experience, understanding and knowledge. Age, experience, and possibly wisdom too, effects to what degree new perceptions and learning are applied or computed, but the fundamental principal of learning through trial and error, experimentation and imagination, is something that at its very purist infants, given the frequency and intensity at which they are engaged in this, probably do better than adults. But as adults, we never stop learning – thankfully.

In looking to develop theatre for the very young, adult artists and educators have a huge amount to learn from this youngest audience, as well as from each other. Before expanding on this, I want to be clear that, without entering into a whole debate of its own, I am not looking to suggest that creating theatre for the very young should be seen as a means to supplement or complement children's learning. Nor is it a prerequisite that adults creating theatre for such young audiences need detailed knowledge in how children learn. As artistic theatre and festival director, Paul Harman,[1] reflects, it is more about artists asking what their own unique role is, in relation to children. But, appropriately, it is through playful exploration and discovery, trial and error, research and dissemination that theatre for the up to threes is now developing in the UK.

Before focusing on this very specific age-range, it is worth noting that the UK has a history spanning more than twenty years producing a diversity of well-researched theatre for the three to sixes. Theatre companies such as *Oily Cart, Quicksilver, Polka, CTC, M6*, and more recently, *Travelling Light, Half Moon and Little Angel* Theatres have a proven commitment to early years theatre, along with a host of experienced freelance performers and puppeteers working individually or as part of smaller-scale, often unfunded, companies. Less highly profiled, the long-term dedication from these individuals and companies such as *Banyan, Tam Tam, Garlic, Freehand, Lyngo* Theatres, *Tell Tale Hearts, Dynamic New Animation* and *Indefinite Articles* has been no less significant to the developing status of early years theatre over the last two decades.

---

1 Paul Harman: Artistic Director *CTC Theatre* 1994-2008; Director "Take Off Festival" 1994-2008; member of *Assitej International Executive Committee* 2008-2011.

## "Take Off"

The early work of *Theatre-Rites*[2], in particular under the founding leadership of the late Penny Bernand, and more recently productions by the company *Fevered Sleep*,[3] have further highlighted possibilities in creating theatre, steeped in a visual and poetic aesthetic, that one could argue connects with the imagination of an intended audience whilst transcending parameters to touch all ages. An awareness that the very young are a specific audience need not restrict the artistic potential; it is precisely this creative opportunity, along with the uniquely intense, sincere and uncompromisingly honest response of the youngest audience, that makes early years theatre such a fascinating field in which to work.

Comfortable, yet I trust not complacent, in producing theatre for the three to sixes, theatre artists and performers, directors, designers, dancers and musicians have become increasingly intrigued by the possibilities of creating theatre for babies and toddlers under the age of three.

It was *Oily Cart Theatre* that pioneered an approach to creating work for the under threes at the beginning of this decade, building on their trademark aesthetic, rich in design and musicality, and with an emphasis on a participatory, multi-sensory theatrical experience. Initially realised through their practice in creating accessible theatre for children and young people with profound and multiple disabilities, they acknowledged and explored the similarities and differences of theatrical engagement through similar techniques with pre-ambulant and pre-lingual babies and toddlers.

In recent years, a small but growing number of artists, many already versed in making theatre for three to six year-olds, have turned their interest and attention to making work for zero to threes. Alongside this, significant changes in government policies regarding the structure of children's services, early years childcare provision and frameworks for learning relating to infants from birth has, in some part, revalidated the role that play and creative learning has in the holistic development of babies and toddlers.[4] The expansion of early years and arts networks, in particular *Earlyarts*[5], has supported a growing collaboration between arts and educators and childcare professionals. Collaboration through showcasing national and international theatre productions, including those for children

---

2 See www.theatre-rites.co.uk. The company's work is constantly developing, but no longer with a focus on early years audiences.
3 See www.feveredsleep.co.uk. Unlike the other companies cited, Fevered Sleep also creates theatre for adult audiences.
4 Kathy McArdle provides a detailed account of recent government and education policies, in England, and of the impact of these on early years arts initiatives in her research, included in the pending 2009 publication "*Small Size*: A space to grow" (pub. Edizioni Pendragon, Bologna, Italia). For further details visit www.smallsize.org.
5 See www.earlyarts.org.uk. Originally regional but now a national and international network uniting early years practitioners with multi-disciplined artists.

aged zero to three, have been further supported by festivals and organisations such as "Take Off" and *Birmingham Rep* (England), *Starcatchers* and *Imaginate* (Scotland) and *Sticky Fingers Early Years Arts* (Northern Ireland).[6] Events coordinated by these organisations have assembled artists, educators, carers and parents to further the exploration of early years theatre and the arts in early childhood,[7] with increasing emphasis on the under threes. In relation to developing theatre practice, a significant occasion at the "Take Off 2001 Festival" brought together a group of about 18 theatre practitioners to improvise possible scenarios for performance development. An afternoon's workshop inspired several new ideas, some of which were later realised in production.

## *Small Size*

Since 2006, a key component and supporting player has been *Small Size*[8], a European network that promotes, develops and advocates the cultural significance of performing arts in early childhood. With plans to expand, the network currently comprises seven co-organising partners, centrally administrated by *La Baracca, Teatro Testoni Ragazzi* in Bologna, Italy. Its UK partnership is managed through *Polka Theatre*[9] in London. As one of a handful of theatre venues exclusively committed to producing and receiving theatre for children aged zero to 13, Polka has a dedicated studio for early years audiences and a history of hosting a wide range of European theatre for early years as part of its artistic programme. Since the 1990s, the theatre has received productions from Denmark, Italy, France, Belgium, Spain and Germany, using these occasions to foster meetings amongst UK colleagues. Primarily focusing on theatre for three to sixes, over the last decade this has expanded to meet the wider zero to six age-range.

Recent *Small Size* funding has enabled the profile of early years theatre for zero to threes to be raised across the UK, with Polka working in close association with UK festivals, venues and arts organisations; subsidising two further

---

6 www.ctctheatre.org.uk manages the "Take Off Festival"; *Starcatchers* is undergoing development with a website pending. Currently further information about all aspects of the *Starcatchers* project can be obtained from *Imaginate*.

7 The conference report "Charting Antarctica", following the "2007 Early Years Creative Forum Let's Pretend" co-ordinated by *Birmingham Rep*, expands upon the development of early years theatre (0-6) in the UK from the late 1980s to the present. The report is available for download from the *Birmingham Rep* and the *Small Size* websites.

8 See www.smallsize.org, a *European Network for the diffusion of performing arts for early childhood* funded by the *European Unions* "Culture 2000" programme, co-ordinated by *La Baracca* (Italy). Current co-organising partners are *Polka Theatre* (UK), *HELIOS Theater* (Germany), *Théâtre de la Guimbarde* (Belgium), *Accion Educativa* (Spain), *GOML* (Slovenia) and *Teatrul Ion Creanga* (Romania). See Appendix „Supporters".

9 See www.polkatheatre.com.

workshops and laboratories for artists through which individual theatre practitioners have continued to spawn ideas for new productions, enabling diversified artistic and creative partnerships, hosting showcase performances with discussions and directly supporting the development of two new productions for zero to threes. Throughout all this activity there has been a keen sense of investigation, exploration, analysis and above all, curiosity.

Five years ago I would have suggested that we were beginning to "scratch the surface" in this field of theatre for the very young. Now I believe we are a small team of excavators, working not just for our own development but with a collective interest, digging the ground to see what lies beneath. Like the innately curious child or the reflectively intrigued adult we still have more questions than conclusions.

Seeing theatre produced by our own peers remains a primary source of inspiration. Over the years it has often been producers and programmers, whose remit it is, viewing the work. It is not always so easy for practising artists, performers and educators to take this opportunity. But this situation is changing. Over the last five years we have had increasing opportunity to look outwards, as well as reflecting upon our own work. And, significantly, not only has the range of visiting productions and our attendance at overseas festivals and conferences fed our curiosity, but the more inclusive composition of practitioners accessing this work has increased, thus expanding our collective points of reference and experience. This can only be a healthy situation.

From a wealth of work many UK colleagues have accessed during this period, I refer here briefly to just three; the productions by *Théâtre de la Guimbarde*[10] ("Terres") and *HELIOS Theater*[11] ("Earth, Stick and Stone" and "Woodbeat"), all of which explore the relationship between artists – sculptors, puppeteers, musicians – and the raw, natural materials of clay, earth and wood in direct a association with air and breath, rhythm, sound, music and song.

My somewhat clumsy but intuitively sensed analogy of unearthing the potential of theatre for zero to threes arises from these pieces of work. Rooted within these productions is the winning essence of discovery combined with the licence to imagine. When presented with an aesthetic, an artistic intent executed with precision and skill, it offers the audience an experience that captivates and challenges. In much the same way as we have seen theatre practice in the UK, exemplified by companies such as the aforementioned *Theatre-Rites* and *Fevered Sleep*, the above work of *La Guimbarde* and *HELIOS* illustrates that playful exploration and discovery are experiences that young children know about and understand, and affirms that emotional and symbolic resonances, when unearthed, can strike a chord that almost defy definition, whilst fuelling the imagination.

---

10 See www.laguimbarde.be.
11 See www.helios-theater.de.

## "Starcatchers"

What is emerging from the work that we are creating in the UK? Appreciating the increasing opportunities to enter into an exchange with our European counterparts we are also nurturing a richly diverse collection of home-grown theatre; work that is benefiting from the practice we are building of constructive peer support amongst a core group of artists interested in the diversity of creative approaches being explored and realised. Although still limited in number, the range of work and the nature of collaborative partnerships are expanding.

Pivotal in our recent development has been the work generated by a pool of artists through *Starcatchers*, the Scottish-based project running since 2006, that was funded to support the actual and researched work of artists in early years nurseries and children's centres in north Edinburgh, which has led to new productions and published research. Alongside this has been the continuing success of freelance director, Sarah Argent, whose initial foray into directing for nursery audiences was channelled through her work for Cardiff-based *Theatr Iolo*.[12] Both Sarah, and *Starcatchers* producer Rhona Matheson, have embraced the challenge of developing work for zero to threes, and both have been recipients of the *Small Size* development funding, resulting in the 2008 production "Out of the Blue" (Sarah Argent with Kevin Lewis) and pending for 2009, "Archaeology" (Rhona Matheson with Andy Manley and Rosie Gibson).

Beyond this, there are other examples of work being created, but as valid as the work itself being realised is the focus of attention and interest amongst a growing audience of UK children's theatre and early years professionals. This was recently exemplified by the early years programme at the "Take Off 2008 Festival", involving six pieces of work for zero to fours including three new, experimental pieces. Through some brave experimentation and willingness to present work in varying degrees of progress to theatre peers, early years educators and childcare professionals, babies, toddlers and their parents, we continue to raise questions, seek solutions and endeavour to keep creating worthwhile theatre experiences. We continue to discuss what it means to be age-specific, and to what extent, or at what point in the creative process, this becomes relevant. We continue to reflect on the role and function of the artist and the art forms used to convey meaning and emotion, and the relationship between theatre and play.

What have we discovered? We are aware of the enormous demand for theatre for zero to threes, but this mostly amongst the more privileged parents who are willing and able to come to a theatre venue. The economics of venues subsidising a programme of work for audiences of a limited capacity (20-40 on average) and the provision of a suitably intimate, safe and conducive environment remain an issue for many venues now becoming interested in presenting theatre for such young children. We know that an increasing number of early years professionals

---

12 See www.theatriolo.com.

value the opportunity for their children to experience this work, within the time that the children are in their care. Part of their challenge is to persuade the parents of this, parents who have an increasing role in partnership with the early years settings, for example locations that serve the professional care and education of pre-school children[13]. These can in many cases dictate how certain funds are prioritised. There is still work to be done in demonstrating the possibilities and value of the arts in early childcare, particularly to the large sector of our society to whom theatre and live performance is an alien experience. And for those who are willing to endorse the opportunities, the practicalities of visiting a venue can be prohibitive, so housing a performance within the nursery or early years setting is the obvious, and often successful, resolution. This leads us to question the issue of the environment for which the work is created, the composition and location of the audience, the differences imposed by this and the impact of this experience, delicate as it can be and which is dependent upon this.

Over and above the very essential contextual questions of audience relationship and environment – physical, social and emotional factors that deeply affect this fragile audience – are our findings and queries about the structure and content of the work.

Clearly there is beauty in simplicity, with an appreciation that this is not easy to achieve. Rediscovering the sensorial pleasure of 'material', whatever that may be, and having the performer/s or artist/s communicate the joy and wonder of discovery through the integrity, focus and skill of their approach as a performer, leads us to question the dimension of theatre. What is it that takes the shared experience beyond play and into performance? Where do these overlap? The issues here lie in the artistic and aesthetic delivery that transcend child's play, yet acknowledges the recognition and sense of ownership young children have of their own play, and indeed, their expertise in it. And what of the material – be it the physical fabric, or indeed, the more abstract sense of content? Are there limits to what will interest and engage a baby or toddler? And what age-ranges within these broad 36 months, should we choose to define these, are most appropriate? Is this to do with the material/content, or the emotional subtext, or the structural design and dynamic? Perhaps it has to be a combination of all three.

I would suggest that we tend to veer towards physical, often natural, material – light, water, sand, clay, earth. We know that discovery, burial, gravity, transition – and most definitely feathers and food – engage and delight. And although we recognise the baby's innate multi-sensory response to environment, we also have a tendency to more readily explore, first and foremost, the visual – with the other senses, not so much in isolation of course, but following on. Yet it is clear from recent discussions that there is still more scope and interest to explore

---

13 For example nursery schools and day care nurseries, children's centres and the private homes of professional childminders.

sound, vibration, music, voice and language and through this, the relationship between the human body and the space it inhabits.

## "My House"

With regard to emotions and feelings, we are not shy in addressing these, but it is possibly a more challenging and less familiar route down which to journey. I would suggest that Andy Manley in "My House" (2007)[14] succeeded with great charm, delicate eccentricity and warm sensitivity in capturing the essence of loneliness, belonging and friendship and has paved a way for others to follow to explore the possibilities of addressing emotions for toddlers aged around 18 to 36 months.

Shaping the theatrical experience is the structural design and dynamic of the piece. Artists and performers experienced in making theatre for children, including zero to sixes, will appreciate the need to focus on the shaping and pacing of their work for a young audience. For those skilled in this the transition to zero to threes may seem awesome, and although it requires delicacy and conviction, it is not, I believe, so great. As apparent from performers in tune with this age-group, it is not so much in the breadth of the smile but in the warmth and intensity of the eyes. The tempo of breath, the rhythm and the integrity of non-verbal communication speak volumes – but all this should be a natural part of a performer's tool box. There is enormous significance in the communal dynamic in the relationship between the audience and performer in terms of environment in which the work is being experienced. Wherever this takes place, the dynamic is very intricately, very delicately a three-way relationship between performer, child and accompanying adult (although arguably different in a venue to a nursery setting).

What remains to be further explored is the physical staging. Beyond the comfort and close proximity between audience and performers, there remains the issue of staging. With the exception of *Oily Cart* and *Lyngo Theatre*, performances for zero to threes have tended to be presented 'end on' with the audience usually seated on a cushioned floor and the performers facing them, full frontal. Maybe this is the most direct way of maintaining that all-important eye contact? Despite different arrangements of cosy enclosure, there seems little variation in this. Furthermore, there is the significance of that contact, and to what extent the parameter is drawn between the audience area and the performance space. How that defined space is established, and to what degree if and when the performers enter the audience space and vice-versa, clearly holds resonance with, in particular, the audience. There appears to be a trend in expectation – being that the audience remain in their space until the 'end' when they are gently invited to enter

---

14 Produced in association with *Starcatchers*; see footnote 6.

in to the performance area. This is then their time to explore, and play; the payoff for having sat and watched for 25 minutes. From my experience this is, more often than not, time spent willingly, absorbed and engaged in watchful observation; the child fixated by the experience, the accompanying adult both by their own engagement and the fascination of watching their child in response.

Although at times the performers may extend into the audience area, and breaking down this fourth wall can helpfully support the audience's sense of belonging and engagement with the communal experience, the opposite is not encouraged. Of course audience intervention, physical or vocal, may come from the spontaneous reaction of the audience, and how this is acknowledged and affirmed is down to a range of choices that have to be made by the performers and director in structuring and presenting the work. *Oily Cart* and *Lyngo Theatre*, however, notably design their productions to actively involve the audience experientially and with hands-on participation. This is a different approach, which requires particular skills on the part of the performers, and clearly succeeds in engaging its audience. Seeing what is possible, and believing there is more to explore, I would not suggest that this approach is necessary in order to engage, but both companies have developed a style that invests in design and detail with meticulous care and expertise and that has worthily met with great professional and public acclaim.

An emerging piece of work that takes the notion of theatre, installation and play into a different direction with the collaboration between visual artist Rosie Gibson and actor/director Andy Manley, is "Archaeology", produced by *Starcatchers*. The performance centres on a large cardboard play-structure during which babies and toddlers enter into a world of discovery and exploration, digging up hidden wonders from the crevices of this landscape. Currently undergoing research and development, this work exemplifies our ongoing desire to cross boundaries and explore the possibilities in creating theatre for the very young. There is a keen sense here that through experimentation, peer support and international exchange, we are beginning to unearth the potential. Through our digging we are, I believe, finding some treasure. We are happy to share this, and trust that, given the resources to continue our excavations, more could be unearthed.

## "I was struck by the difference in age between us, but by the similarity in hairstyles"
### Journeying out of the blue

*by Sarah Argent and Kevin Lewis*

In an Arts centre in Darlington, in the north of England, a 52 year old man with very little hair sits on a carpeted floor, surrounded by a dozen or so babies and toddlers aged between six and 24 months, many of whom also have very little hair – as he said of this experience, "I was struck by the difference in age between us, but by the similarity in hairstyles".

They are all, young and old, actively playing with paper: shredded white tissue paper and sheets of shiny blue paper that make a wonderful scrunching sound. Prior to this, the babies, toddlers and their parents and carers have spent 25 minutes watching this man playing with different forms of paper; focusing intently on most of his actions, giggling and gurgling with delight at others, occasionally being distracted by their mother's silky hair or another child in the audience.

This article aims simply to describe the journey by which this man came to be here. It is the story of a director and a performer, both of whom we are for the first time creating a theatre piece for an audience of babies and toddlers and, we hope, it captures the challenges we faced and questions that arose for us during this process. The piece is entitled, "Out of the Blue" and, being our first foray into the world of theatre for such a young audience, is something of an experiment, an exploration into an area of work still very much in its infancy (!) across Europe, but particularly so here in the UK. To this end, we were delighted that both *Polka Theatre* in London and *CTC Theatre* (the organisers of the "Take Off Festival" in Darlington) were happy to programme "Out of the Blue" on the understanding that it was work-in-progress rather than an artistic fait accompli. These performances were an opportunity for us to observe the responses of babies and toddlers and to gain feedback from colleagues which, along with our own reflections on the work, will determine what changes we make to the piece prior to its next series of performances in May 2009.

S.A.: As a director and workshop leader, I have worked extensively with and for three to four year olds, while Kevin Lewis, the performer, has almost 30 years experience of working with older children and young people.

In 2006, I was one of three theatre practitioners to receive a "Creative Wales Award" from the *Arts Council of Wales*. This wonderful scheme guarantees artists a livelihood, enabling them to take time out to research, experiment and innovate. The award paid for approximately five months of my time and the travel and accommodation costs of visits to the "Visioni di Futuro, Visioni di Teatro

Festival" in Bologna, to *Helios Theater* in Hamm, to festivals and performances in Scotland and England, to observe babies and toddlers at play, to read about their development, and to participate in workshops set up by both *Small Size* and the "Starcatchers" Project in Edinburgh.

Inspired by the people I had met and talked with during my research and the productions I had seen, Kevin and I worked together with two other performers, a designer, and a lighting designer on a week-long exploratory workshop which aimed to create fragments of potential shows for the under threes.

## Our inspiration

The words of Charlotte Fallon of *Théâtre de la Guimbarde* about the starting point for any piece for young children have always stuck in my head: "What interests me? What do I want to share? What do I like most?" So the focus for this workshop was the life and work of the Portuguese artist, Paula Rego. During the workshop we explored:

- The stark light and shadow in Rego's work, reminiscent of her native Portugal. To this end, performers dictated the source of light – playing with hand held light-bulbs, anglepoise lamps, etc.
- Luminescence – bottles, beads and other glass objects with light shining through them acquiring an almost magical aura.
- The white and intense blue of azulejos (Portuguese tiles)
- The properties of paper – ripping, scrunching, unrolling, folding etc.
- The image of a character sitting cross-legged on the floor drawing and humming. "I'd sit on the floor; I'd have a piece of paper, and coloured pencils ... when the point of the pencil scratched on paper, it was utterly thrilling ... And I became completely absorbed in what I was doing. I'd sit on the floor and draw hour after hour". (Paula Rego)

I was then lucky enough to receive a *Small Size Seeding Fund* award to create a new show from the ideas explored in this workshop. I originally intended to create a piece for children only slightly younger than those with whom I had previously worked – perhaps two year olds – but eventually I rose to the challenge issued by my dear friend and mentor, Jo Belloli, and decided to devise a piece for an audience aged six to 24 months. Having agreed to this, it then dawned on me that, while I had spent a significant amount of time during my "Creative Wales" research in the company of the under twos in my local *Children's Centre*, I had in fact seen very few productions for this age-group, so this new show was going to be a real journey of discovery.

I wanted to work with Kevin, whose performance in *Theatr Iolo's* "Are We There Yet?" – a show for three to four year olds – had been much praised for its simplicity, gentleness and honesty. One of the characters Kevin had discovered during the workshop was a man who enjoyed playing with paper (there is an autobiographical element to this character, as Kevin enjoys making collages, so is regularly to be heard and seen ripping paper). The character had also developed in response to the vast number of videos on *You Tube* of babies chortling and giggling with delight at the sight and sound of sheets of paper being ripped or paper bags being scrunched. We wished to explore this character further, and to retain several of the design elements from the workshop – the muted blue and white colour palette and the strong use of light and shadow.

## The material – paper

We gathered together many types, weights and sizes of paper – from giant sheets of tea-bag paper through sheets of ordinary A4 paper, to tiny circles of fine tissue paper. Kevin played with these papers, exploring the visual, aural and sensual properties of each: playing peek-a-boo, disappearing and reappearing from behind a single sheet; pulling at it with a concertina-like movement with growing ferocity until it ripped; playing keepy-uppy with a ball of scrunched-up tissue paper which emitted a wonderful sound on each hit; dropping a series of sheets of paper to the floor, watching them wafting in the breeze as they came down to earth and echoing their downward trajectory with sound. The joy of playing with this material is that the paper's movement cannot be predetermined, so the element of chance plays a large role. The performer has to become entirely engrossed in the movement and in the moment, something which, as Kevin describes later, is essential when performing for babies and toddlers. Kevin played with each piece of paper until he felt he had exhausted the idea, until he grew bored with it or until he spotted something else – thus we arrived at a series of exciting images.

## Story and character

The main challenge we encountered, and which caused us much soul-searching, was how to engage such a young audience from moment to moment while ensuring that the piece has an intelligent dramatic through-line. While it may be argued that this is not necessary for babies and toddlers, we were keen to achieve a piece which is not merely a series of random images strung together, but in which the character goes on some kind of emotional journey and which has a coherent narrative progression in order to satisfy both the adults who would comprise a large percentage of the audience and ourselves as artists.

Initially, Kevin's character was a clown called 'Blue'. He was very endearing and very naïve and was discovering the world and the properties of the paper in the way that a baby might – i.e. this was his first encounter with each of the objects with which he came into contact. We tried out the material in a nursery and, while we were heartened by the way in which Kevin's performance captivated the children, our desire for Kevin to have a clown-like naivety seemed to be limiting the things he could do within the internal logic of the piece.

That night we sat rather despondently, discussing the piece into the early hours something was amiss, what was it? Then it struck us – an adult, when playing with and for a child, can choose to have and/or feign this sense of delight and discovery but is also knowledgeable about the properties of paper etc. This gave us more options in the way Kevin could interact with the material. Now that we had decided to abandon the clown, we wanted to find a new character/persona for Kevin. Who might be surrounded by paper? An artist – and an artist with a baby might play with that paper for the amusement of his own baby – so we returned very directly to our source material of Paula Rego.

The structure of the piece now came together quickly, and we began to realise what the piece was really about; an artist sits in his studio surrounded by his materials, but is frustrated at being creatively stuck. His partner brings his baby (personified by all the babies in the audience) into his studio for him to entertain for a period of time. In the process of amusing this baby, using the paper and objects which litter his studio, he comes up with an idea and finally creates a 'painting' using light – we therefore see him, at the end of the piece, with a sense of achievement both as an artist and as a father. Whether this would be immediately discernible to an audience remained to be seen, but it gave us the dramatic through-line and the emotional journey for the character for which we had been seeking, while allowing the performer to engage with any and all of the materials in a variety of ways.

**How much emotion?**

Our other major concern was how far we could go in expressing those 'negative' emotions (anger, frustration, fear, sadness) which are the stuff of drama, without unhelpfully and unnecessarily upsetting the audience – or alarming and unsettling their parents. This time, Barbara Kölling of *Helios Theater's* voice rang in my ears, reminding me not to,

> "fight shy of the violent or aggressive. We don't actively want our audience to cry, but if you're exploring things, sometimes you have to be quite violent or heavy. Don't reject an idea (such as chopping wood), simply because it is violent or aggressive, instead try and find a way of presenting it that works".

Our character starts from a place of sadness and frustration and we were concerned that it would be problematic if the character's emotions transmitted themselves to the babies. On the other hand, if we avoided these emotions and invested the piece with too much softness and loveliness, would it become too anodyne?

Questions remain about this aspect of the piece and opinion is still divided. Some colleagues felt the piece focussed too much on the sadness and frustration of the character while others exhorted us to go further. In the current structure, the character's progress from sadness and frustration to creativity and elation sees him only momentarily being lifted from the emotional and artistic doldrums, before repeatedly returning there, prior to finally lighting on his artistic inspiration and consequent joy. It was suggested that his interaction with his baby should lift his spirits and clear his creative block incrementally, building inexorably to a climax.

In terms of the overall rhythm and tone of the piece, we personally feel that, despite being intellectually conscious of Barbara's advice, subconsciously we veered on the side of caution in our desire not to shock or startle the audience. Babies and toddlers are actually more robust than we had given them credit for and, perhaps, on balance, the piece could be more boisterous.

**Language**

Debate rages about the role of and need for language in theatre for babies and toddlers. In the workshop, we had played with text in both Welsh and English, even including sections of Shakespeare's "The Tempest". However, within the context of "Out of the Blue" – a piece about a solitary man – words felt alien; his demeanour, states of tension and physicality seemed much more eloquently to speak of his mood. We did experiment with finding words to describe the sounds of the paper, but again we felt that the sounds themselves were more interesting than the words.

The only section of the piece where words are used in the performance is a song. In taking variously-sized and coloured bags out of a large white paper bag, the performer describes these bags. On realising the rhythmic quality of these words, he begins to form these words into a song with a strong jazz lilt. We think that the appeal of this song, rather than being the intrinsic beauty of the singer's voice, is perhaps the repetition, being present at the moment of creation, observing the process of trial and error involved in the coining of a song.

The audience, particularly Alys, aged two years and one week, thoroughly enjoyed the song, "Big Bag, little bag, blue bag, blue". In fact she asks us [her parents] to sing it over and over and over again!

There was a very positive response from babies and adults to the jazz-based recorded soundtrack we used – a mixture of Shostakovich's Jazz Suites and rather sweet, mournful ambient jazz.

## Staying and playing

We knew that we wished the actor/audience relationship to be broken subtly at the end of the piece and for the children to be encouraged gently to join the performer in playing with paper, but precisely what kind of paper the children should play with was quite problematic.

In order to avoid any children receiving paper cuts, we initially distributed squares of the soft-edged tea-bag paper which had been used throughout the performance. However, at our first try-out one parent commented that it looked rather like toilet paper. We also distributed bunches of shredded paper; this turned into something of a soggy mulch when several of the babies placed it immediately into their mouths, so one parent suggested that we use a more shiny, harder-wearing paper. We purchased shiny blue paper which made a wonderful sound as it was crumpled and was less inclined to disintegrate when wettened by spit but, while the majority of babies thoroughly enjoyed playing with this, several colleagues noted that this paper had a different aesthetic to that used in the performance. The shredded paper made a re-appearance, when it was agreed that it was the parents' responsibility to prevent the children putting it in their mouths but that, actually, it would do no harm if chewed and swallowed and it is probably fighting a losing battle to expect little ones of this age not to put things in their mouths!

So, this playful encounter with the children became a joyful and slightly anarchic session in which the children and their adults explored the properties of the different types of paper – playing peek-a-boo, placing shredded paper on one another's heads (and sometimes on Kevin's head) and crumpling and uncrumpling the sheets, all in imitation of Kevin's actions during the performance. It left the floor strewn with strands of shredded paper – thank Heavens for vacuum cleaners! This session allows Kevin an unparalleled opportunity to talk with the parents about the politics of this type of theatre experience and to ascertain what they believe their children gained from the performance. Several parents requested copies of the photos I took of their children at their first theatre experience, clearly seeing it as an important milestone in their cultural development.

## Observations about the audience

As is often the case at festivals, we gave one performance to an almost entirely adult audience. There were two three year olds in the audience and one little girl who, at ten months old, was the correct age for the performance. Initially, she laughed heartily at Kevin's actions. However, I thought we had lost her attention when she suddenly climbed down off her father's lap and appeared to be turning away from the onstage action and looking into the auditorium. Within seconds, however, I realised that she simply wanted to watch the action from a different vantage point and to show off the fact that she was able to stand and walk! Clinging onto her father's thigh for support, she walked round to the far side of the bench on which he was sitting, leant forward, placed her elbows on the bench and her chin on her hands and intently watched the remainder of the performance from this position. With the security provided by her father, she felt safe to venture away from him.

**Performing to this audience**

> "To be in contact with a little baby means, for an actor, to find an equilibrium between 'telling' and listening, trying to privilege the latter." (Charlotte Fallon)

*K.L.*: Interacting with an audience whose attention can come and go is a little like the drama exercise where you stand in a circle and throw a number of balls simultaneously; you have to develop eyes in the back of your head in order to be aware of balls coming at you from different directions. You certainly need to be able to 'see' with your whole body, to sense if a baby's attention is held, even if you are not looking in its direction.

In aiming for a quality interchange/relationship with every child in the audience, I have to make a judgement about when to hold individual contact to take the relationship with that particular audience member onto another deeper level; weighing up that individual child's needs with the needs of the audience as a whole; I run the risk of losing the attention of other children while engaging intimately with just one, unless I can manage to share my attention again in time.

On first engaging with the audience, it is clear that some children are immediately more at ease, more animated and engaged; they are your gifts, as it is easy to get responses from them. Other children are initially a little timid and slightly uncomfortable; the challenge is whether you can get them to engage by the end of the piece. With these more wary babies and toddlers, you want to try and draw them in by paying them attention and enticing them, at their own pace. It is necessary to tune into their body language, their energy, their state of being in order to get a response. It is very similar to an improvisation exercise we call 'The Yes Game', which involves locking onto your partner and through a mixture of copying, amplifying and responding creating invisible threads between you and them.

The challenge in performing "Out of the Blue" is to engage in this complex and rich interchange while pursuing my own storyline. This entails real active listening, being very much in the present moment. It's a very fine balance and there's only me on stage! It is important to be emotionally truthful, not to smile unnecessarily nor indicate what the audience should be thinking or feeling at a particular moment, simply "being" in front of them. As director Martin Staes-

Polet has declared, "Too much energy from the performer can create too much tension in the baby".

You also need to be aware of all the constituent parts of the audience. Unlike with adult theatre, or even, to a certain extent with theatre for older children, an audience of babies and toddlers is not a homogeneous unit, but a series of 'islands' – pairings/groupings of child and adult/s. Performing to them involves a three-way communication between me and the child, the accompanying adult and the child, and me and the parent. If the adult is uncomfortable or is not excited by the performance, this transmits itself to the child, so we need to put them at their ease too – they can only tune into their baby's rhythm if they're relaxed and calm. The adult can also become excited by the intensity of the child's response; this may be the first time the parent has observed its child experiencing this specific emotion in this way.

## Future directions

On the whole, we have been delighted with the response to "Out of the Blue"; there has been very positive feedback from parents and colleagues alike and invitations to perform the show at a number of festivals and theatres. We have also received insightful, honest and very useful constructive criticism, which is being filtered into our thinking about how to rework the piece.

Now that our confidence in both the paper's and Kevin's ability to engage the audience has grown, we are aware that we can cut some of the material we created and explore the properties of the paper more fully. It has been suggested that we lose the back story about the artist and his baby in its entirety, but we are loathe to do this as we feel there must be a way of retaining it, while more fully exploring the paper – we do not want to believe that the two are mutually exclusive.

There were sections of the piece without music, in order that the sounds of the paper itself could be heard, and we will retain these. There were, however, other moments where the absence of music made the piece feel rather flat. We hope to find more music to provide a near continuous soundtrack. With additional resources we would certainly look to employ a musician who could play live. We would also employ a stage manager, as the downside of me operating the sound and lights for the show was that I was unable in performance to concentrate on the faces, bodies and breathing of the audience in order to gauge their responses moment to moment.

## Taking other people with us

We have also realised, however, that there is more work to be done in convincing people of the value of this type of work. Despite our best endeavours to explain the process to the staff at one of the nurseries in which we tried out the material for the performance, one nursery nurse had clearly preconceived ideas: "It will only hold the children's attention if it's full of bright colours and there is lots of interaction and participation"!

I tried to explain that, based on my research, blue and white would predominate and that, while the performer would be in constant contact with the audience, there would be none of the sort of "interaction and participation" she anticipated. I attempted to reassure her by describing productions I had seen during my research, to which her reply was "Well, we'll have to see if *our* babies are the same as Italian and Belgian babies!"

To the surprise of some parents, the babies responded best to the simpler moments, where the performer engaged more directly with the material and with them. More complex and more rigidly-choreographed sequences, e.g. transforming a tailor's dummy into a ball-gowned woman with whom he dances, were less successful. "Starcatchers" had experienced something similar when microanalysis of a video trained on the audience during one of their performances showed that the babies were not particularly engaged by a dance sequence that many parents asserted was their babies' favourite part.

With limited resources, we have attempted to create a piece which we find aesthetically pleasing, which uses music to which babies are not regularly exposed and which requires the audience to sit without actively participating for 25 minutes. We were, at times, anxious that we had been too ambitious but, thankfully audiences have so far responded favourably. So we look forward to our future travels.

# Appendix

# Credits

*Megan Alrutz*: First published in: *TYA Today*, Vol 23, n.1, 2009

*Gabi dan Droste*: First published in: *IXYPSILONZETT, Magazin für Kinder- und Jugendtheater* (Beilage zu *Theater der Zeit*), 2/2008, p. 12-15

*Agnès Desfosses*: This article was first given as a presentation at the symposium "Theater von Anfang an!" ("Theatre from the Very Beginning!") in Berlin, 24 November 2006. See also: www.theatervonanfangan.de/texte/TheatervonAnfangan_Vortrag_Desfosses.pdf, January 2009

*Melanie Florschütz and Barbara Kölling*: First published in: *IXYPSILONZETT*, 1/2008, p. 20-23

*Dan Höjer*: First published in: *Opsis Kalopsis* 2007/1, pp. 7/8

*János Novák*: Published in the internet: www.dansdesign.com/gb/articles/28_10_05_5.html, and: www.theatre.org.hu/kolibri/Glitterbird_english.doc, January 2009

*Ute Pinkert*: This article was first given as a presentation at the symposium "Theater von Anfang an!" ("Theatre from the Very Beginning!") in Berlin, 24 November 2006. It was first published in *IXYPSILONZETT* 2/2007 and second published in: *Theater von Anfang an!*, edited by Gabi dan Droste, Bielefeld: transcript 2009

*Wolfgang Schneider*: First published in: Dokumentation des Symposiums „first steps", *HELIOS Theater* Hamm, 16.-18. September 2005. See also: www.theatervonanfangan.de/texte/Dokumentation_First_Steps_Schneider.pdf, January 2009

*Gerd Taube*: First published in: Dokumentation des Symposiums „first steps", *HELIOS Theater* Hamm, 16.-18. September 2005. See also: www.theatervonanfangan.de/texte/Dokumentation_First_Steps_Taube.pdf

*Geesche Wartemann*: First published in: *Theater von Anfang an!*, edited by Gabi dan Droste, Bielefeld: transcript 2009

# Plates

*Compagnie Acta* (Villiers-le-bel, France): "ReNaissances", director: Agnès Desfosses (Photograph by Agnès Desfosses)

*Toihaus Theater* (Salzburg, Austria): "FÜR DICH! ...oder doch für mich?", director: Myrto Dimitriadou (Photograph by *Toihaus Theater*)

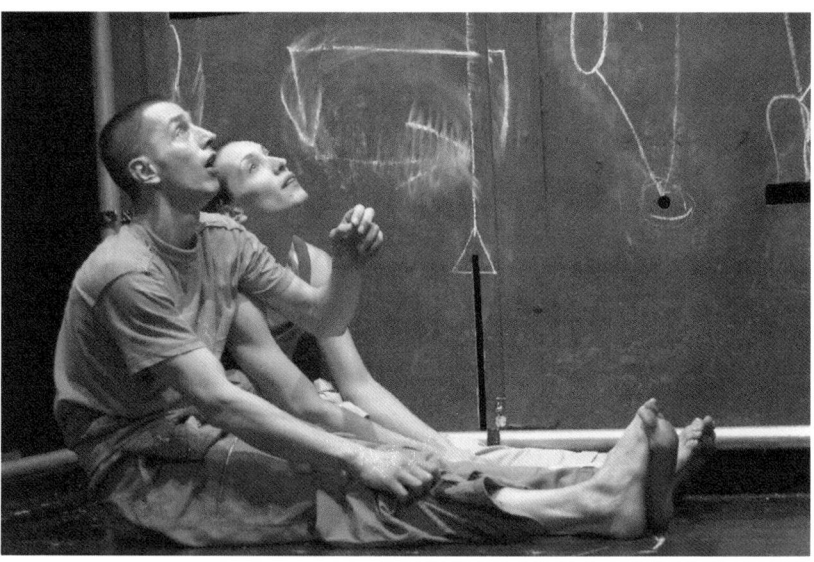

*Mala Scena* (Zagreb, Coratia): "The Parachutists, or On the Art of Falling", director: Ivica Šimic (Photograph by Ivica Šimic)

*Dschungel Wien* (Vienna, Austria): "Überraschung", director: Stephan Rabl (Photograph by Meike Sasse)

*Windmill Performing Arts* (Adelaide, Australia): "The Green Sheep", director: Cate Fowler (Photographs by John Schiller)

*Unga Klara* (Stockholm, Sweden): "Babydrama", director: Suzanne Osten (Photograph by Lesley Leslie-Spinks)

*Théâtre de la Guimbarde* (Charleroi, Belgium): "Bach...à sable", director: Charlotte Fallon

*Theater o.N.* (Berlin, Germany): "Rawums" (above), director: Werner Hennrich and "Hase Hase Mond Hase Nacht" (below), director: Andrea Kilian

Valeria Frabetti in "Pietra Piuma", *Teatro Testoni Ragazzi* (Bologna, Italy), director: Roberto Frabetti

Roberto Frabetti in "Cikeciak", *Teatro Testoni Ragazzi* (Bologna, Italy), director: Valeria Frabetti

*Theater der jungen Generation* (Dresden, Germany): "Funkeldunkel", director: Ania Michaelis (Photograph by Juliane Mostertz)

*Starcatchers* (Edinburgh, Scotland): "My House", director: Andey Manley

*Theatr Iolo* (Cardiff, Wales): "Out of the Blue", director: Sarah Argent (Photograph by Arthur Molyneux)

*The Children's Theatre Company* (Minneapolis, USA): "Cat's journey", director: *Dockteatern Tittuts*

*TAM Teatromusica* (Padova, Italy): "Al di LA", director: Laurent Dupont

*Kolibri, Children and Youth Theater* (Budapest, Hungary): "TODA – miracle in children's language", director: *Kolibri* (Photograph by Judit Szlovák)

*Polka Theatre* (London, UK): "Under One Roof", director: Roman Stefanski (Photographs by Robert Workman)

*Association 16 rue de Plaisance* (Rennes, France): "The garden of the possible", director: Benoît Sicat (Photographs by Benoît Sicat)

*Helios Theater* (Hamm, Germany): "Holzklopfen", director: Barbara Kölling (Photograph by Walter G. Breuer)

Hanne Trolle of the *Theatre Månegøgl* (Copenhagen, Denmark), director: Peter Hesse Overgaard (Photograph by Vibeke Toft)

# Authors

*Megan Alrutz* is a professor of theatre at the *University of Central Florida*. She is a board member of *ASSITEJ/USA* and currently serves as the managing editor for *TYA Today*.

*Sarah Argent* is a freelance director specialising in theatre for the very young and has been instrumental in developing *Theatr Iolo's* work for early years. She is also lecturer at the *Royal Welsh College of Music and Drama*.

*Jo Belloli* is associate producer and programmer at *Polka Theatre* in London with specific experience in early years theatre spanning twenty five years. She currently serves the UK partnership of *Small Size*.

*Gabi dan Droste* was 2006-2008 project leader of the German project „Theatre from the beginning! Networking, models, methods: impulses for aesthetical learning in early childhood" at the *Children's and Young People's Theatre Centre in the Federal Republic of Germany*.

*Agnès Desfosses* is an artistic manager, author and photographer, creating *ACTA* – a stage company. Since 1994, she is creating plays for very young children (under four years).

*Myrto Dimitriadou* works in Salzburg/Austria as the artistic Leader of *Toihaus Theatre*. She specialized herself in theatre for the youngest since 2003.

*Charlotte Fallon* is a Belgian pioneer of baby and toddler theatre. Since 2000 she created four internationally renowned toddler plays. She has been teaching artistic training to day-care nurses for three years as a part of the urban project "L'art à la crèche".

*Melanie Florschütz* is a freelance theatre artist from Berlin: a dramatic and character actress, playwright, puppeteer and performance artist.

*Cate Fowler* is youth and family program manager (*Adelaide Festival Centre*), and director of education services (*Queensland Arts Council*) and founding director of *Windmill Performing Arts*.

*Roberto Frabetti* works in *La Baracca – Teatro Testoni Ragazzi* of Bologna as director, author, actor, workshop leader, writer and theatre's manager. He is also project manager of *Small Size*, the net-development of the *European Network for the diffusion of performing arts for early childhood*.

*Ana Lúcia Goulart de Faria* is professor in the *Faculty of Education* at the *State University of Campinas – UNICAMP*, São Paulo, Brazil.

*Carlos Herans* is stage director and set designer, artistic director of the *Semanas Internacionales de Teatro para niñas y Niños* (*International Week of Theatre for Children*), author and playwright adapter, co-founder of *ACCIÓN EDU-CATIVA Association*.

*Dan Höjer* is a Swedish author and journalist.

*Barbara Kölling* is a theater director and, together with Michael Lurse, co-artistic director of *HELIOS Theater* in Hamm, Germany.

*Kevin Lewis* has worked for almost 30 years as a director and actor in theatre for children and young people and community theatre. In 1981 he joined *Theatr Outreach/Theatr Clwyd* in North Wales as an actor, and became artistic director of the company in 1987. Since 1990 he has been artistic director of *Theatr Iolo*.

*János Novák* is artistic director of theatre *Kolibri*, Budapest (Hungary), and president of *ASSITEJ*/Hungary.

*Ute Pinkert* is professor for theatrical pedagogy at the *Universität der Künste* in Berlin (Germany).

*Stephan Rabl*, formerly a clown and an actor, founded the *SZENE BUNTE WÄHNE* (*SCENE OF COLOURFUL ILLUSIONS*) in 1991, with festivals in Vienna and Lower Austria. Since 2002, he has been artistic director of the *SCHÄXPIR*-Festival, and since 2004, a founding director of the *DSCHUNGEL WIEN* (*VIENNA JUNGLE*), a theatre for young audiences in Vienna's Museum District.

*Wolfgang Schneider* is professor for *Cultural Policy* and dean of the *Department of Cultural Studies and Aesthetic Communication* at the *University of Hildesheim*, chairman of *ASSITEJ*/Germany, and president of the *International Association of Theatre for Children and Young People*.

*Ivica Šimić* is artistic director of *Theatre Mala Scena* and secretary general of *ASSITEJ International*.

*Sandra Regina Simonis Richter* is professor in the *Department of Education* at the *University of Santa Cruz do Sul – UNISC*, Rio Grande do Sul, Brazil.

*Gerd Taube* is director of the *Children's and Young People's Theatre Centre in the Federal Republic of Germany*, he is visiting lecturer at the *Goethe University*, Frankfurt am Main (*Institute for Research in Children's and Young People's Literature*).

*Michel van Loo* is artistic director of *Théâtre de la Guimbarde* in Charleroi, Belgium.

*Geesche Wartemann* is professor for theory and practise of theatre for children and young people at the *University of Hildesheim*, Germany.

# Supporters

## *Small Size*

*Small Size*, the net is a project for the development of the *European Network for the diffusion of performing arts for early childhood* (0-6 years, with a special attention on 0-3 age group).
The Network was founded in 2005 with the support of the *European Commission* and the "Culture 2000" programme. It was established by four professional theatre and educational arts organisations, *La Baracca* (Italy), *Théâtre de la Guimbarde* (Belgium), *Acción Educativa* (Spain) and *GOML – Gledališče za otroke in mlade Ljubljana* – (Slovenia). Later in the same year, three additional partners were invited to become co-organisers to support the development of *Small Size*: *Helios Theater* (Germany), *Polka Theatre* (UK) and *Teatrul Ion Creangă* (Romania). Further funding from the *European Commission* and "Culture 2000" programme was subsequently awarded in July 2006 for the three-year project, to allow an extension of the network across Europe and beyond.

*Small Size* provides a structure through which to meet, share expertise and exchange knowledge; to develop collaborative projects and disseminate information and research. Through its networking, it aims to promote an awareness of the significance of performing arts for early childhood with objectives that include increasing children's creative potential along with the comparison of different European cultural traditions. In addition, it aims to give value to projects and events that support the development of training and educational programmes for early years educators and artists, and for producers and artists creating productions for the early childhood audiences, through widening opportunities for research and collaboration.

The key tool through which the Network operates is the expanding website www.smallsize.org and the integrated database which allows anyone interested in to openly share expertise, support development, endorse and advocate the role of performing arts in early childhood. The website can also serve as a link connecting colleagues and organisations immediately and directly. This, of course, without forgetting the growing opportunities for colleagues to meet each other in person given by festivals and showcases, conferences and seminars across Europe – meetings that enable a broader exchange of professional insight and personal inspiration.

The principal inspiration of *Small Size* rests in the children themselves, and our value of them. Through the network we trust the beneficiaries will be these children, alongside artists, teachers, early years educators, carers and service managers, parents and grandparents – in effect, everybody involved in performing arts, education and care of young children.

The several activities *Small Size* project organises and promotes can be grouped in three areas: production, training and diffusion-exchange.

Productions and artistic research have a lead role. During the project, the partners have realised many productions, co-productions and artistic performances for children from zero to six years, and supported the production of new pieces of theatre for children from zero to four years by other European companies through "*Small Size* seeding fund". Furthermore, a common artistic research path has been undertaken: this workshop-based research is led by three directors belonging to three partner companies (*Helios Theater* Hamm, Germany; *La Baracca*, Bologna, Italy and *La Guimbarde*, Charleroi, Belgium).

The several training activities are different for kind and structure – workshops, research groups, stages – and are addressed towards artists, teachers and children. These activities are fundamental, especially when thinking about an improvement in expertise and a wider diffusion of the idea that arts are a right for the youngest ones too. Among these activities there are the "*Small Size* workshops": addressed to young artists and playwrights, or nursery nurses and teachers coming from several European and non-European countries, these workshops are thought to give them the chance of sharing a common artistic experience.

Diffusion activities have a key importance for an expanding network, and this because of their capacity to create relationships, occasions for sharing and an active memory. These activities are publications, multimedia, research and exchange among the partners, but also events such as Festivals and Showcases. *Small Size* Festivals – the key exchange stations of the Network – deal with theatre, arts and culture for early childhood, with a special attention on zero to three-age group. They host shows produced both by *Small Size* partners and by other companies, round tables, workshops for teachers and educators together with artists, workshops and ateliers for children.

For any information about *Small Size* and its activities contact:

*La Baracca – Teatro Testoni Ragazzi*
via Matteoti 16
40129 Bologna, Italy
tel. 0093 051 4153713
info@smallsize.org
website: www.smallsize.org

## KINDER-, SCHUL- UND JUGENDTHEATER
### Beiträge zu Theorie und Praxis

Begründet von Charlotte Oberfeldt † und Heiko Kauffmann
Herausgegeben von Wolfgang Schneider

Band 1  Charlotte Oberfeld, Heiko Kauffmann: Kinder- und Jugendtheater. Werkstattberichte. 1983.

Band 2  Ruth Kayser: Von der Rebellion zum Märchen. Der Etablierungsprozeß des Kinder- und Jugendtheaters seit seinen Neuansätzen in der Studentenbewegung. 1985.

Band 3  Irene Batzill: Vom Frust zur Selbstbestätigung. Beeinflußt das Jugendtheater die Persönlichkeitsbildung? 1986.

Band 4  Daniel Meyer-Dinkgräfe: Englisches Schülertheater - Black Comedy. Theorie und Praxis einer englischsprachigen Theater-Arbeitsgemeinschaft in der gymnasialen Oberstufe. 1988.

Band 5  Andreas Linne: Bearbeitungen klassischer Stoffe für das Kindertheater. Medea - Hamlet - Metamorphosen. Dramaturgische Untersuchungen zu drei schwedischen Kindertheaterstücken. 1990.

Band 6  Jugendclubs an Theatern. Herausgegeben von Herbert Enge, Marlis Jeske, Wolfgang Schneider. 1991.

Band 7  Klaus Doderer / Kerstin Uhlig: Geschichte des Kinder- und Jugendtheaters zwischen 1945 und 1970. Konzepte, Entwicklungen, Materialien. 1995.

Band 8  Gerhard Eikenbusch: Sozialdemokratisches und kommunistisches Kinder- und Jugendtheater in der Weimarer Republik. 1997.

Band 9  Martin Vogg: Die Kunst des Kindertheaters. Analyse des künstlerischen Potentials einer dramatischen Gattung. 2000.

Band 10  Manfred Jahnke: Kinder- und Jugendtheater in der Kritik. Gesammelte Rezensionen, Porträts und Essays. 2001.

Band 11  Kirstin Hartung: Kindertheater als "Theater der Generationen". Pädagogische Grundlagen und empirische Befunde zum neuen Kindertheater in Deutschland. 2001.

Band 12  Christel Hoffmann: spiel.raum.theater. Aufsätze, Reden und Anmerkungen zum Theater für junge Zuschauer und zur Kunst des Darstellenden Spiels. 2006.

Band 13  Wolfgang Schneider (ed.): Theatre for Early Years. Research in Performing Arts for Children from Birth to Three. 2009.

www.peterlang.de